D0861350

TYLER'S LAST

A NOVEL

DAVID WINNER

Outpost19 | San Francisco
outpost19.com

Copyright 2015 by David Winner.
Published 2015 by Outpost19.

Winner, David
        Tyler's Last / David Winner
        ISBN 9781937402785 (pbk)
        ISBN 9781937402990 (ebk)

Library of Congress Control Number: 2015912527

OUTPOST19

PROVOCATIVE READING
SAN FRANCISCO
NEW YORK
OUTPOST19.COM

TYLER'S
LAST

Chapter 1
La Porqueria, Spain

September 5, 2001
4:00 PM
Tyler

"My wife has gone to Marrakesh with her little French girl-friend, my car has broken down, and the villa we've taken for the summer is right up this hill." Tyler repeats what he plans to say if he runs into someone.

He limps over a plastic bag overflowing with garbage and a dead seagull, also odorous with decomposition. The uneven stones make him stumble into the bushes where that heady eucalyptus smell has been replaced by a long history of middle-class Spanish urine.

Jangled from the long walk back from his *poste restante* and disappointed that there hasn't been even one postcard from Ornella, he stares blankly at the shrubbery before willing himself forward.

The path, which starts a few feet up the hill from the last restaurant on the beach, pains his knees and strains his lungs. If someone were to crop up, he doesn't have to explain why he's here, in this dreary Spanish beach town, when he's generally summered—falled, wintered, and springed at Bel Vento, just below Naples on the craggy Amalfi coast. No one has to know that he'd had to sell it in order for him and Delauney to return money to their investors before their long-running scheme was publically exposed. Tyler can just smile tranquilly, wave his cane, and continue up the hill.

He builds momentum, despite his ailments, a faint breeze caressing his cheeks. But relief from the boiling heat just makes him fret about the cooler Italian summers and the obsessive financial cops who'd stolen them away.

Blood pounds so dangerously through his veins that he has to stop to catch his breath. He calms himself in the usual way, by remembering his arrival on the continent, after ditching those dreary digs back in Queens, back in the early days of the Kennedy administration. Cal in Sicily flits through his mind, of course, a business that had ended badly. But the sun had shone so brightly, the water so blue, the martinis so cool in the winsome way of one's first time abroad. America and its bedevilments had been banished from his life.

A loud mechanical rumbling interrupts Tyler's reverie. The speeding Alfa Romeo would have knocked the remaining life out of him if he hadn't slipped off into the bushes. Which is all pretty offensive, and now one of his favorite Italian shirts is entangled in vines. It rips slightly when he gets himself back on the road, and his underarms are soaked in sweat. When Ornella had been so desperate to marry him in the 70's, only months into their leisurely liaison, he had driven his own Alfa and had no stains under his arms.

He lowers his head and stares at the ground as he approaches what passes for home, but those hooligans are still out guzzling lager on the veranda next door.

"Cheers, mate," slurs the louder, fatter one, wearing ridiculous American-style long short pants and a painful-looking sunburn.

Tyler hardly feels cheerful and is certainly not their mate. How they so effectively ruled the world, he can hardly imagine, as their loutish lower orders have no notion how to hold their drink.

He raises his head and looks murderously back at them. When he was younger, the flat-edge razor he kept in his breast pocket would scare off any miscreant. But he's now too old to risk unnecessary tussles.

"Fucking poof," says the fatty, "haven't seen your old lady lately, have we, who she banging now?"

A moment later, feeling notably worse for wear, Tyler enters one of Delauney's spare villas, into which he'd moved with Ornella after losing Bel Vento, enjoying its cool, dark (if gloomy) refuge from the blazing heat. A martini with a twist would hit the spot but a quick tug on the vodka is more convenient on such a lonely nervewrack of a day.

He grabs the bottle, but tipping it into his mouth feels crass and alcoholic, so he pours it into a jigger and from the jigger into a highball before tossing it down.

The slight elation from his first drink of the day is enhanced by the happy sound of the telephone, *La Moglie*, his wife, Ornella.

He rushes across the room but slows down about halfway in order to enjoy the anticipation. As he reaches for the receiver, a pleasant image of Marrakesh fills his mind, the first stop on the *Tour Nostalgique de L'Afrique Colonial* his wife has taken with her little French lover. *La Moglie* drinks mint tea on the balcony of the Hotel Foucault, gazes at the snake charmers, beggars, and tourist item vendors of the *djemaa el fna* and suddenly misses him. Dominique, the girlfriend, is pretty in her small-faced way, but Ornella must finally have tired of her frilly conversation.

"*Ornella, mia cara!*" he booms ridiculously on the phone, sounding like the vulgar American he might have remained had he stayed in the United States.

The silence on the other line alarms him. Is there something wrong with the connection or with Ornella herself, he wonders, the thought of having to go after her making his knees ache.

There are plenty of people with perfectly terrible feelings about him, the Delauney investors to whom he still owes money, for one. Many would harm *La Moglie* if they could locate her in Africa, but why would they have waited until now? Her romantic idyll has been going on for weeks.

"Ornella," he asks warily, "*sei tu?*"

"Nope," goes an American voice, middle-aged and patrician. "*Non sono, Ornella.*"

Something insidiously familiar, a tad sarcastic in the tone, slips through Tyler's skin into his innards, making him burp and fart.

"Who the hell are you?" Tyler demands. If it isn't *La Moglie*, he really can't be bothered. A jigger or two more and a nap now are in order.

"*Un bruciato*," goes the voice, sounding suddenly weary.

"A burned one," it repeats in case he hasn't understood.

Tyler can't quite make sense of it, and an unpleasant sensation in the back of his throat is starting just where he can't scratch it.

"I was on fire when you left me," the gruesome voice goes on, "but you couldn't burn me away."

4:45 PM

Minutes have slipped by, nearly a quarter of an hour, but Tyler still clings to the phone, frantically reassuring himself that he can't really be talking to Cal Thornton.

"Are you still there?" he finally asks. "Are you there?" he demands, more edge to his voice. He wants to explain to the false Cal Thornton that the real Cal Thornton had *absolutely* been burned away—blazing petrol from their motorboat plus several bottles of burning booze.

A scratching sound on the phone, then a dial tone. The caller has hung up.

Tyler slams it down and storms over to the bar to pour himself a stiffer drink than he usually allows himself this early in the day. As he sits on the scraggly armchair that Delauney got from God knows where and stares at the bushes out the window (the only sea view being from the bathroom upstairs), he breathes in long yogic breaths and exhales them out again, trying to empty his mind of distraction.

"Ohm…" he says, his voice deep and superficially calm, "ohm."

But the memory of the real Cal gets caught in his throat. Cal hasn't smiled his pretty smile for many decades, but Tyler still sometimes aches for it.

He'd met Cal at the bar of the Taormina Hotel not long after first arriving on the continent. The man had been skipping out on his girl for the evening, and, soused and joyous, the two of them were soon punching each other's shoulders and dreaming up whispery conspiracies against the sour-faced Italian waiters, Cal's father back in stuffy old Greenwich, Connecticut, and most of all the heavy, literal-minded American he was mercy-fucking.

They left her behind to take the Milazzo ferry to Stromboli, inspired by Bergman and Rosselini's recent exploits, and took a small villa on the remote far end of the island.

It wasn't that Tyler was homosexual. Young men had all sorts of feelings. It's just that Cal had tricked him so brazenly, after the pitchers of martinis and the dark red wine. Lounging languorously back on the divan right below the open ocean window, his tousled hair splayed out against the pillow, he had looked straight into Tyler's eyes like he suddenly had something serious to say.

Then he patted the area of the divan right next to him like he was summoning a domestic animal.

"*Vieni qui*," he drawled seductively, "come over here."

No fool, Tyler refreshed his drink and kept his distance, figuring the old fellow was too pickled to know what he was doing.

But Cal banged his hand on the divan again and gazed into Tyler's eyes, determined and insistent.

Tyler can still hear the distant waves, smell the dank, salty air, and feel his body lumbering hesitantly across the room.

And what he feared did not come to pass. It was not like the nasty girl removing the football just as the foolish boy was about to kick it in the American comic strip. Cal didn't jump to his feet, or wave his hands in front of his face, pushing him off at the last minute. Instead, he grabbed Tyler's head and welcomed Tyler's tongue with his warm, sour lips.

They slurped and clawed at each other, ripping off each other's polo shirts and squeezing each other's erections. After knocking an old lamp off the coffee table, they landed on the floor themselves, fondling more and more greedily.

They had to pause and pull themselves up from the ground in order to catch their breath and gulp down more wine, but then they solemnly twisted back together again as clouds covered the sun and cool air punctured the room.

Until Tyler suddenly found himself spinning awkwardly away from the divan.

He caught the angry glint in Cal's eyes and saw that the

man had shoved him away. And was slapping him fiercely across the face.

A *"finnochio,"* Cal was calling him, the Italian word for fag, "a fucking *finnochio.*"

Seeing only loathing on Cal's snarling face, Tyler replayed the last several moments, then replayed them again. Then he felt his cheek, still stinging from Cal's hand.

The negro fleet-week sailor with whom Tyler had spent a night the year before had given him a case of crippling regret. But Tyler hadn't hit the man or pretended the thing hadn't happened. And no one could slap Tyler like a girl no matter how drunk they got. They'd get punished like a man when the moment was right.

Pouring more scotch now, Tyler limps up the stairs, through the hallway and into the bathroom. Sitting on the toilet, he stares out the window as the sun slips down the horizon line. Across it somewhere lies Ornella in Morocco, much farther and in a westerly direction is the rugged coast of Stromboli.

Tyler's left hook sent Cal careening, the splintery edge of the tile coffee table denting his forehead.

His heart still racing, Tyler paced to the window, then guzzled the last of the wine. He wouldn't have minded winding things back just a bit, but that wasn't in the cards, and when Tyler finally turned around, he found that Cal was only shallowly breathing.

Tyler kneeled and peered into Cal's unconscious face. Then he placed his mouth back on Cal's mouth, blew boozy breath into his lungs, and pumped his soft chest with his muscular hands. And kept on going until color returned and his breathing no longer sounded so labored.

Climbing back to his feet, Tyler looked around him at the empty bottles lying on their backs in the vestibule, the cigarette butts and ashes on the table. He had to consider more seriously what Cal would do when he opened his eyes and shot back into the world. He needed to soberly assess his options.

Cal would hardly admit to having amused himself by tricking Tyler into his arms.

There was really no chance that he would tell anything other than a fairy tale to the fat girl in Taormina and anyone else who might care to listen, molested by a homosexual, and a low-class one at that.

Tyler imagined rumors spreading like a medieval contagion, from the fat girl to the bellhops at the Hotel Taormina to the boys shining shoes across from the Roman temple. It was true he'd left America in a cloud, but that involved only two-bit fraud, not an accusation of homosexual assault. He preferred to imagine his cold-hearted mother envying his brave new European life (to which his parting postcard had alluded) rather than eventually catching wind, as the Nosy Parker was bound to, of the awful rumors rushing across the Atlantic.

Tyler hated nothing more than the thought of people whispering about him, but there were other, even more serious considerations. Cal would cut him off the moment he came to his senses, and the money Tyler had brought with him to Europe had run out in Taormina.

Together, they'd gone to the Western Union in Milazzo on their way to the Aeolian ferry station, and Cal had cashed over a million lire wired to him by his buffoonish father in America. It was still in his valise in the other room.

Tyler heard a faint groan coming from the body on the floor, but Cal just arched his back and slipped back into sleep. He'd be conscious soon enough, and Tyler needed to take care of business.

Less than a decade had passed since those masses with mother at Saint Peter's on 159th Avenue, so he mumbled a "Hail Mary" to calm himself. Then he ran into their bedroom, found the valise under the bed, and easily located Cal's money and passport. He also changed into one of Cal's white suits, in order to look less recognizable when he returned to civilization.

Next, he dashed out the front door and spun around the villa to make sure no one was walking by, unlikely as they'd seen nobody during their several-day sojourn.

Then he ran down the tricky stone steps to the landing and found the two-gallon can of petrol just where they'd left it across from the motorboat.

It took him several minutes to drag it up to the villa, but Cal was still knocked out by the time he returned.

He poured it carefully over the divan and the floor, and he was lugging it towards Cal, but had to stop short. He couldn't bring himself to pour gas on the lovely young man lying wounded in the late afternoon light.

After emptying liquor in the same places, he grabbed his satchel, which now included both of their passports and Cal's cash.

After taking one last look at Cal's surprisingly peaceful face, Tyler had reached towards him, a farewell kiss in mind, but he stopped short again, his lips only inches away. It was too gruesome a gesture, unnecessarily *grand guignol*.

When he located Cal's gold lighter, a dull ache started in

his stomach, and he knew he'd gone too far to turn back then.

So he lit a *Corriere della sera*, and lit the fuel and booze with the *Corriere della sera*.

He did not stay to watch the blue flames spread through the cottage as he was no pyromaniac, and there seemed little chance that the unconscious young man would get out alive.

He arrived on foot several hours later on the other side of the island just in time for the evening ferry back to Milazzo. Then he caught a train to Catania.

There he stayed for several days in a grubby out-of-the-way *pensione*, spending his mornings drinking coffee, his nights drinking whiskey, and all other times translating the local papers word-for-word in search of a story about a burned cottage at Stromboli, which never appeared.

His last act before leaving Sicily was to wire Cal's father in Connecticut, in Cal's name, claiming to be in trouble and in need of more funds.

That absurdly rich (and usually knackered) old man sent over another million lire, which Tyler had no trouble picking up with Cal's passport at the *Banco di Sicilia*.

Soon he would meet Delauney, a master of creating new identities and making money by marginally illegal means. After that, he would be set up in Rome running numbers and slitting the occasional throat. Several years later, now named Tyler Wilson (after two American presidents), he would meet Ornella. A few years after that, now *Direttore Responsabile* of one of Delauney's best Ponzi schemes, he would save enough to purchase the Amalfi villa just outside of Sant'Agata, Bel Vento.

But it was on Stromboli that he had first taken some-body's life, and there may have been psychic repercussions of which he has not been aware, repercussions that still blur his memory. In these magical days, information can be so much more easily had. At the *poste restante*, they have computers with the Internet, the World Wide Web they call it now. Tomorrow, he can look up some of the papers from that time to see if anything had happened after he'd left Sicily. He can search for any evidence to suggest that Cal Thornton might somehow still be alive.

September 6, 2001
9:55 AM

The morning light blares in through the inefficient blinds, Tyler's heart pounds arrhythmically, and a peculiar taste fills his mouth. Has he vomited again? He'd rather not look at the dent he made in the Johnny Walker bottle while attempting to calm himself the night before.

But while closing the old European window slats, he sees the old Fiat he'd purchased in *Sant'Agata* after having to sell his beloved Alfa.

His watch, which he'd failed to remove the night before, tells him it's ten a.m. The garage has fixed the transmission and dropped it off with him as promised. He's also braced by the fact that the phone hasn't rung since yesterday af-ternoon. Cal, or his impersonator, appears to be leaving him alone.

After showering in cold water and forcing down some toast and coffee, he dons a recently pressed shirt and slight-ly frayed Chinos and jumps into the car. A few easy min-utes later, he's rolling down La Porqueria's main drag.

There was no reason not to stop at his regular *chiringuito* for an order of grilled sardines and a half bottle of cool white Rioja.

A few sips later, he realizes how unnecessarily anxious he's been. He's grown jittery late in middle age. His pre-occupation with the false Calvin Thornton has been typically alarmist. Tyler's barely functioning mobile had been forwarded to the landline at Delauney's Spanish villa, so anyone who called that number wouldn't necessarily know where he actually was. And it's hard to imagine the bourgeois Spanish families would be setting themselves up for a another beach day, the sun flirting with the clouds, if they inhabited the sort of world in which people survived blazing fires and came back decades later.

If the man were somehow still alive, he would hardly show his face in dreary *La Porqueria*. He would have confronted him decades earlier in Rome or at least gone to Bel Vento and made a nuisance of himself in that more attractive environment.

La Porqueria has its pleasures, even if they are déclassé, thinks Tyler while gulping the last of his wine. Ornella really should have given it more than a few days before telephoning her little French girlfriend and taking off to North Africa. Tyler and she could have lunched and dined companionably on paellas and grilled fish. She could have read her Italian-translated British murder mysteries under a shared beach umbrella and occasionally tugged his hand. They've never been much in the bed department but have been plenty fond of each other, still are as far as Tyler is concerned. Perhaps "in sickness and in health" is too much to ask of someone, but one shouldn't disappear at the slightest sign of trouble.

Several unnerving missives greet Tyler at the Internet Café where he has his *poste restante*. The brief postcard from Ornella is written in halting English.

Caro Tyler (He can hear her musical voice. "Teelor" is how she pronounces it.)

Dominique and I go to Casablanca after now, and, perhaps we fly more into the beautiful Africa to Senegal. Having a marvelous time.

Hope this finds you well.

Ornella

The "*Caro*" is the only thing resembling affection, and she seems to be going farther away rather than returning to him. She sounds more like a casual acquaintance than a wife of many years. Though she surely won't pass the rest of her days in Africa, so chaotic since the Europeans left, she might well return to her aging mother in *Sant'Agata* without giving further thought to Tyler sweltering in Spain.

Suddenly, he's hacking painfully, an allergic reaction to some vile Spanish flower, which is the real explanation for the tears creeping down his face.

At the bottom of the pile are two more postcards. The first, from Delauney, makes him sigh in exasperation: no doubt another favor, another ridiculous errand—removing microfilm or a diskette from someone's toiletry case and sending it parcel post, taking a mobile phone from a train locker in some inconveniently located city, dialing a number and leaving a coded message. At least Delauney hasn't asked him to rough anybody up since Tyler has entered late middle-age. He owes the man more than ever for the use of the villa, but at some point enough was enough.

I must ask for a New York errand, dropping something off and coming right back. Ticket departing Malaga in two days, papers, money, and mobile phone arriving in tomorrow's post. Just dial its voicemail for further instructions once you've landed at JFK. I'll come over to LP (La Porqueria, Delauney was a compulsive acronymist) *myself upon your return and pick up the phone.*

Thanks in advance,

D

Despite all these years and all these favors, Tyler doesn't entirely trust the man. He's also bone tired of being Delauney's errand boy, but it wouldn't be a bad time to catch a plane out of town.

New York, he thinks to himself. He hasn't been in decades. Cal passed his youth in nearby Connecticut at Thornton Hall. Tyler can't help but remember that.

Tyler, old chum, goes the last of the postcards, *just met up with Samuels, who sends his regards. Will catch you soon.*

Cal

His heart racing, Tyler jumps to his feet and looks through the window, immediately plotting how far away he can get without stopping for gas. He throws down a few coins and dashes towards his Fiat. Cal and Samuels can have *La Porqueria* to themselves.

But in the humid air, painting for breath, it occurs to him that the real Cal Thornton couldn't possibly know about Samuels, the big black American who'd refused to keep his nose out of the Delauney fund and had to be smothered with one of *La Moglie*'s mother's pillows when he'd visited Bel Vento in the middle of the eighties. If Tyler keeps hitting the panic button like this, he'll give himself angina and never learn who's been harassing him.

Back inside the café, it takes quite a bit of help from the

long-faced Spanish girl but soon Tyler finds himself on the World Wide Web, delving into the distant past.

He puts quotes around "Calvin Thornton," as she has suggested, enters it into the computer, and finds several stories dating from after he'd left Sicily: a small villa on Stromboli, two missing Americans. No article refers to the closing of the case, but he supposes the police don't like to advertise their failures.

He's about to close out when he decides to try Cal instead of Calvin and notices something more recent, only a few months before. "Clicking" on it, as the Spanish girl had suggested in her perfectly idiomatic English, Tyler sees it comes from an American cable television network called Court TV. The program is entitled *Unsolved Mysteries*.

In 1962, says the come-on, *two Americans take a villa on the far side of the famous island of Stromboli and are never heard from again. The villa was burned in a fire, but no bodies were identified inside. Did John Burnette* (Tyler's alias at the time) *really murder Cal Thornton and take his money? Did Cal Thornton escape the fire, as some have suggested, and change his identity?*

Then it lists several times when the show will be aired. Maybe Tyler can find it on his hotel television in New York.

7:00 PM

Back at the villa, Tyler flips a cheap cut of beef onto a rusty frying pan and realizes it would be perfectly perilous to show up in New York using any of his usual identities. He needs to find a fresh one and promptly communicate it to Delauney or risk scrutiny at emigration. Delauney may have forgotten the minor crimes Tyler committed in America decades ago, the consequences of which may have ballooned during his absence.

It was that quaint little mortgage refinancing scheme, *a folie de la jeunesse*, that earned him enough cash to make it to Europe. Rather than leave Jackson's crummy apartment in Woodside, where he'd been staying, he'd gotten on the horn the minute he was alone in the house and called people at random in the phonebook, offering them a better rate if they financed their mortgage through American Mortgage Values.

They were encouraged to send their checks, at the new reduced rate, to the particular P.O. box that he'd taken out in his name. Most callers either didn't pick up or hung up on him or told him to mind his own business, but on about every fortieth call he'd reach someone excited about saving cash.

What happened to abandoned P.O. boxes and their fraudulent contents? It must have filled with checks soon after his departure for Europe. They had been so difficult to cash anyway, even with the slick-looking American Mortgage Values ID card made for him by a dubious Italian type in a copy shop around Times Square. He had been running out of check-cashing places in negro neighborhoods as it seemed risky to go to the same one twice.

It was soon after plain clothes detectives had shown up at Jackson's place when he was off cashing checks that Tyler left for the continent. One could well assume, therefore, that Terence Richards (his identity at the time) and Johnny Conlon (his actual name) might be in hot water in America, depending on how much the police bothered with petty crimes. They may even have tied Richards and Conlon to Tyler Wilson, his primary identity since then, but couldn't be bothered to extradite him. Traveling to New York was beyond risky even if he comes up with a new identity. Was there really no one in Delauney's entire staff of operatives without an American criminal record?

But it was no good grumbling. Tyler can fret all he wants, but Delauney will take the villa away if he refuses to go, and if Ornella returns to *La Porqueria* and finds him living in a flea-bitten hovel on the outskirts of town, she will turn right back to Africa or Italy, any place he was not.

Tyler pours lots of salt on the pathetic excuse for a steak and carries it over to the tiny dining alcove. It looks entirely unappetizing, and the frying smell now permeates the house.

While dumping the plate (the miserable meal on it barely touched) into the sink, he hears the phone ringing again.

He's gulping down scotch when it finally stops.

Only to start back up again after a minute of reprieve.

What's most galling is that it's certainly not even Cal: just some *low-life, scumbag, bottom-feeding* imposter. He's searching for more old American insults when the phone finally ceases for a tender moment. But then it starts again, louder and more obnoxious than before.

That smarmy little voice comes back into his head, its dreadful drawled syllables. Cal had a bit of a society accent but never sounded quite that much like a *grande dame*. Of course, the pompous "*bruciato*" reference had to be considered uncanny, but he could have learned the damn story from the web of the world.

And the nerve to call himself Cal, like he had some sort of right to it, when it's Tyler who had shared his last moments on earth and understood, more than the fat American girl or anyone else, what the poor chap had been through in stuffy old Greenwich with that awful drunk for a dad. Men didn't reveal much to each other in those days, but Cal had spilled it all out in the wee hours of their first evening on Stromboli, his mood turning inward and angry, his lovely face shaking voluminously from side to side.

When the ringing stops and starts yet again, Tyler pulls himself to his feet, grabs the receiver so hard that the phone almost comes out of the wall, and claims Cal for himself.

"Cal Thornton here."

Silence on the other end as Tyler's words sink in.

"No," that same aggrieved-sounding voice childishly insists, "*I* am Cal Thornton, and Samuels and I will teach you a lesson you won't soon forget."

"You can't be Cal Thornton, and you can't be with Samuels," Tyler growls, though he'd just claimed to be Thornton himself and the caller has obviously hung up. "They're both stone cold dead."

Tyler's heart pounds, the room spins around him, but he feels the first modicum of self-satisfaction in months, confusing the hell out of that cocky asshole, the False Calvin Thornton, from whose name he's just created an acronym *a la* Delauney, the FCT. He doesn't know who the FCT is or where he's calling from, nor does he have any real sense of what he might want (though money in some form or other was never a bad guess), but he can safely assume he's been thrown off his game.

Since the collapse of the fund, he's sounded deflated when answering as "Tyler Wilson." "Cal Thornton," on the other hand, had popped resoundingly off his tongue like a bottle of decent champagne.

He'd only used it as an identity for a few brief weeks

right after returning from Stromboli. Nearly four decades later, it's the perfect alias for his New York errand. He would have no trouble remembering it, and it would be good fun to steal it away from that terrible telephoner.

He stands immobile with the phone in his hand, wondering if the impossible were true, if the man with whom he'd been speaking had escaped the blaze on Stromboli. It couldn't be ruled out. Martini had survived that lethal blow in the men's room of the Regency and had to be dispatched later on a train. One had to remember that.

His trusty intuition may no longer be reliable, but these phone calls confirm his hunch. He had heard neither the roaring traffic of the *Autovia del Sol* nor the high-pitched screeching of the Malaga Train. And he catches only eucalyptus and fried steak when he sniffs the air. FCT nor his real dead friend were likely in Spain.

Tyler thinks of Thornton Hall, Cal's grandiose Connecticut birthplace, and wonders if Cal might be calling from the place where the whole bloody business got started.

In Bel Vento, his mobile phone would tell him who was calling and from where, and if he could get just a little more life out of the broken old thing, it might contain a clue.

He finds it under some magazines and an undershirt along with the charger. The screen had busted when he'd tossed it at the wall the night before he left Italy, but he might be able to make out a few numbers if he can bring it back to life.

A few moments of charging later, a little bit of light returns to its dusty screen. The next time the FCT calls, it

19

should ring once before forwarding itself to the Spanish landline.

Within moments, it's ringing, but he can see on its screen it's just one of his contacts, his Italian tailor demanding to be paid.

The next call, only seconds later, doesn't turn out to be one of his creditors. He can barely see the screen but the preponderance of numbers confirms that his gut hadn't been lying to him: it is an international call.

Picking up the house phone on the next ring, he hears the sound of the FCT and knows he was right about the man not being in Spain, and Thornton Hall was as good a guess as any.

Cal had described it so vividly that night on Stromboli: wing after rambling wing, ballrooms and gardens.

Acquired by Cal's great-grandfather around the turn of the last century, the web of the world at the *poste restante* claimed the remaining Thorntons still live there, Cal's nephew Christopher having inherited the place.

Back when *La Moglie*'s tedious conversation had tried his nerves, Tyler had imagined moving there himself. Cal had invited him before things went off-kilter.

Tyler can still hear Cal's diatribe when he closes his eyes and concentrates hard enough. Cal's "pompous and hateful" old man would eventually get his way and drag Cal home, but he, Tyler, could come back with him.

"If you came with me, it wouldn't be as frightfully dull."

Not dropping by, passing the night, or even spending the season, but actually staying, moving in.

A policeman's son from Howard Beach.

It had made Thornton Hall seem like Tyler's birthright. After taking care of Delauney's business, he can go there and see it for himself. He'll tell Christopher and his family that he's Cal's long-lost friend. No, he'll tell them he's Cal, like he'd told the FCT on the phone. He'll have the passport to prove it, and to hell with them if they don't believe him.

And if they bring out the real Cal from some hidden wing of Thornton Hall, so much the better. It was a confrontation several decades in the making.

Tyler closes his eyes and pictures it once again: the blue flames creeping through the villa, himself dashing off into the distance down the hilly path towards the ferry to Milazzo.

It's not difficult to imagine Cal waking from his slumber and gasping for breath, not yet dead from the head wounds, the burns, the smoke inhalation.

Then running out of the beach villa just before it collapses and searching uselessly around the place until he's figured out that Tyler had fled the scene.

But what would he have done next? He hadn't come after Tyler seeking immediate revenge and would hardly have returned home with his awful father still in residence. Tyler imagines him spending his father's last years wandering the earth like a mad Dutchman, then landing back at Thornton Hall after his awful old man gave up the ghost.

Tyler's heart palpitates as he thinks about going there, blood coursing through his body. His fingers tingle. His privates harden.

Rather than waiting around for him in Spain, he'll show up at their doorstep, getting under Thornton skin, jangling Thornton nerves. The thought of entering his personal hornet's nest, the place that spawned Cal, gives him a devilish thrill. He slaps his cheeks to stop himself from giggling.

And the place will be chock full of answers if he figures out where to look. He'll stomp through hallways of gilded-age furniture until he reaches the children's wing, unchanged since Cal left for the continent. Gently, he'll rock on his old friend's rocking horse, maybe turn on the Lionel train set if it's still set up on the floor. He'll tear through the period pornography hidden in one set of dresser drawers and find the mediocre grades Cal received in school in another, sniffing the sweet residue of the boy's tender scent.

A bit calmer now that he has a plan, a gleefully incoherent one, he shakes out the leg which had gone stiff from standing, tosses the broken phone down to the ground, and limps up the stairs to the walk-in closet where much of what they'd taken with them from Italy had been stored. Naturally, he'd rather sit on the veranda with a cocktail, waiting for the evening to cool, but now that he's decided to enter America as Cal Thornton, he'd better find his impersonation gear.

The first few boxes are removed easily enough before the dull pains begin in his back, and his breathing becomes labored. Thank God he had been stronger in his youth or he would never have been able to bury dead old Samuels in Bel Vento's dirt cellar, back in the hectic period when the Delauney fund first almost unraveled.

A box or two comes open when he removes them, and he's surprised not to find the winter clothes of *La Moglie*, which should make up the majority of their storage. Now curious, he opens several more to find some dress shirts and trousers of his own but mostly the sheets and blankets from Bel Vento, which he thought had been given to the local convent to be distributed to the poor.

Ornella's winter clothes are nowhere to be found. He

must have been too preoccupied with the whole moving business to notice that she'd managed to store them someplace, perhaps her mother's house. Another box contains more useless sheets, the next old newspapers reeking of mold and deception. The absence of her clothes revealed her plans for the future, her stay in *La Porqueria* always intended to be brief.

Well, he can't think about that now. After he's returned from America, recharged his back account and his confidence, he can go to Africa and collect her.

Once he's caught his breath again, he manages to make his way through several old suitcases and boxes of newspapers until he gets to the metal tin with the combination lock and the words "inessentials" scrawled in black magic marker. The combination is his birthday, a date no one other than him can be counted on to remember.

The top layer is full of documents from the seventies when he worked on Delauney's early schemes: a British passport under the name John Woods with an image of himself wearing the excessive sideburns of those times, a Canadian one with a handlebar mustache and curled hair. He digs through the eighties, past the nineties into the new millennium. Underneath everything is the instamatic that makes passport-size pictures, and the machine that laminates it and stamps the USA motto, its three telltale stars. As forging only part of a document was in theory less illegal, Delauney has been sending Tyler passports without photos and letting him finish the job.

But if he's going to enter America as Cal Thornton, he'd better get to Delauney quickly to tell him which name to forge.

Their primitive communication system has worked well

over the years. Delauney has two voicemails. You call the first number and leave a message with the first of every third word. Then you call the second number and leave a message with the second, then the first number again with the third.

Bearing the disguise box, Tyler walks downstairs to the kitchen phone.

"Make the passport in the name of Calvin Thornton."

"Make in of," Tyler leaves on Delauney's first machine.

"The the Calvin," Tyler leaves on Delauney's second machine.

"Passport name Thornton," he leaves on the first again, which actually seems rather incriminating.

But how he can transform himself into Cal, he wonders, without knowing how the man has aged, what he looks like now? Or would have looked if he'd survived, he half-heartedly corrects himself. The magical Internet may offer some answer. The Spanish girl at his *poste restante* would most certainly help.

It may be pointless and daft, not up to the standards of the schemes of the past, but at least he has some idea how to respond to the madness into which he has fallen.

Done in by the long and complicated day, he gulps down the rest of his drink and walks upstairs to the couch in Delauney's old study where he usually passes the nights.

Sleep descends rapidly but soon tires of him. Wide awake at one in the morning, he closes his eyes only to find them opening again of their own accord. The smell of rancid olive oil occupies his nose from the dreadful meal he'd cooked himself, and disgust wracks his body from his recent series of terrible life choices.

Stretching his arthritic joints, he rises to his feet, and

wonders what he can do to tire himself out. His eyes skim quickly past the Graham Greene paperbacks on the bookshelf and the cheap radio on the coffee table to settle upon the photographs filling the walls, which he hasn't yet properly scrutinized.

Delauney kept framed snapshots of all of his operatives in each of his houses, some obscure protection against the double-cross, but Tyler sees only family images in the room where he had been failing to sleep. Just one glance at the enlarged portrait of Delauney's great uncle, the baron, smiling sardonically at him from the wall, has Tyler fleeing the room.

On the way down to the ground floor, Tyler finds several images from Delauney's mother's more criminal side of the family—*pieds noirs*, Algerian Jews, they'd been up to mischief for several generations. In a neat row right below them were the photos of the operatives, including himself looking dapper with the rather homosexual mustache he favored during the seventies.

Downstairs in the tiny living room/dining room, he finds several more formal portraits of not necessarily family members, a bulky society matron wearing an enormous pearl necklace, a skinny negro in a top hat. The only photo that looks at all recent is of a ridiculous-looking fellow about Tyler's age with dyed blond hair, a white summer suit, and a face he can't quite place but which looks eerily familiar.

September 7, 2001
9:00 AM

The long-faced Spanish girl at the internet café blinks

her bright brown, slightly triangulated eyes the following morning, takes the photo of the young Cal Thornton that Tyler has just printed from the Court TV pages of the World Wide Web, and puts it back on the screen of the printer. Money is tight these days, but Tyler has plenty of room on the debit card just sent to him by Delauney to pay the 75-dollar fee required by the *What They Look Like Now* webpage, which is supposed to allow a glimpse of the son who died young or the lover who left long ago, but can also reveal what people passed out in burning Sicilian villas might look like decades later.

"Now, we must scan, Mister Tyler."

"How long should this take?" he asks the Spanish girl.

"Very fast and then we will see."

The printer beeps jarringly to indicate that the scan has been successful, and the Spanish girl goes back to her computer. She has a few questions for Tyler before they can continue.

"How many years we add to the photo?"

The picture of Cal he'd found on Court TV must have been from his undergraduate days, a few years before Tyler ran into him.

"Forty," he replies, horrifically long ago.

"Okay," she confirms without commenting on what must be twice her lifetime.

"Does he smoke and drink the alcohol?"

It takes Tyler a moment to consider the question. Cal hadn't been much of a smoker but could keep up well enough in the drinking department. No reason to think he's given that up.

Apparently, that's all the information the computer requires. It plays a cloying electronic version of the William

Tell overture over and over again, trying to build suspense. Three or four minutes later, the overture stops, and they hear a shrill bing.

"Is complete," says the Spanish girl.

According to the computer sketch, the Cal Thornton of today is nearly bald, just quaint fluffs of down around the crown. His nose is a little red, and his cheeks are pudgy and indistinct, the computer adopting the modern, more puritan view of the deleterious effects of drink.

Grabbing the computer sketch from the girl, Tyler traces Cal's nose with his index finger, then his cheekbones, his sardonic face. Closing his eyes, Tyler conjures the awful voice he's been hearing on the phone. The same man? He just can't say.

Tipping the Spanish girl over-generously and grabbing the plane ticket, partially completed passport, mobile phone, and debit card that had arrived in his *poste restante*, Tyler jumps back into the Fiat and heads towards home.

Back at the villa, he heads straight upstairs, where he's stacked the dusty boxes. As luck would have it, the first one he chooses contains his metal disguise kit.

He takes it into the bathroom and is about to open it when he realizes that he must first rid himself of his hair. Unlike Cal's, it is quite resilient though he's had to dye it black. Finding a pair of trusty scissors that used to reside at Bel Vento, he goes in front of the bathroom mirror and clips away, then he shaves it with an electric razor until the floor is covered in hair and only a dim circle remains on the crown of his head. Checking the computerized image of the contemporary Cal, he sees that he's pretty much gotten it right.

He comes across a minor problem when he discovers

that his dye collection lacks peroxide or anything else that might turn his remaining hair white. Of course, he could take the Fiat back down into *La Porqueria* and poke around the *farmacias*, but he already feels depleted.

Next he must apply the nose putty. He stares at the computer print-out and then his own face in the mirror and back and forth again to isolate the exact difference in their noses. He determines that Cal's is broader and a bit thicker. The carefully applied putty on the sides and the top disappears into his nose without appearing so noticeable and changes the shape in just the right way. *Does the world really have room for two Cal Thorntons?* he wonders as he appraises himself in the mirror.

When he takes a final glance at the computer image of Cal, he sees that they're not actually so similar. But he's achieved what should be his main priority, making himself less recognizable. No one in America has likely seen Cal in decades, so resembling him is hardly crucial.

Before he allows himself a drink, he'd better take care of the passport. Tyler sets up the instamatic on timer mode, shuffles his face close to it, flicks it on, and waits for the flash.

The picture that develops a few minutes later looks reasonable enough, so he fits it into the appropriate area in front of the passport, and stamps it together with the embossing machine.

Presumably, Delauney has remembered to contact that brainy tech specialist in Bangalore and gotten him to hack into the US government passport system to make the magnetic strip read Calvin Thornton when they run it through the machine at immigration.

He has not eaten since the awful meal he'd made for himself the evening before. He also remembers the debit card that Delauney had loaded with expense money.

Tyler sips more white Rioja and chews spicy grilled squid at his favorite *chiringuito* a half an hour later, watching the Mediterranean waves dance in the lights, a sense of contentment washing over him. Why was he against this town, anyway? To hell with *La Moglie* and her nattering opinions. Thank God she's not there to ruin the evening he's enjoying with himself.

But just as the wine is magically mixing with squid tentacles, the brakes of an automobile slam down on the street, followed by the piercing sound of skidding. Metal doesn't smash into metal, but Tyler's heart has already jammed up into his throat, the FCT springing back into his mind.

Just because the man wasn't calling from Spain doesn't mean Tyler can waltz blithely around town. The next gulp of Rioja only helps a little, and the next bite of squid tastes so bitter that he spits it out—and suddenly his stomach rebels. Limping on his bothersome knees across the restaurant, he makes it just in time to the fetid *baño*, where he feels dangerously exposed. *La Moglie* would never show up for the funeral of a husband who died so disgracefully.

Back up the hill at Delauney's villa, the moment he turns the key into the lock, the phone starts to ring, twelve times before stopping. He's managed only one swallow of the scotch when it starts again.

Then again and again until he takes it off the hook at midnight.

Whoever the man is, he won't leave Tyler alone. He

reaches instinctively into his breast pocket for the blade he no longer keeps there, then roots around for a rusty steak knife instead. He feels a bit better with it clutched in his fists and positively exultant once he's started to stab the air around him, imagining what it would be like to knife the torso of the man whose picture was spit out by the *What They Look Like Now* computer program, his bright summer whites turning vividly red.

Once Tyler has exhausted himself, he lies down on the couch. His bags are packed and his documents prepared, but sleep steers carefully clear of him. The photograph of Delauney's great uncle, the baron, stares down on Tyler while he tosses and turns until he surrenders the room to him.

On the stairs, he catches a glimpse of himself, a confident smile under that handlebar mustache, and he wonders how he's managed to lose touch with himself so entirely.

While appraising the photo of the odd-looking fellow with dyed-blond hair again downstairs and wracking his brain to figure out where he's seen him before, he loses his remaining patience with Delauney's dark, cramped villa that Ornella had been right to complain about.

His flight doesn't leave until noon, and Malaga is only two hours away, but he's out the door and on the road by three in the morning.

Chapter 2
La Herradura, Spain

September 6, 2001
3:30 PM
Eve

Telephones ring with unpleasant people on the line, post-cards demanding favors pile up on her doorstep, and a nagging sense of being due someplace else wracks her fuzzy little mind as she slips in and out of an uncomfortable afternoon slumber.

A car honking brings her abruptly back to her senses, but she can't get her swollen little legs off the musty green sofa. They finally break free only to send her tumbling down towards the tile floor. Her hands find the three-pronged cane right by her side just in the nick of time, and, after shaking back and forth for a moment like a Virginia poplar in a windstorm, she steadies herself.

These exertions in the Spanish heat make more sweat drain through her armpits into her dark blouse and trickle down her cheeks from her dyed black sideburns.

Has Tyler followed her here, she wonders, looking around the room for signs of him, or has she been stalking him? They've been dancing their eerie tango since she first assembled him decades before. More than just her favorite character from the thriller books she writes, he was her ideal man. If only she had been able to pull him out from the page into the world, she would not have needed to trifle with those decades of girls.

Of course, it was perfect good fortune that, just as she was making poor Tyler begin her last book about him in her least favorite European country, she got word from Elizabeth Smalls that one of her friends had a beach villa available for a few weeks in *La Herradura*, which she has appropriately renamed *La Porqueria*. It is more than enough time for one of her research trips, but she's had to suffer alongside poor Tyler.

It's not just the heat she dislikes. That ancient Moorish blood, which is responsible for their triangulated eyes and easily tanned skin, makes them ruder than Frenchmen. Pedro (who is actually South American) is to drive her slowly down from the villa into town and back up again as many times as it takes for her to describe Tyler's path, but, rather than ring the bell, he beeps impatiently from outside.

After a quick tug on the Johnny Walker bottle in the bedroom bar, she descends the stairs with surprising alacrity and makes her way out to the parlor to find the driveway empty.

The scotch has improved the world, even this imperfect corner of it, and as she's in no hurry now that Pedro has failed to materialize. She has time to pour another jigger from the bottle in the downstairs bar and savor it while considering her next move. It is well on in the afternoon, and since Parkinson's has capped her likely lifespan, there's no reason to limit her pleasures.

It goes down all too quickly, however, and she knows better than to refill it before Pedro arrives, or she won't be able to write cogently in her *cahier* while being driven up and down the hill.

Another sound, this one off-key and electronic, pings mildly through the house. It isn't the tinny doorbell nor the shrill telephone. A few moments later, she identifies its source: the new computer Elizabeth Smalls and her awful Spanish girlfriend have installed for her to do research. Loosened by drink and her descent down the stairs, she manages to get herself moving again across the parlor into the dark study where it's located.

The cloying noise suggests it's broken, but the message on the screen displays the words "new mail."

"Aha," she shrieks, her heart leaping out from under her sweaty cotton blouse, "Tab!" Her lovely *Nederlandse kutjehas* has written back.

That moniker, "Dutch cunt," seems no less appropriate now that she's finally heard back from Tab, as Tab had flushed her from her mind the minute after brutally abandoning her.

In the first week or so after the affair was over, she'd heard Tab's breathy outgoing message when she called ("you know what to do"), but it didn't take the girl long to disconnect her machine. For a while after that, she'd get a dour Dutch voice, needing no translation, announcing that the number was no longer in service. Her letters came back "address unknown" in English as well as Dutch, as the little cunt wanted to make sure she understood that it was no good chasing after her.

It takes several minutes to figure out how to read the electronic mail. Her creaky fingers move that infernal rodent in useless circles only to learn that rather than her Dutch cunt, some American asshole is offering to enlarge her penis. The American requires no response, and the jitters that creep over her skin like the pox whenever she thinks about Tab (what Elizabeth dismisses as her "tiresome obsession") must be scratched the only way it can —by writing another electronic message.

It has been almost a decade since Tab vanished into the Dutch ether, but she's only been in any way reachable for the last five and a half days. Of course, when Elizabeth Smalls and her equally bossy young Spanish girlfriend had shown her how to enter names onto the "research engine," they expected her to look up the impressive pages that emerged when she put in her own name as well as anything that might help with *Tyler's Last*. She giggles as she imagines the sour expression bound to appear on Elizabeth's face when she figures out who was "researched" the minute she and her girlfriend were out of the house.

As well as acquiring Tab's electronic address, she'd managed to delve a little further into Tab's world and found that nothing much had changed. One photograph caught her in a black leather version of a space suit, her carrot-red dyed hair high above her head. In another, a young Tab sat erect in a metal chair, her pink Mohawk juxtaposed ironically against her ill-fitting American Girl Scout uniform.

She couldn't look at images of Tab without remembering the way the girl had made love to her after they'd first arrived at her garret apartment in Rotterdam, how she'd tossed the mattress onto the floor, grabbed her by her underarms, and pushed her back against the bed frame. After tying her tightly to it with some kind of cord, Tab had stormed out of the room and slammed the door, but just as the waves of annoyance, followed quickly by despair, had started surging through her tired old body, the girl had returned from wherever she had been, torn off both of their clothes and made vehement love.

The next image she clicks on, the classically rakish one of Tab wearing a top hat, a penciled-in mustache filling her mischievous face, reminds her of how Tab had repeated the bed frame bit the next afternoon but wandered out of the house after tying her up and did not return until evening.

At some point during the excruciating hour spent freeing herself, she'd wondered how Tyler would have managed, not that he would have ever been caught like that by any cunt, Dutch or otherwise.

Her first electronic messages to the girl came out startlingly sentimental—she would never have called her "my dearest Tab" when they were actually together—but when the girl still wouldn't respond, her mind got caught up again in their last encounter at the American-style bar where she'd waited with such airy stupidity, agonizing over whether they should live together in her house in France, return to Virginia where she grew up, or stay in Rotterdam, however little she liked the place.

Dabbing her finger at the beginnings of a tear, she remembers how nonchalantly Tab had shrugged her shoulders when she'd finally shown up. Then she gazes at the top hat on the screen, pounds the computer table with her arthritic little fists, and recites Tab's last words to herself.

"The old lady," she sighs, approximating the girl's blasé tone, "can stay in Rotterdam if she likes but this little frolic has gotten dull."

Her electronic messages to Tab have gotten darker, but sexier too, as she's kept writing them, the not at all dull things she plans to do to the girl. Lately, she's been raging like one of her edgier characters, Owen Sinistra after Eliza took a lover. Things cycled out of control pretty quickly for old Owen, she notes to herself, like they'd actually met.

The doorbell interrupts her reverie, the obsequious sort of sound that one expects from an Ecuadorian driver. She'd rather let the man wait outside while she writes Tab again but knows he'll leave her in the lurch if she doesn't get to him immediately.

"Good evening, *señora*," says Pedro when she opens the door. Having never done anything as indecent as marrying, she deserves to be called *señorita* despite her age.

"Good afternoon," she says back, giving him a quick look over. Short, dark, and slight, he looks simultaneously middle-aged and prepubescent, a little worse for wear in any case with his black hair matted like a street cat and his eyes crusted over and bleary. His button-down waiter's shirt and grease-stained flannel trousers look slept in. *A typical Indian*, she thinks, *the man can't hold his drink*.

She sits in back of Pedro's flimsy little jalopy as they descend the hill, inhaling gas, sweat, and cheap cologne.

After instructing him to turn around at the bottom of the hill and drive back up again, she gets out her pad and pen and starts to scrawl notes.

The grimy footpath begins in the sandy parking lot of the last *chiringuito* on the beach and meets the road just above its second floor patio.

They drive very slowly, but it's not really like walking. Getting out and trying a few steps might get her into poor Tyler's shoes, but it looks too steep, and she feels too frail. She feels even worse for the man when she remembers the inexplicable phone calls shattering his already dislocated world, something she won't really be able to sort out for him until she gets Tab out of her system.

As the road winds slowly uphill, she glimpses the ocean, the beach, the taller, uglier of the new *Herradura* condominiums but mostly just the mud-stained eucalyptus bushes overgrowing the road, and the tacky mission-style villas even more offensive than their Southern California imitations.

Poor Tyler, she thinks, *no proper shoulder to protect him from the sports cars roaring up and down the road.* Walking can make anyone feel like an outsider. Elizabeth Smalls's car wouldn't start one winter in Los Angeles, and they'd had to walk the mile from her house to the multiplex on the side of an interstate to see the offensive movie that German had made from one of her Tyler books, only to suffer legions of indignities, exhaust in their lungs, dirt in their clothes.

Pedro consents to driving down the hill and back up again a second time, but they get immediately stuck behind a delivery truck backing out of one of the villas.

When she looks back down the hill, she sees a shadow emerging around the bend.

He wears dark trousers and an elegant light-green shirt.

With a disorienting jolt, Pedro accelerates back onto the road once the delivery truck has passed, apparently having lost patience with the slow pace she'd requested.

About five minutes later, Pedro drops her off and wishes her a cursory good afternoon before speeding back down the hill as if he's remembered that he's due somewhere else.

Now exhausted and desperately needing to pee, she pulls herself up the stairs to the bathroom. Her limbs manage not to freeze along the way, but her heart beats worryingly, and she loses her breath. Piss spurts powerfully down into the toilet water like in the old days until it sputters to a close, leaving an uncomfortable sensation in her bladder.

The journey downstairs is easier, of course, and she moves straight into the room with the computer without even stopping to fortify herself with another drink. The electronic mail Tab has written in her absence will be plaintive, urgent, and will automatically disappear if it's not read immediately.

She finds no messages, not even from strangers trying to sell her things, but before she gives up and shuts down the computer, she puts Tab's name back into the research engine and discovers the following.

Fuck Death: Een installatie: Opening by invitation only. The Van der Horne Warehouse. Boomgaardsstraat 2343, Rotterdam: Featuring de kunst en: Elizabeth Jongens, Cliens Van Der Storle, Elizabeth Von Schinjnde, Anton Jongens, and Tabitha, the Fuck Witch. September 10, 2001.

What year is it now, she grasps for it, her mind and body shaking together, *what day, what month?*

Slowly, it comes to her, September 6, 2001.

She hasn't missed it yet.

September 7, 2001
7:00 AM

After lying uncomfortably awake most of the night, the old lady drifts into dreams in the early morning hours.

A voice from downstairs slips into her sleep.

"Wish fulfillment" was the proverbial dream interpretation of the irritable French psychiatrist she'd seen after her breakdown, who'd had dandruff on his collar and onions on his breath.

A blond girl sits on an Eames chair somewhere in northern Europe, reading a yellow index card just spit out from an enormous old computer.

Even without her reading glasses, the old lady can catch the gist of the SOS note from Tyler, but, before she can mull over the dangers lurking for him in America, it morphs into Tab's handwriting. An eerie apprehension grows in the old lady's gut as the voice from downstairs penetrates further into her dream, speaking American English but sounding cuntly Dutch.

Suddenly awake, the old lady pulls herself to her feet, stumbles across the bedroom to the staircase and descends, hanging on to the banister for dear life. Tab will disappear if she doesn't get to her fast enough.

Before she knows it, a firm young hand has grabbed her elbow, and a long narrow face with black hair has popped up out of nowhere.

Elizabeth Smalls and her awful Spanish girlfriend have made another one of their early morning raids.

Her little body shaking in disbelief, she starts calling the Spanish girlfriend by Tab's name, stuttering, "T…T… T…"

Then Elizabeth Smalls, resembling Margaret Thatcher in one of her many tweed skirts, guffaws pityingly and corrects her. "Her names is Lourdes. Can't you keep anything straight that doesn't involve yourself?"

The old lady bows her head but not in shame. She's considering how best to rid herself of them.

Elizabeth Smalls—naïve, no-nonsense, New England-born—cleaned up the old lady's stale Morton Street apartment and forced her back out into the world when she had been at such loose ends after Oriana had returned to her husband in the middle of the fifties. The old lady had cut things off with Elizabeth the moment she returned to some semblance of herself, but that gawky, hopelessly smitten girl stuck around after the romance had fizzled. Elizabeth, accompanied these days by that awful Spanish girlfriend, has been caring for her and invading her privacy ever since.

The old lady looks across the room and sees that the Spanish girlfriend (having adopted Elizabeth's intrusive habits) has checked the scotch bottle in the downstairs bar to see how much has been consumed since their last invasion and is now walking towards the computer in the other room to figure out what she's been up to.

The old lady is now awake enough to remember the traces of Tab all over the screen, which, if discovered, would cause an unbelievable hullabaloo, as Elizabeth Smalls has never forgiven her for falling so desperately in love with a Dutch girl years after they'd been together. Worse is that they'll see the invitation to Tab's opening and imprison her in Spain until it's come and gone.

"Lourdes," she says, urgently waving her three-pronged cane in the air, "I need you right now."

The Spanish girl beams with pleasure—as the old lady generally ignores her—and dashes back.

Once the old lady has gotten the attention of both of her visitors, she announces that she's feeling quite peckish and absolutely insists on taking her guests immediately to lunch at one of the *chiringuitos* in town.

To prove her point, despite the fact that she's wearing only a grubby sweat and pee-stained nightgown and the *chiringuitos* won't be open for another hour, she grabs the scotch, takes a significant sip, and stumbles out the front door into the humid outside, where it's threatening to storm.

After only a few breaths of fresh air, she feels one of her elbows being grabbed by Elizabeth Smalls and the other grabbed by Elizabeth Smalls's girlfriend. They are steering her back inside.

While it's true she's feeble-bodied and needs their help, she's nearly eighty, unless she's passed that already, and should be able to do as she pleases.

What she pleases to do is to yell at the top of her lungs, raising the same sort of ruckus she had as a child when Mother was doing something reprehensible.

And while her mother would have slapped her silly for such an outburst, Elizabeth Smalls and her Spanish girlfriend frown furiously but agree to be taken out to lunch once she's changed into more presentable clothes.

On their way out about twenty minutes later, after the old lady has put on one of her many pairs of blue jeans and a cotton sweater, Elizabeth attempts her usual bag trick, leaving it behind so she'll have to come back for it afterwards and stay God only knows how much longer poking her nose into the old lady's business.

"Elizabeth," says the old lady, firmly pointing to the drab blue backpack of the kind used by impoverished students in the United States.

Elizabeth shoots her a dismissive glance but gives in, putting the bag over her shoulder as they walk out towards her car.

Down the hill at *Linda Mar*, the only *chiringuito* open before noon, they sit at a table looking out over the turbulent sea.

The old lady sips the Spanish beer, which is all she's ordered, as she turns out not to be hungry after all. Elizabeth and her girlfriend exchange disapproving glances as they munch on olives and manchego.

"How does Tyler fare these days?" asks the girlfriend, who has heard the old lady refer to her character like a friend.

Not very well, she thinks to herself, looking gloomily out towards the water, then back at Elizabeth's Spanish girlfriend still looking at her expectantly.

"None of your business," she finally responds.

"We're pleased you've reduced your scotch consumption at least," says Elizabeth Smalls stiffly.

The old lady takes a big gulp of beer and smiles wryly at her. Elizabeth Smalls only knows about the downstairs bar.

"We've been having a hoot up at *Marina del Este*," says Elizabeth not very convincingly.

"*Fantastico*," chimes in the Spanish girlfriend.

"Just us two girls," rejoins Elizabeth Smalls.

"But we are very preoccupied of how you are alone," says the girlfriend.

"Worried," corrects Elizabeth.

Which means, of course, that they plan to move in with her. The two of them act all lovey-dovey but can't stand to be alone with each other.

She has to act fast, or they'll detain her indefinitely.

Helplessly, she looks around her at the waiters still setting up tables at the adjoining *chiringuito*, and the middle-aged couples in rain togs walking down the beach.

None of them will help her, but just as she's wondering how best to escape her jailors, she happens to look over her shoulder and see Pedro walking down the sidewalk on the opposite side of the street.

She gulps down the rest of her beer, jolts to her feet, and, without explaining herself to her stunned luncheon companions, manages to make her way out of the restaurant with her cane.

She almost gets run over by a couple of Spanish teens speeding on a Vespa but crosses the street while Pedro is still within yelling distance.

Unfortunately, her weak little lungs have given out on her.

"Pedroçito," she screams once she's got her breath back, as that was surely the little fellow's nickname, "I've got a job for you."

Pedro stops and turns around.

"Good money," she yells, which gets Pedro ambling towards her.

"You've got to take me someplace," she says when he's gotten close, "but it's far away."

7:00 PM

After Elizabeth and her awful girlfriend finally return to Marina del Este late that afternoon, the old lady gathers together her belongings for the long drive with Pedro the next day—several of her signature cotton sweaters, two pairs of blue jeans, and her only dress, a black one that has seen better days but will have to do.

Once her travel whiskey, pistachios, cash, and passport are in hand, she pulls out her *cahier* from the bottom desk drawer and tries to get Tyler to the airport as quickly as she can in order for him to wait impatiently for his plane to New York.

But each time she summons the concrete-block tourist hotels and limey retirement complexes on the road to Malaga, they turn into dank Dutch streets, and she sniffs rotting fish and toxic chemicals. Sighing plaintively, she abandons poor Tyler to his own devices and allows her mind to wander as it pleases, that momentous fortnight in Rotterdam ten years before.

Before Parkinson's, when she was barely in her seventies, practically a baby, she had been called upon to judge their annual film festival. She was an expert, they surmised, as her work had so often been filmed, all those terrible men impersonating Tyler.

She'd always liked the idea of travelling to the Netherlands, as she saw traces of her father in people's faces there. That poor man, treated unconscionably by her mother, came from Dutch stock. The weather always bothered her, though, so often raining and bitter, the food as well, pickled fish that lay heavy in one's stomach.

The judging turned out to be a dreary affair as she felt little about any of the dully experimental European films with their melodramatic montage and absence of good sturdy plots. For several long afternoons, she'd sat at the head of the long table in the antiseptic conference room assigned to the festival, sipping bitter Dutch coffee and wishing all those critics would leave for the lavatory at once, so she could slip her flask out of her black purse and pour scotch into her Styrofoam cup without provoking disapproval.

After the decisions were finally made with very little input from her, the stout German woman who had been staring at her quite abrasively throughout the deliberations grabbed her shoulders firmly with her meaty hand and asked if she wanted to go out and "take a beer."

"Or three," she jested with a hearty burst of Teutonic laughter.

The old lady's plan (worked out in detail during the endless meeting) had been to go back immediately to her hotel, delve into her stash of salted pistachios, pour a stiff drink, and take a scorching bath in the spotlessly clean and mod black-tiled tub.

"I really can't," she said to the fat (probably lesbian) movie critic.

"Of course you can."

It was true. She could, and maybe she shouldn't always be such a bad sport.

"Only for thirty minutes," she finally answered, "no more than that."

"As long as you like," said the German, her accent comically broad, more like the villains in old movies than the svelte, accent-less northern Europeans one tended to meet.

She was told to wait on a street corner outside, as the fat lesbian went off to get her car. Watching everyone slowly trickle out of the building until she was alone in the dreary drizzle, she considered ditching the woman and going straight home by herself, but before she could think to look for a cab to get her there, one of those kooky old Volvo minibuses emerged in front of her. The front seat opened, she climbed in, and played unsuccessfully with the broken seatbelt during the short drive to the bar.

That was the beginning of the nineties when darkness was still the rage. Every place was lit by candles scented with musky oils in imitation of some primitive era that one was lucky enough not to live in.

Not only was this place pitch black, but it had on some awful disco music that rumbled through her bowels as she went inside. She had to grab the fat Kraut's hand in order to avoid bumping into someone or tripping in the loud darkness.

As her eyes gradually adjusted, she saw a wooden bar on one side of the room, *à la Americaine*, with stools in front of it and bottles lined up below a long mirror in back. Delicate little tables, mostly occupied despite the early hour, filled the opposite side of the rectangular room. Many of the women wore old-fashioned flapper-style dresses, reminiscent of the era in which she'd first been taken from Winchester, Virginia, to New York as a child. Most of the men dressed with that same antiquarian formality—button-down white shirts, black jackets, with black ties. A few oddballs were dressed more like her—in jeans and cotton sweaters—so she didn't feel that desperately out of place. In fact, she rather enjoyed the genteel, old-fashioned atmosphere, what all of Rotterdam must have been like before the war.

While the fat Kraut found her a seat at an empty table and went off to get her a beer, she observed something peculiar about the nearest man in one of the old-fashioned suits, namely that he was not a man at all. All dykes, it occurred to her. She had been taken to a Sapphic bar. Yes, she had written that book under a *nom de plume* in which two women French-kissed, and she preferred them in bed however much they bored her at dinner, but that didn't mean she had to be taken to a place for lesbians. A beer was a beer.

Of course, she had frequented them in New York in the old days, even the rough ones the mob used to run, but there weren't many in Europe, at least not ones she knew of. And none of them were places one simply walked into from the street, particularly not in the bright light of the middle of the day. Going required careful preparations, elaborate subterfuge, so as not to be noticed by the police.

One could never just open a door and find only queers.

The fat Kraut returned, bringing several of her friends and a dark beer in a marvelously long tall glass.

After gulping quite a bit of it down, she turned to see who else she might be required to talk to: two older ladies in ill-fitting flapper dresses and a striking young woman with a shock of blond hair like people in the punk rock bands still popular at the time. Dressed unlike anyone else there in a black tee-shirt and gray flannel pants, she snarled alluringly around her at a scene that must have seemed woefully old school.

The two old dykes immediately engaged in Dutch conversation, but between the fat Kraut, the punk girl, and herself, there fell an uncomfortable silence.

It was exactly the point at which people generally asked some ridiculous question about Tyler. What was he really like? Well, he was just like in her books if they bothered to read them. Or (if they really lacked social graces) they'd ask if fooling around with Cal Thornton on Stromboli meant that Tyler was homosexual. She was quite prepared to look disgruntled and evade questions, but none were forthcoming.

She was happy being left alone but still felt uncomfortable. The place was loud, dark and increasingly packed. The judging had been more than enough human contact for the day, and it had been a mistake to allow herself to be dragged to a bar when there was plenty to drink in her hotel room.

An urgency in her bladder provided an excuse to stand up. She'd make her way to whichever dark place in back that they kept the lavatories and, rather than sit back down with the ladies afterwards, she'd nod distantly at them, find the front door and look around for a taxi.

Of course, the lavatory proved difficult to find. There were no doors with anything resembling Dam or WC when she searched in the back of the bar, so she slipped past the group of women, keeping her eyes safely away from them, and looked around the front. Still no signs indicated anything useful, but the second unmarked door she tried turned out to be it.

Once she'd left the blaring light of the lavatory, she had to stagger carefully forward with her hands in front of her until her eyes began to readjust to the darkness.

Almost immediately, she smelled a butch cologne and felt herself being yanked by the arm back into the bathroom.

She caught only a glimpse of Tab's blond spiked hair before the lights were cut off, and she felt her jeans being unbuttoned and yanked down her knees like she was a little girl about to be spanked. A harsh, almost feline sandpaper tongue overwhelmed her lower parts and she lost her balance while starting almost immediately to climax. Tab had to grab her ass to stop her from falling backwards against the toilet.

"Hurry, Mr. Tyler, hurry up," the girl commanded.

She searched around the wall for the light switch. Not wishing to kill the sexy brutality still shuddering through her body, she gave up on the light, went down on her knees and managed to find her pants and get them on without toppling over. She couldn't cope with the buttons, so her old-fashioned white underwear went on display as Tab dragged her through the bar into the still rainy Rotterdam evening.

From there, she was shuttled into the sour-smelling

back seat of a battered old Volkswagen. Tab was taking her home.

The French Border
September 8
11:00 PM

Torpid vehicles crawl forward through impenetrable border traffic, French and Spanish drivers gesturing melodramatically with their hands. After less than a week in *La Porqueria*, her name for *La Herradura*, the old lady has not only wrenched Tyler free (to New York) but has nearly escaped Spain. Pedro has not just taken her down the hill in order to bring her back up again more slowly. He's driven her all the way through the north of the country to the edge of France, which they'll need to cross along with Belgium to reach Rotterdam and the opening of Tab's show. It will take them a little more than a day with only a brief sleep stop, as Pedro assures her that he's a fast and efficient driver, having trucked from Lima to Guayaquil and back again many times when he was in his teens.

She's booked rooms for them in an American-style motel outside of Bordeaux for a brief nap about two-thirds of the way through their drive. Though she hardly relishes all that time with Pedro, no one else she knows will help transport her without reporting the matter back to Elizabeth Smalls, who can be counted on to nip the expedition in the bud.

The delicious thought of Elizabeth's palpable disapproval when she gets wind of her departure makes the old lady snort so loudly that Pedro yanks his head sharply around, worried that she's having some sort of seizure.

Along with the requisite scotch flask, she's brought a spiral notebook to keep up her cahier along the way.

September 8 11:30 PM Finally crossing into France.

I'm writing in my cahier, chewing the salted green pistachios that are all my stomach can take, and peeing, simultaneously. Except for my guffawing fit several hours ago, Pedro has kept to his agreement not to look back at me as I may have the kitchen funnel from the villa under my black skirt and be straining to pass water into the empty Johnny Walker Black bottle. Of course, I shake while I'm doing it, spilling pearls of pee.

I'm not too worked up about hygiene, though, as I'm preoccupied with poor Tyler, the question of what will become of him now that I'm so dotty and infirm. I've got him safely out of La Porqueria, but I don't know what lies in store in America. I sense his presence, not the living specter I'd seen climbing the hill the other day, but his troubled mind and failing intuition, as Malaga grows smaller and smaller below him through the plane window. Once I've dealt with my Dutch girl, I'll concentrate on Tyler. I can't let him loose unprotected in a lion's den like Thornton Hall.

"Dearest Teelor, (as Ornella had lovingly called him before she grew tired of his indifference and discovered the almighty taste of pussy) I incant as we build up speed now safely in France, trouble may be on its way, but your last can't come before my own, and we both have a little more in store."

1:00 AM Darkness approaching Bordeaux

I can see lights off the sides of the long straight highway but no particular sense of the landscapes surrounding us. Cars zip blithely by in both directions, these modern European highways nearly American.

The doctors say the nerve condition will get me within the year, and Elizabeth tells me I should be reflecting upon the choices I've

made, the person I've become. "Carpe Diem, Carpe Diem," the ole-
aginous headmaster of that awful school in Winchester would tell us
girls, and while not every day is available to be seized, what I don't do
now will never get done. Perhaps it's the scotch into which I have been
dipping as the car roars forward into the night, but I feel a dangerous
sense of possibility. Tab will hardly thrill to see me, and I have no
plan to change her mind. Once I get to her, though, I can finally spit
out the taste she left in my mouth. I can teach her the lesson that I had
been too besotted to teach her before, that you can't call yourself Tyler
then hang his mother out to dry.

A few hours later, now deep in the night, she listens to Pedro snore in his adjoining motel room, knowing she too must sleep to steel herself for tomorrow.

But whenever she closes her eyes, they open reflexively back again. The scotch-driven optimism has soured into hung-over despair, the devilish problem of what to do when she gets to Rotterdam. She can't just show up at the girl's opening and expect her to stand idly by and let herself be confronted. The old lady has to come with some kind of plan. Resolving to get out her *cahier* tomorrow and work that out makes her breathe more easily, but she's still too keyed-up to sleep.

She flips on the lamp at the side of the bed and concentrates on the languorous nude in the Renoir reproduction on the wall until its nipples turn into Tab's nipples, its thighs turn into Tab's thighs, and its far fleshier abdomen recalls the skinny girl prancing naked around her barely renovated tenement apartment.

Lightheaded suddenly, the old lady grabs hold of the bedpost but the motel room still fogs before her eyes. She gazes longingly at the rumpled sheets and musty carpeting as they become less and less distinct while she gets whisked back to the American-style bar, and from there, to the girl's apartment.

Where they had been drinking beer all afternoon, red wine all evening, and hitting the schnapps as the hour grew late, a habit Tab had picked up during a residency in Vienna.

The old lady had only managed a bite or two of stale croissant and a rotting pear from the refrigerator, and all that drinking on an empty stomach quickly got her ears buzzing, a tinnitus that would take months to get rid of.

She hadn't discussed the ongoing rain with the girl, nor the film festival she'd spent the last several days attending. Not a word about the elections raging in the Netherlands at the time, nor the nonsense in the Balkans. Everything was all about Tyler. Tab, who seldom looked at anything as bourgeois as a book, had read her Tyler novels and loved how bold he was, how lawless—hardly the first dyke to fall in love with the man. Tab's blue eyes wild, her bangs tumbling down her face, she'd carried on about his early days taking care of business for Delauney to the old lady like she'd been there herself, using that awful American expression, "kick ass," to describe him.

And Tab insisted on interrogating her about him.

First, she wanted to know if Cal Thornton had died from the blow he received or the smoke inhalation or somehow not died at all. But then had the gall to change the subject and question whether Tyler had actually ever "fucked the wife," wagging her finger in the air like she'd nailed him.

The invasion of Tyler's privacy sent shivers up the old lady's spine, coming up acidic in her mouth. And asking wasn't enough. The girl had to make something up herself, describing the poor man driving powerfully into Ornella doggy style as his mind went out the window and his wife went through the motions.

"You left all that out," she bitterly insisted, "but I figured it out."

Tab had looked so adorable saying it, though, her eyes wide and intoxicated, her lovely pink tongue enthusiastically licking her chops.

She'd called the old lady "Mr. Tyler" in the bathroom of the American-style bar, but claimed the role for herself the minute she got the old lady into her bedroom, referring to her as Ornella and fucking her voraciously with a chocolate-colored dildo found discarded on the dusty floor. None of her previous lovers (Elizabeth Smalls, God forbid!) had seemed anywhere near worthy of the man, but closing her eyes and letting her hands lie limply by her side, the old lady couldn't help but imagine that Tyler was the one inside her—some lovely blond incarnation of her ideal man.

But what ruined the tender moment just after their lovemaking was the sure knowledge of how irate Tyler would be if he found himself in bed with the likes of her. Even Ornella had become too old and female for him, and the old lady's withered body with its gray hairs, wrinkles, and odd smells would sting the hell out of him if he got too close.

And how much worse she is these days—she thinks, as she stares glumly at the Renoir nude—losing her continence and her mind.

Crawling deep into the sheets, she sinks into the sour-smelling pillow and calls out for Pedro next door, trying to make him come take her back to Spain. The little man won't listen, and soon the whole bloody business starts back up again, Tyler's ears still ringing on her second day with Tab. They talked about him constantly with none of the respect he was due. The old lady had pictured him smoking his morning cigarettes at Bel Vento, looking down the cliffs at the sea and feeling the acrid taste of betrayal in his gut.

But those irrepressible gap-toothed smiles that shone from Tab's face whenever she got more dirt on him made the old lady's compressed little chest ache and got her asking unwholesome questions about being someone's mother and lover at the same time.

The old lady would remind herself that the flimsy door of the garret apartment was unlocked and all she had to do was slip out when Tab wasn't looking and keep on going until she found a cab. But her not-unpleasant old life already seemed impossibly dismal.

Meanwhile, the girl got harder to please, making the old lady infringe even further on Tyler's privacy.

Immediately after the suffocation of Samuels, he'd climbed up the stairs to Ornella's bedroom, where she lay deep in sleep, lifted up her nightgown, and pushed himself inside her the same way he'd pushed the pillow over Samuels's mouth, making her climax indecently despite her upper bourgeois Italian Catholic inhibitions.

Unimpressed, Tab insisted that the old lady wasn't giving her the full picture. Tyler had to be cuckolding his prudish Italian wife since he was still a potent young man when he met her and a queer one at that.

Unsatisfied that the art-fraud and money-laundering business were "all encompassing," she insisted that if the man wasn't cheating with boys, he had to be engaging in onanism.

Grumpy looks creeped over her face when Tab didn't get the details she wanted. It broke the old lady's heart, the way she checked the large plastic clock above the rust-stained refrigerator whenever she started feeling bored.

After another rotten pear lunch on their third full day together, the old lady found herself spilling embarrassing secrets, Tyler's journeys down the dark streets behind *Napoli Centrale*, his humiliating encounters with those train-station trollops.

And later that afternoon, why should she resist the rush of acting out the roles, sometimes a boy, sometimes a girl, but always fucked dismissively, and paid cheaply for it, with a crumpled Dutch Kronen she later returned to Tab?

"How'd you like that, whore?" Tab asked once she was sated, smacking the old lady's face with her hand though she had to know that Tyler would have never said anything of the sort and was gentle with his prostitutes.

The vibrant pain in her cheek exhilarated the old lady, another new sensation flickering through her body. But the girl was careful to keep her off-balance. After raising her hand again, she went into her freezer for some oily ice cubes and gently applied them to her bruises, then started making her cup after cup of weaker and weaker sugary tea from the same cold leaves in her old black pot.

What hooked the old lady most of all were the melancholy mornings when the sleepy, hungover Tab—softer and kinder early in the day—would let her ramble pointlessly, mostly about Father, who'd been much on her mind since Mother had given up the ghost that fall.

When the old lady was a young child—on the infrequent visits that Mother would allow—Father would take her for hot chocolate and pie a la mode at the big restaurant in the old hotel in downtown Winchester, then sit her on his knee in his new Packard outside and tickle her cheeks with his scratchy whiskers. The old lady was much more fortunate than her leading man, she would explain to the Dutch girl, as Tyler's policeman dad had jumped ship before the boy was even born.

Tab would look sadly over at her when she woke up each day, sympathizing or just lost in her head, until her patience evaporated all at once in the middle of their last night together.

That awful morning, the girl woke up glaring poisonously and kept it up all day. The old lady tried to come up with something even more humiliating about her leading man but drew only blanks. "You know when Tyler," she began, but the girl just rolled her eyes and shuddered. Pounding her thighs with her fists, Tab cursed under her breath, a whole week of her young life wasted on a fictional man.

Who was just, she declared while slamming her bedroom door, "a closeted little deviant."

Shaking and sweating, the old lady camped out on the battered easy chair right across from the bedroom door and trembled each time she heard Tab curse inside.

She shouldn't have been so surprised by Tab's cruel last words about their *frolic growing dull* when the girl had stormed so furiously from the house that afternoon, insisting on her way out the door that they meet later outside of the house for a drink at the same American-style bar.

Tab had ditched her as effortlessly as Tyler's dad had ditched Tyler and what made it worse was that she had begun to feel Tyler slipping away himself. By the end of that pungent week spent embarrassing him with Tab, she could no longer summon him to the page. For nearly a decade, she suffered fruitlessly in France rehashing other old thriller characters while receiving lousy advances and even worse reviews. She had finally caught up with Tyler again only a few months before, just as her own last was starting in earnest.

Back in the cloyingly soft motel bed, the old lady slips into a state close to sleep, but the ridiculous question Tab once asked her wakes her wide up again.

"So who is he anyway?"

The obnoxious little Jew on the BBC had wondered the same thing.

"Your father?" Tab had demanded.

A handsome fellow, victimized by Mother, but with not one quarter of Tyler's balls.

"Your mother?"

Cruel and strong like Tyler, but brutish and inelegant.

Tyler was brilliant, tempestuous, powerful, and suave. The absence of real men like him had forced her down the Sapphic path.

And the person most like him was not like him at all.

Who else had his excruciating beauty, his bloodthirsty energy, his absence of fear? Who else could call herself by his name without looking like a fool?

"My father," she had lied to get herself off the hook.

"Thought so," the obnoxious girl had declared.

The next time the old lady wakes up, it's morning and Elizabeth Smalls fills her mind. She giggles as she imagines

Elizabeth's crestfallen look when she deduces she's been off seeing Tab, then frowns when she hears Elizabeth's little snicker, convinced the girl would rebuff her again.

But this time, the old lady won't just take it like a wallflower, weeping dismal tears while her Dutch cunt strolls out of the American-style bar. With Tyler as a model, she will find a way to force the girl's hand. Pedro is already on board to help, and she can hire others. Immigrants come cheap, and she's got plenty to spend. Eventually, she'll allow Tab to get on with her life, but she can't let her just slip away, not after all the turmoil she's caused. Fair is fair.

Chapter 3
Mid-Atlantic

Delauney could have paid for business class or at least found Tyler a decent seat assignment. The Iberian flight across the Atlantic has him cramped into the window surrounded by a large American and her young son.

As a young man, he preferred window seats, staring at the hills and valleys of unfamiliar foreign cities, but now, having been everywhere he wanted to go, he can only abide planes when he can freely kick his legs out into the aisle.

He wishes he had thought to fill his flask with whiskey and bring it along. The few weak drinks they are likely to serve him will be far from enough to knock him out, but at least he's made it safely out of *La Porqueria*, driving the Fiat to Malaga without incident.

The little American boy in the middle seat next to him has the good grace to fall immediately asleep. But he wakes up wailing when the rattling old plane reaches cruising altitude. The mother, monstrously obese in the contemporary American manner, is too busy to tend to him, going through her enormous brown purse in search of useless makeup items.

The boy stops wailing but starts flailing his little hind legs instead. Mostly, he hits the seat in front of him but occasionally twists around and nails Tyler's arthritic right knee.

"Madam," says Tyler to the American lady, now in the process of applying some gruesome mascara, "can you tell the little fellow to stop kicking?" The words, once out of his mouth, sound terribly stentorian. "Uptight" was the word Americans used for anyone fussing about anything.

"John Edward, stop bothering the nice man," says the lady with the type of broad southern accent one rarely encounters abroad.

Which gets John Edward kicking so frenetically that Tyler has to squeeze his body against the window to avoid being maimed. The child finally exhausts himself about fifteen minutes later, at which point Tyler sees the stewardess slowly approaching with the drink cart.

"Could sure use some wine," announces the American woman.

"Me, too," admits Tyler, allowing frustration and politesse to get the better of common sense. If one talks at all to such creatures, one risks getting stuck talking for the whole flight.

So many years out of the country, but he can still recognize her type: chatterbox, probably a busybody. Those old terms come back to him.

Except she's doing something unexpected. Rather than carry on about her recently completed European tour and life in the provinces, she starts asking him questions.

She wants to know what his name is. She wants to know where he lives. She wants to know why his family isn't accompanying him on the return voyage to America.

"My name is Calvin Thornton, and I live at Thornton Hall in Greenwich, Connecticut," he says stiffly.

Tyler explains to the obese American that he works as a salesman for a vacuum cleaner outfit, mostly on radio and television campaigns since the door-to-door angle stopped working in the crime-ridden 70's. His two children (Amy, eight, and William, six) are travelling to Paris with his wife, Joanne, but he could only participate in the Spanish part of the trip, as he's due back at work in Stamford the next day.

He may have made his kids too young, Tyler realizes, as he looks more his age (just past sixty) without his hair, but it would be just about par for a vacuum cleaner salesman to live in a place with a lofty name like Thornton Hall. It could be a pretentious middle-class housing development.

"What do you think of the old country?" she now wants to know, but, before he can dream up what this incarnation of Cal would say, she launches into her own opinion, the part of the conversation in which she felt required to express interest in him thankfully over.

She complains bitterly about the restaurants that never bothered to open until several hours after dinnertime and then served only spicy, garlicky food. People drove miles over the speed limit and, despite the beastly heat, could not be counted on to air-condition their business establishments. Suddenly, she's moving her face close, overwhelming him with her flowery perfume and whispering into his ear about the devastating experience they'd had at the beach the other day, "ladies with their boobies out."

"Despicable," agrees Tyler, slithering into the skin of this provincial Cal Thornton, so different from the sophisticate he'd encountered in Sicily. "Reprehensible."

Claiming the the same view of the old country as the woman and feeling his third glass of white wine wash over him, he soon drifts off to sleep.

Tyler wakes up a few hours from New York, feeling achy and claustrophobic, but he locates one of the last Ativans from the Sant'Agata pharmacy in his wallet, and everything is made bearable again.

4:00 PM Eastern Standard Time

With companionable grace, he says goodbye to his new-found friends and limps as quickly as his knees will allow him through the long series of JFK corridors, so he won't have to wait forever at the passport line.

After picking up his baggage and carrying them through the "nothing to declare" line without being questioned, Tyler slips into the bathroom. After a jittery pee in a good old American urinal, he gets out the kit to touch up the nose, which doesn't turn out to be as misshapen as he feared.

Several people come in and out of the bathroom during the process. A group of short indigenous-looking people who look as if they've arrived from Ecuador or Peru, some Italian tourists carefully combing their hair and applying sugary perfume, and a handsome negro who wishes him "good day" in an African accent. This was the positive side, he remembers, of the New York experience. One might be put off by the solitary life among the decrepit buildings, but no one particularly questioned another's behavior. He remembers the Italian type making his fake American Mortgage Values identification card without asking a single question.

An enormous vehicle the size of a small van picks him up on the taxi line, a modern version of the checker cabs of old. He provides the driver the name of the dingy midtown hotel that Delauney has booked for him, but before he can settle in and enjoy the ride, observing all the changes the decades have wrought, he checks in to get his instructions.

The mobile phone takes about a minute to come to its senses. It beeps once it does, the words "new message" appearing on the screen. Tyler gets out the little paper provided by Delauney and follows directions: the number sign, then 72, then 4233, probably a meaningful password in Delauney's numerological universe.

A brusque-sounding Russian voice gives him directions.

He's not allowed to go to the hotel and rest up. He must proceed immediately to the subway as "yellow cab from airport may be watched."

What follows are subway directions: the Howard Beach A train, changing to the F train at Jay Street to the Brooklyn Aquarium stop, almost the end of the line. A walk along the boardwalk will take him to Café Tatyana, but "not to go to Tatyana but to turn left instead" onto Brighton Beach Avenue.

A half block down, he must enter the glass door of an establishment called The Love Club, which makes Tyler recall the difficult 1970's when one felt required to make love not only to one woman but several at the same time.

In the entrance area of The Love Club, he is to ask the "fat man" if he can speak to a woman named Eve, an unlikely-sounding alias.

"The Eve," concludes the Russian's message, will tell him how to proceed.

The subcontinental cabbie, who had already started to grumble about taking him on that most standard of routes, JFK to midtown, curses in his tribal tongue when he learns he is being redirected to the nearest subway.

Quickly and sullenly, he drives, slamming the brakes periodically and dropping Tyler off ten tense minutes later in front of the Howard Beach station.

Tired and confused, Tyler can't quite grasp what the

young Hispanic MTA official in the dirty blue uniform is trying to explain. Tokens are a thing of the past. New York City, in imitation of the slicker European metros, now has a plastic card on which one can electronically stamp money to gain access to the train. Tyler only buys one ride as he hopes to taxi to his midtown hotel once his errand is complete.

Thankfully, there are only two choices of trains, and since he knows the Rockaways, where he spent many the clammy and uncomfortable summer afternoon with his mother, lies further into Queens, he figures he'd better head the opposite way, as that should eventually lead him to Brooklyn.

The A Train
5:30 PM

The air tastes pungent down on the tracks, familiar after decades. But what's happened only hits him after several gloomy minutes with no sign of a train: Delauney has been toying with him. Knocking away his entire adult life on the continent, he's stuck Tyler now right where he had the misfortune to grow up. The A train of the Billy Strayhorn song is in Harlem at least an hour northwest, but the Howard Beach station is only minutes from where Tyler had lived with Mother in a gloomy post-war apartment building that no one would think to tear down. He feels it nearby, radiating harm.

Not a sense of nostalgia, nor even exactly contempt, but a bad memory from when he was nine years old sneaks into his head and won't allow itself to be dislodged.

They'd gussied up the station—fresh plaster, new tiles

—but it's the same place where he waited with Mother one afternoon to go to a big street called Grand Concourse. In the faraway Bronx, Aunt Millie was dying.

Previous subway journeys had been short but exciting—dark crowded staircases moving deep into the earth, machines zipping forward underground faster than buses. But once the train arrived that afternoon, they'd stayed on for many more stations than ever before, and the swaying back and forth had made him sick to his stomach. Proud of himself for keeping it together after it was finally over, he was dismayed when they didn't climb back up to the street it but got on a different train instead. A few stops later, Mother could tell he was going to vomit and handed him the supermarket bag she'd brought along just in case.

The elevator was out in Millie's building, and Mother let him rest on the seventh floor before yanking him up to the fourteenth.

A negro nurse ushered them into a cluttered apartment smelling of medicine and old age.

Plump and capricious when she'd visited them in Queens before the cancer, Millie lay emaciated and drawn on the bed, her face like a mask. She'd stopped eating, the negro nurse told Mother, and it was only a matter of time.

"Say goodbye to Aunt Millie," Mother had commanded.

Johnny (his name back then) obediently mumbled, "goodbye Aunt Millie," but that didn't turn out to be good enough. He was required to get up close and kiss her paper-thin cheeks. It was lucky he'd lost all of his cookies on the train as the death in her breath made him gag.

Next, he was supposed to wait outside with the negro nurse while Mother said her own goodbyes, which he could hear through the door while chewing the stick of cinnamon gum the nurse had given him. A low muttering, almost a moaning, was how Mother sounded when she was most upset.

When she finally emerged from the sickroom, she wiped tears from her eyes with her shirtsleeve, nodded disapprovingly at the negro nurse and started the long descent down the staircase, pulling Johnny so fast he kept nearly tripping.

Outside the building, they were catching their breath before hiking back to the train when Mother suddenly stiffened, the hand holding Johnny's tightening like a vise.

Johnny looked up and down the street and back into the lobby but didn't see anything out of the ordinary.

Mother's body was fluttering, her teeth were chattering.

"Go Johnny," she stuttered, "go back in there and hide."

"There" meant the lobby, and Johnny did what he was told.

The lobby door had windows, though, so he could watch her from inside.

First, she walked up to Grand Concourse and perched on its lip, rattling back and forth. Then, after finding a break in traffic, she plunged into the street. Brakes squealed, a car in the second lane stopping just in time.

When another got so close that Johnny worried she'd been hit, he slipped out of the lobby and walked up to Grand Concourse himself. His heart beating quickly, he only saw only buses, trucks and cars, until he caught a glimpse of Mother, already on the other side, grabbing hold of a tall man in a blue uniform.

Which didn't make sense, until it did. The only policeman that Mother could be trying to kiss was his father.

Johnny couldn't tell if this was a good thing or a bad one. Sometimes Mother said that his father would come back one day and make everything okay, and other times she would say that his father would return to give him the proper beating he deserved.

Johnny stared as hard as he could at the gray moustache and the beginnings of a gut but couldn't focus on the man's face. Was there anything soft in it, or was it as hard as Mother's?

Stepping into traffic, he tried to cross like his mother had, but several cars beeped at the nine-year old trying to jaywalk the big street in the neighborhood far from Howard Beach, where his father had got himself reassigned once he'd learned there was going to be a baby.

Johnny made it back to the sidewalk safely, and when he looked across the street again, he saw that his father was walking briskly away. Mother was trying to follow him until he stopped, waved his fists in her face and said something which made her crumble to the dirty ground.

Johnny stepped out into Grand Concourse again to try to get across to her, but a bus zoomed by, scarily close, and he lost his will.

Slipping back into the lobby of the building where Aunt Millie was dying, he watched as best he could from there. A few minutes later, Mother got up, wiped the sidewalk off her dress and walked away, probably in the direction of the corner where she could cross with the signal.

When Mother finally arrived back to the apartment building, Johnny could see she was inflamed. Her eyes were red from crying, and her mascara was running down her cheeks. Motionless, she glared down at him for the longest time before shaking her head, grabbing his hand and leading them both away towards the subway.

It was all his fault, and he would never be able to live it

down. His best shot was to get as far away as he could as soon as he was big enough to get the chance.

The A Train
6:00 PM

Fifty odd years later, the characters on the train are mostly the same, except along with negroes and Puerto Ricans, there appear to be several grimy Central Americans, a subcontinental family in shabby western clothes, and a tall man in blue robes who looks African. Senegalese, Tyler wonders to himself, recalling *La Moglie*'s colonial nostalgia tour.

A few steps into the long ride, an old orthodox Jew gets on the train dressed in a filthy version of their traditional regalia: nineteenth-century black clothes, ridiculous sideburns, silly cap. Tyler remembers them being rather well put-together, but this one is an absolute disaster. His pants are unzipped, his shoes untied, and his beard grows wildly down his chest. He smells terribly of alcohol and indigestion.

After staying seated for a stop or two, swaying back and forth on his hips and muttering to himself, the Jew stumbles to his feet and does a sort of awkward lap around the subway car. His unpleasant odor, overwhelming as it gets closer, almost makes the chicken and rice served on the plane come back up Tyler's troubled esophagus.

After exactly two laps, the man grabs hold of the subway pole and stares sourly around the car. Tyler, letting his curiosity get the better of him, looks the Jew in the eye, and, as a result, becomes the primary audience for the following monologue.

Apparently, everyone has been stealing from the Jew. The Nazis have been stealing from the Jew. The Russians have been stealing from the Jew. All *goyim*, as a matter of fact, have been stealing from the Jew. But worst of all, the Jews have been stealing from the Jew, this Jew at least. The Jews, he claims, have "jewed me out of everything."

Tyler gets spotlighted as, apparently, he "thinks he's better than us" with his "fancy bald head" and "dirty Dolce and Gabbanas." The surprisingly fashion-conscious Jew informs Tyler that he's as bad as an "SS commandant" or "communist Arab," a "dirty peasant" in any case. *Not true*, Tyler thinks to himself, lower-middle-class Howard Beach to be sure, but then years on the continent.

The Jew, Tyler gathers, must have more or less taken over America. He wouldn't be surprised to find men wearing peculiar nineteenth-century clothes in Congress or the boards of Fortune 500 companies.

Words to that effect form deep in Tyler's throat, but he swallows them back before they get to his tongue. He won't be able to do his errand for Delauney, nor go on his fact-finding mission to Thornton Hall tomorrow, if he gets mauled by a crazy Jew.

Whose accusations still ring in Tyler's mind after he gets off at the next station. He'd stared into Tyler's eyes like he knew who he was. *Could he somehow be connected to the FCT?* Tyler wonders for a paranoid moment.

At an enormous station called Jay Street, Tyler climbs down a flight of stairs onto a dingy platform underground where he must wait for the orange line to take him to the ocean.

About fifteen minutes into the F train ride, the train

limps out of the tunnel onto an elevated track, slowly rocking forward in the direction of the sea. Tyler sees legions of clapboard houses and the occasional Soviet-style soulless apartment building looking empty in the middle of this workday. Only orthodox Jews walk the streets with their black clothes and long beards.

They pass over an enormous cemetery, which reminds Tyler of the ones he grew up near in Queens, the sort of place he had been destined to spend eternity before escaping to the continent. He has no idea where he will buried now that *La Moglie*'s family plot in Sant'Agata is presumably no longer available to him. Pretty much anywhere would be preferable to the colorless graves and pompous mausoleums passing below him with their faded flowers and Irish names.

Tyler gets off the train at the penultimate station and takes a concrete ramp over the Coney Island aquarium that lands him on the boardwalk.

He wheels his bag as best he can over the uneven wooden planks, taking in the wizened old Russian men in their Speedos and muscle tee-shirts and the round-shaped old Russian women in their bikinis and sundresses, who make him feel out of place in his travel suit and terribly hot in the merciless sun.

The directions turn out to be spot on, except it's difficult to pass by Café Tatyana without stopping in for at least one drink. The European-style café tables point towards the Atlantic glimmering in the distance.

A buxom but muscular bottle blond grabs him by the arm when she sees him gazing enviously at the café and tries to steer him towards an empty table.

He tries to pull away but can't quite match her strength.

The harder he tries, the more she hooks him in, smiling merrily all the way as if it were a normal way to do business.

"*Ostav' menyu v pokoye*; leave me in peace," he finally says, recovering a bit of the Russian he'd learned for one of Delauney's early errands, which confuses her enough to loosen her grip.

After making his escape, he takes a right turn, as instructed by the phone message, onto a murky side street, then a left onto a large boulevard with another elevated train running above it. A couple of blocks later, he sees a concrete one-story building with a giant sign dwarfing its tiny entrance. Its enormous red letters blink "love" and "café" over and over.

The door opens easily enough, bringing him into a foyer covered head to toe with mirrors. Above, below, and across from him, he's confronted with his shaved head and pouchy eyes. He zips the zipper that he'd forgotten to zip in the international urinal at JFK and gazes warmly into his weary, handsome face.

"Dear old Tyler," he whispers lovingly to himself.

Of course, the fat man who is supposed to instruct him is nowhere to be found, nor is anyone else for that matter, but, after several minutes of careful inspection, he sees an indentation in the glass that turns out to be a door.

Which opens into a room much larger than he would have thought possible in such a small building. Long, oval-shaped tables are set up with fruit plates and bottles of vodka and Coca-cola. Disco balls light the ceiling, and there is a dais in back for entertainers to perform. Nobody plays now, but what sounds like Russian hip-hop blasts loudly from the distorted stereo, shaking his delicate bowels.

He sees only waiters bringing fruit and vodka to the non-yet-stocked tables, but just as he's beginning to worry he may be in the wrong place, an enormous fat man with a bushy black beard (classic bear, if one likes the type) emerges from the back with a frustrated look on his face.

He mutters something in Russian, and when Tyler appears not to understand, repeats it in English, "not open for thirty minutes."

"Or perhaps thirty-five," he adds with a dour frown.

"But I want to speak to EVE," Tyler tells him.

Nothing changes in the fat man's disgruntled face. He does not go in search of this EVE nor explain to Tyler where she might be.

Instead, he shows Tyler to a table in back of the restaurant just below the dais and promptly disappears.

A few minutes later, another waiter, tall and muscular with commandingly chiseled features, emerges from the back and hands Tyler an enormous menu with both Cyrillic and Roman lettering.

The thought of shish kabob or even Chicken Kiev makes Tyler's stomach growl. All he can think to order is smoked sturgeon and a glass of cold Stoli. He's been reduced to cheaper vodka in recent months, but this will surely be on the house.

The sturgeon is too salty, and he can tell from the first bite that it will go straight through him, but the vodka is cool, pleasant, and comes in a large, half-full glass. After the anxiety of the day, he can hardly blame himself for downing it quickly. Before he can get the waiter's attention to order another one, an unpleasant surprise arrives at his table, the check.

The sturgeon (at $12.95) is twice what the menu had

claimed, and though drink prices had not been listed, charging fourteen dollars for a glass of vodka is absolutely criminal. How much will the Russian mobsters pay when they arrive later in the evening with their tawdry girlfriends? Two dollars? Nothing at all?

Fortunately, he can put it on Delauney's debit card.

"Cash only," says the waiter when he sees it.

This gets more and more ridiculous, but Tyler puts down two of the elderly American twenties he has brought along from what remains of his foreign bill collection.

What is this about, anyway, he wonders, the excessive mysteriousness making him cranky. Should he ask for EVE again?

The change arrives a moment later along with a thick white envelope. The waiter scolds Tyler with his index finger when he starts to open it.

"Wait until car," he says.

Sure enough, only a few minutes later, Tyler finds himself in a black Town Car being driven towards Manhattan.

A few blocks into the long drive, he rips open the envelope and finds an Amtrak ticket for Union Station in Washington, leaving the day after next, and another ticket for a parking space in the garage right above it, where, undoubtedly, he's supposed to go once he's arrived.

Also in the envelope is a strange electronic device about the size of a woman's pinky. On it are the words "Travel Drive."

"EVE" was indeed only some sort of code. Given Delauney's acronymic obsession it probably stood for something. Tyler must take the train the day after tomorrow and deliver the "travel drive" to whomever or whatever would be waiting for him in the appropriate garage space.

Shuffling the envelope and its contents into the breast pocket of his jacket, he concentrates his attention on the Brooklyn landscapes passing by: the boulevard with its grand buildings aging honorably on either side and its park in the middle with more old Jews and Russians seated austerely on stone benches.

Hotel Pennsylvania
8:30 PM

It's after dark by the time the black Town Car drops Tyler off at seedy Hotel Pennsylvania. A group of odd-looking women in matching gray and brown uniforms with the insignia of the Turkish airlines is emerging from a van outside.

His tiny room has the dusty drapes and sour-smelling bathroom one would expect from a hotel housing obscure airline personnel. At least the water bug in the sink disappears down the drain before he's required to assassinate it.

What the hell is he doing here anyway, performing some cloak and dagger errand best entrusted to a local? He wonders about Thornton Hall as well, why he's got himself so set on finding the pretentious place Cal carried on about when his poor wife is adrift in Africa with that small-faced French girl.

Lacking appetite for dinner in the Macy's tourist zone, he sets up shop at the empty hotel bar and drinks more vodka.

The ramshackle lair deep within the bowels of the hotel has miniature leather armchairs on poles attached to the bar and greasy, cramped booths in back that look like they haven't been sat in for decades.

Tyler is congratulating himself for having discovered a setting gloomy and isolated enough to match his mood when a pudgy, inebriated Chinaman in tight jeans and a New York Yankees tee-shirt staggers back from the bathroom.

After attempting unsuccessfully to mount a stool, he leans against the bar and orders a rum and coke.

Once the drink has arrived and the Chinaman has taken a thirsty gulp, he turns to Tyler as if they'd already been in mid-conversation, and demands to know (in an off-putting nasal Midwestern accent) what kind of vodka is in Tyler's cocktail.

Tyler looks away as he mumbles his not very top-drawer answer, but the Chinaman has already launched into his dreary life story.

Apparently, his wife had left him the year before for the lady they'd hired to re-plaster their upstairs bathroom, and he's been reeling ever since.

He's visiting New York from Cleveland to take his thirteen-year-old daughter, Dawn, who he barely gets to see, to *The Lion King*, but, plugged in constantly to some newfangled electronic musical device, she's hardly spoken to him the whole time. So when "you get right down to it, man," he's just as lonely as he is at home. Dawn's gone to sleep, giving him the opportunity to go out on the town, his version of it, at least, the hotel bar.

Tyler half listens, his eyes wandering around the faded New York tourist photos in back of the bar, his mind focused on his journey tomorrow to Thornton Hall. Just as Tyler's second glass of vodka on the rocks and the drunken Chinaman's latest rum and coke arrive simultaneously, Tyler feels something thick and awkward in the air.

He looks over to find an aggrieved expression on the Chinaman's puffy face, his flimsy right arm wiggling poignantly in search of a handshake.

"I said I'm Frank Kim," he repeats again, "what's your name?"

"Ty...," begins Tyler before thinking better of his answer and staging an extensive coughing fit.

"Cal Thornton," he says once the pseudo fit has run its course, grabbing Frank Kim's hand and pumping it manfully.

"Where's your old lady?" asks Frank Kim, giving him a chance to tell his own sad-sack story.

And Tyler feels just buzzed enough from his various vodkas to consider the question.

Ornella and her little French girlfriend would have left Morocco by now. Where was she headed next? Senegal, one of the few civilized places left in Francophone Africa.

"Well, Frank," Tyler finally replies in his roughest, most masculine tone, "my old lady flew the coop. Also with a girl."

Frank Kim looks at Tyler expectantly, so Tyler tells the following story.

Calvin Thornton, a vacuum cleaner executive from southeastern Connecticut, had been having a pleasant early retirement, mornings on the links, afternoons around the large house in Greenwich with the lovely younger Mrs. Calvin Thornton when the prissy little bitch announced she was going on a European tour with the French spinster down the block who was a ...lesbian.

But how can Tyler bluntly blurt something out that had been so elegantly implied, his weakness in the lovemaking department, her failure to return until late in the morning after nights with her *amici femminile*.

The word "lesbian" feels awkward in Tyler's mouth, unfairly damning. *La Moglie* was indeed in Africa with her little French girlfriend, but one needn't draw such bald conclusions.

And the very sound of the word sends tears dripping down the Chinaman's round face, his newfound friend in the same miserable predicament.

Tyler's eyes dampen, too, as he's getting drippy in late middle age. Sentimental images of *La Moglie* at Bel Vento crop up all over his mind: drinking coffee in her nightgown in the kitchen, the morning sun flooding her lovely Roman face; beside him in the front seat of the Alfa, Jackie O glasses on her eyes, her latest silk scarf flapping over her shoulders while they peer down at the heart-wrenching Amalfi coast.

Despite the panoply of odors—rum and coke, cheap cologne, sweat, and garlic—Tyler pulls Frank Kim close for a warm and fuzzy man hug. He can't wait to reach Thornton Hall—if he can even find the place—then knock off the ridiculous Delauney errand the next day so he can concentrate on what really should be his main priority, getting poor Ornella out from the clutches of the girlfriend who must surely be getting on her nerves.

Just as he's extricating himself from Frank Kim's damp arms, Tyler hears the sounds of someone new shuffling into the bar.

His heart skips a beat, but it's only an old lush with dyed blond hair and overwrought perfume.

She looks away when Tyler catches her eye, and he realizes what they must look like—middle-aged homosexuals getting gushy with each other after too many drinks, unimpressive-looking fellows in any case. Is he really so different from the drunken Chinaman, he wonders to himself. Both were drowning their sorrows in dingy surroundings. Both their wives had fled into the arms of girls.

Frank Kim excuses himself to go puke in the bathroom, and Tyler doesn't wait for him to come back to settle with the bartender and slip upstairs.

Tyler plans to flip on the creaky television and search around for Court TV in hopes of catching that Stromboli business, but he can't seem to rouse himself from the lumpy leather chair. It is nearly seven in the Spanish morning, and he's had too much to drink and too little to eat to stop his foolish old body from caving in on itself.

Just as he slips into sleep, a bright red light irradiates the room. He's peering warily around him, looking for its source when he sees *La Moglie* standing in front of him, an oddly determined look on her regal face.

It doesn't surprise him that she's arrived in the middle of the night, and without warning, but he can't fathom how she knew where to find him. Apparently, she hasn't made it to Senegal yet. She appears to be wearing some sort of Moroccan native costume: a white *djbellah* over her body and what looks like the top of a *burkah* over her head.

Shrugging off her robes with magnificent ease but keeping on the headpiece, she jumps naked into bed with him, even though he remembers going to sleep on the chair. She rubs her body ravenously against him like a dog scratching its back on a tree, the damp of her genitals unpleasant on his pajamas, like he's pissed himself in the night. An unintended glimpse of her female parts reveals an alarmingly overgrown gray bush. Bits of milky cellulite spread through her legs, varicose veins bulge painfully right under the surface of her thighs and stray unshaved hairs sprout all around her body like a time-release movie of degeneration. *How long has she looked like this*, he wonders, realizing he hasn't seen her birthday suit since that messy part of their marriage had petered out.

She rubs herself against him with greater and greater vehemence, and once she seems to be reaching her climax, an eerily familiar concatenation of urine, alcohol and decrepitude pierce his stuffed-up nostrils.

When he wakes up only an hour or so later, the misguided phantom, who was awfully familiar but didn't quite seem like his wife, has disappeared, leaving only an empty glass that smells like Johnny Walker on the table and a few strands of jet black hair with greyish roots on the bed.

Once Tyler's pulled himself to his feet, he feels sober enough to see if he can catch a glimpse of the crime show he'd seen advertised on the World Wide Web while still in Spain.

He finds the remote, points it at the television, then presses the power button uselessly for over a minute. He's considering dashing down the stairs to fetch Frank Kim, as he might be able to help with the thing, when it turns itself on.

It's finally functioning, but Tyler can't get it to Court TV. He passes a baseball game, an inexplicable cult movie with half-dressed Americans on a tropical island, then a middle-aged man in a white dress shirt a couple of sizes too small complaining incomprehensibly in an upper-crust accent. Tyler stops switching channels to observe the man's veins bulging out through his bulky neck and his weak fists shaking impotently.

The words "Upcoming on Court TV" appear on the screen while the man carries on about someone torching someone else on a foreign island. That someone (who Tyler realizes could well be himself) had better "watch his step."

How the ridiculous creature knows the story and why Court TV deems it worthy of coverage are perplexing questions, but if Tyler's only dangers come from effete little assholes, he'll live to a ripe old age.

He turns off the television, lies back in bed, and watches the room sway giddily around him.

Hotel Pennsylvania
4:15 AM

Tyler opens his eyes in the dark room. Another nightmare he can't remember has taken him deep into the past, and the journey back is slow and unsteady.

Tyler dreams of Queens in black and white—his rickety cot in the alcove of the 12th story apartment, the dusty curtains perpetually drawn. His routine comes back to him, eighth grade mornings in Flushing where they'd moved from Howard Beach to be nearer the laundry where Mother worked.

He'd feed Freddy, the goldfish Aunt Mary had given him, drink apple juice, scarf toast and dash over to Saint Joseph Academy, the awful place his mother paid for him to attend as she didn't want him at public school with the "niggers and the spics."

"Complain all you want about working weekends at the butcher, but that don't pay nearly half of that school of yours," she liked to tell him, a bit of brogue overtaking her voice when she nagged even though it was only her father who'd been born in Ireland.

"That coat'll have to do you another year. That school of yours has got me by my purse strings."

Saint Francis had added a seventh and eighth grade after the war when Father Swenson's till-taking had left them deep in the red. The longer limbed early teens (Johnny was nearly five and a half feet by eighth grade) were forced into tiny wooden desks built for eleven-year-olds.

The nuns scrawled screechy sentences on black boards, and the nooks and crannies of the school had weathered sculptures of the Virgin and chipped marble crucifixes —Christ's perfect stomach confusing and arousing poor Johnny.

Tyler climbs out of bed now, gulps down water and reminds himself where he is, but when he looks out his dark Manhattan window, he sees 1950's Queens.

A terrific food fight during an eighth grade lunch period lays siege to his mind, baked beans flying through the air, nuns screaming and smacking, a sensory overload from which he had to escape.

A warm April day, Johnny need not find his coat nor hat. He just has to rise to his feet, duck a flying hotdog and a nun reaching for someone's collar, then slip into the hall, from where it is only a quick jog to the Saint Francis's unlocked front door.

Feeling the long climb up to the 7 Train platform in his arthritic knees, Tyler remembers the decision not to waste any of the dollar and fifteen cents in his pocket and hop easily over the turnstile just in time to board a Times Square-bound train.

Agitated and excited, Johnny paces from one end of the car to the other as it passes by apartment buildings, warehouses and factories. Peering into windows, he sees the old people, babies and housewives home in the middle of the day.

Many minutes later, they plunge into the tunnels below the river and resurface in Manhattan, a land (his mother's words) of "fat cats, pimps and queers," that he's hardly seen.

At the last stop, he gets off and climbs many moving staircases to reach the light of day in Times Square.

Where there are enormous marquees announcing shows and movies, neon signs advertising alcohols and airline companies, and negroes, Jews and prostitutes walking briskly by.

On a murky side street, he sees a marquee with the words Lusty Lady and the admonishment, "adults only." It has not been Johnny's particular intention to follow the path of Frank Marotta, Teddy Weiler and the other boys in his homeroom who snuck regularly into the city to see dirty movies, but after a look to his left and then to his right to make sure neither Mother nor her spies are on his tail, he slips inside.

The ticket-taker, an obese negro wearing a soiled white dress shirt, looks him over sternly before taking his dollar. The curiously musty odor does not at all resemble the fragrance of popcorn and candy of the Palace in Flushing.

Seating himself in a cold, damp aisle, he turns his attention to the movie just beginning. First the words, "Peeping Tom," waltz across the screen, then an oddly devious-looking man in a bowler hat peeks his head through a filmed theater curtain and smiles archly at the audience.

The scene switches to a frumpy brunette only a few years younger than Mother lying on a rumpled bed in only her underwear, rubbing her pussy and groaning hysterically.

A minute or two later, the same man, now hatless, enters the room, strips off his shirt and pulls down his pants to reveal a veiny Johnson. Ripping off the woman's brassiere, he suckles her matronly breasts like an oversized baby.

Spellbound and appalled, the thought of Saint Francis, the 7 Train, Times Square and even the theater surrounding him fade so completely that Johnny barely notices that the little man with dirty black hair and an unattractive odor in the next seat has tapped him on the shoulder.

Once he finally gets Johnny's attention, he makes a peculiar gesture. He sucks his finger and peers curiously at Johnny as if he's asking permission. Johnny shrugs his shoulders as the little man can surely do what he wants.

What he wants is to swoop down into Johnny's lap, unzip Johnny's pants with practiced efficiency, and take Johnny's Johnson into his mouth.

A practice that Tyler has never before heard of, which by some unfathomable coincidence is exactly what the frumpy lady has started to do to the man on the screen.

Unnerved and extremely uncomfortable, Johnny still can't help but enjoy the same sensation he's been attaining for himself in the shower. The moment he ejaculates, however, his mood starts to spiral. He thinks of Queens and the consequences of his delinquency and realizes that allowing a man to do the same thing being done by the woman on the screen is probably queer, like Mother warned.

That ugly thought sends the half of a hotdog he'd consumed at lunch barreling back up his esophagus and fills him with fury at the little creature just then taking its own Johnson out of its pants.

Johnny jumps to his feet, desperate to get out of the sleazy theater. Not bothering to check outside to make sure no one recognizes him, he dashes away in the direction of downtown.

His destination is Greenwich Village, which the college kid in the first floor of his building keeps telling him about, the center of what he breathlessly calls "Bohemianism," cafes and cigarettes, poets and revolutionaries.

Queens was shadowy on the brightest of days, the 7 Train dark and constricted, its lights flashing on and off as it lurched from station to station. The thought of what happened in dingy, dissolute Times Square has him aching with shame, but the luminescent sun helps Johnny leave that behind as he strides through the grand arch into Washington Square Park.

His tired legs ecstatically renewed, he bounds towards a playground where wealthy housewives and foreign nannies watch carefully over precious little children frolicking on the slides and swings. Aunt Mary had sometimes taken him to a playground near her summer house on the Island, but he'd hardly ever gotten to swing on the swing sets right off Roosevelt Avenue.

He opens the gate, finds a free swing and starts flying back and forth, trying to see if he can go all the way round. But a woman in a fur coat and a nasty frown approaches him, and he understands that he's missed his chance, already too old.

Farther into the park, he passes chess players pondering the outdoor boards and scraggly men with horned-rim glasses and weird hats gesticulating on benches.

After circling the park a couple of times, staying clear of the playground, he heads westward on West Fourth Street past Sixth Avenue. He pauses for no good reason outside of a townhouse on the corner of Morton Street. A tiny woman with shockingly black hair is dashing down the front steps in the company of a gawky brunette.

Tyler stares at the light just now becoming visible through the hotel window. He skips his memory of the long walk back to Times Square and the uncomfortable rush hour train ride to Flushing. Still, the dread of that return trip makes his stomach fill with acid.

When Mother passed at the beginning of the eighties, Tyler got up to do a victory dance around Bel Vento. But his limbs were limp and his face was drenched in tears, a response he could never fully explain. With her gone, it's easier to re-live that eighth-grade afternoon, taking his time up the twelve flights of stairs. The elevator would always get him there too quickly.

Inch by creaky inch, he opens the front door and, once inside, is relieved not to detect any of Mother's characteristic sounds—soup boiling in the kitchen, the radio going in her bedroom, her clumping glumly from room to room.

Can she really have gone shopping so late in the afternoon? Can God really have graced him by sending her off to play cards with the old ladies on the fourth floor?

Johnny breathes more easily and makes his way into the kitchen, daring to hope that the day's peculiar adventures could be kept to himself.

Except he can tell something is wrong: the fishbowl is missing from the kitchen table. It stands atop the icebox, its water removed. Freddy lies dead at the bottom, already beginning to stink.

Then Mother emerges from wherever she'd been lurking. She smiles savagely. She shakes her head and wags her finger. Each wag means something specific.

I pay good money on school and look what you do.

Spending time with low-lives and queers.

Your father is an officer of the law, but look where *you're* headed.

If you hadn't driven him away, he'd be here to give you the beating you deserve.

Mother gets out the rolling pin and he feels his pants being pulled down for the second time that day. It's hard to imagine anyone can beat him more powerfully than Mother, her forearms strengthened by long days of laundress-work.

Chapter 4
Rotterdam

September 9, 2001
Noon
Eve

The old lady can't stand the thought of poor Tyler twisting and turning on the spongy Pennsylvania Hotel mattress, not while Pedro sleeps royally in the sleekly modern room she's gotten for him at the Rotterdam Park Hotel. She has no notion of lodgings more appropriate for immigrants, and she knows full that well if she didn't find Pedro a room, he'd stick to her like a needy dog.

Which he does anyway, lurking outside her room as she changes out of her soiled black dress and following her downstairs into the elegant bar. All she can do is order him one of those strong and bitter German wheat beers, which he's sure not to enjoy.

Pedro is dark, tiny and badly dressed (another of the white shirts he must borrow from a waiter friend and black cotton pants a size too large), but the young blond bartender seems perfectly willing to serve him anyway. Everyone is absurdly tolerant in this homogenized new Europe.

An odd expression crosses Pedro's face. The beer is utterly different from the light watery stuff he's consumed in Spain and Latin America, and soon he is gulping it like he's dying of thirst.

It's bad enough to drink at a hotel bar with one's driver, but now Pedro is seized with a fit of loquaciousness.

"How is the *señora* feeling after the long journey?" His voice is so urgent and sincere that she actually considers the question. Her stomach is bloated, there is a bad taste in her mouth, and her nerves are so shot that she's dizzy, on the verge of tipping over from the sleek metal chair onto the floor of the bar.

A sense of pointlessness overcomes her. What can she possibly accomplish here, without even a film festival to judge? Her little Indian driver looks crushed by the mood she's unable to disguise.

"*Señora, Señora,*" he says, making nervous fists and losing his grammar, "what can we for do, how can we to assist?"

"Anything, my *señora,*" he pleads, his big brown eyes gazing warmly into hers, "anything at all." For some unearthly reason, the little fellow has grown attached to her.

She has no immediate answer, though in her present state she knows she can do almost nothing without him.

How had Tyler planned everything so smoothly over the years? She tries to recall his methods: the Delauney fund, the Martini affair, the disposal of Samuels. Nothing was exactly planned, of course. Tyler could exploit the situations she thrust him in, the perils she tossed his way, with his remarkable powers of improvisation. But the old lady has no such ability. She can't get to Tab without forcing her hand, which will require working out a plan in her *cahier*.

"Well," she finally answers Pedro, "you can't 'to assist' by yourself; you'll have to hire others."

Naturally, he looks puzzled, as he doesn't know anyone in Rotterdam.

"The bellhop looked like one of yours," she says, meaning to encourage him, though the man was probably Turkish.

"Perhaps," replies Pedro dubiously.

He's too meek to ask how much, so she tries to come up with a figure that would be a lot for an immigrant but not too much for her.

"A hundred Euros for the others, but two hundred for you."

"How many others?" Pedro asks, keeping away from the topic of what she actually wants them to do and how long that might take.

What she wants may not be strictly legal, but she can only let them know that when they're too involved to back out.

The word "two" comes out of her mouth though she doesn't have a real answer. She can't go hiring all of Rotterdam in any case, and four hundred already seems like a lot to spend on this ridiculous charade.

"Yes," he says, trying his best to sound credulous. "Most certainly." If one added the three hundred that he's been paid to drive, it would make five hundred Euros, almost enough to pay for a wife to be sent from home or plenty to blow on a big-breasted girl—or strapping boy if that's what he prefers.

"By tomorrow," she cautions.

"Well…I suppose…okay," he stumbles, troubled by the short notice.

Woozy, achy, and exhausted, she pushes herself up to her feet with the sides of the chair. But after so many hours in the back seat of the car, her legs refuse to cooperate. They twitch dramatically back and forth but stay in place.

She detests them when they act that way. There will be hell to pay, she makes a mental note, when she finally makes it back to her room. She smashes them with her fists when they've been particularly rebellious, making bluish marks that last forever and have been difficult to explain to her doctors.

Pedro, who has witnessed this problem before, knows just what to do.

Grabbing her delicately around the waist, he picks her up with his strong little arms and gives her a shove, just enough to get her moving out of the bar towards the lobby where she can take the elevator up to her room.

She has no appetite for dinner that evening except for leftover nuts and falls asleep before nine after one more drink from her travel scotch.

September 10, 2001
10:00 AM

When she opens her eyes the following morning, she sees a modernist chair, odd-shaped and unsittable, and an equally unfamiliar globe-like lighting fixture looming above her head like a high-tech Chinese lantern. She smells the musty odor of her Virginia mother, though Mother would never have stayed in a room like this, nor would she choose to haunt it now that she's dead.

The air-conditioned atmosphere doesn't seem right either, she thinks, remembering the stuffy room on the second floor of the Spanish beach villa. And she can't catch even one whiff of those pervading Spanish fragrances (eucalyptus, garlic, exhaust) nor the comforting wood and soap aroma, which would indicate she's back home in the house she had built for herself in Normandy. This confusion might be the result of some intricate dream, and she demands to know where she is. A moment later, the idea that she's in the Netherlands hardly seems convincing, the sort of behavior critics question in her characters.

She often wakes up confused, not sure exactly where

she is, but figures it out quickly enough. In fact, the mornings are easier to navigate. Afternoons and evenings are so often poisoned by Tab.

From the time of her morning croissant (the only meal she can still enjoy) to her lunchtime beer, Tab remains a distant figment.

But around mid-afternoon on all too many days, after a drink or two and a dizzying nap on a couch or chair, a bit of Tab-ness will emerge from nowhere, sometimes on the face of one of her paintings or on an unwitting visitor. Sometimes a muffled old car driving by outside will recall Tab's old Volkswagen. It can also be as unavoidable as her own reflection in a mirror or a well-polished table—the same drawn face, the same small, now even more shrunken body that Tab had once desired.

Then the memories rage back. Not so much of the ecstatic week of the affair but of the months that followed after she'd flown home from the Netherlands to France in an agonizing stupor, taken to her bed, and stayed weeping there for weeks. She did not swallow those valiums to escape the world the way everyone insisted, just to (finally, dreamlessly) sleep.

Of course, as Elizabeth Smalls, who immediately came to look after her, and the French psychiatrist she'd hired both insisted on reminding her, it wasn't about the little Dutch girl she'd only been with for a week, but the recent loss of her mother and the problem "with the composition chemical of the brain." That was well and good, but the vibrancy of that week with Tab had shone a permanent light on the pointless wreck her life had become.

Once she recovered enough, she threw out the whiskey flask, torn bra, and Graham Greene book that Tab had returned to her that last afternoon at the bar. But other bras, other books still bring it back.

As afternoon turns to evening on too many days, the memories simmer more and more unpleasantly inside her, making her head spin and innards ache. So many people in her life have died and disappeared, and she's perfectly glad for it. Quite often, she wishes Elizabeth Smalls, her on-and-off late-fifties lover and unremittingly reliable friend, would return to Massachusetts to run the historical society she carries on about, so the old lady can be left alone to lick her wounds.

It's not true, she tries to reassure herself, that she'll suffocate if she can't reach Tab or get hotter and hotter until she bursts into flames like Tyler's villa on Stromboli.

She can hold on, prevent the panic from boiling her insides, if she drinks at just the right pace and frets about other things.

It's only morning but she smells something ripe, which can't be inside the hotel room—cigarettes, rancid pears, leaking gas, and other sense memories from her week with Tab. Looking at her legs through the sheets, she orders them to transport her as far away as possible. After a brief hissy fit, they swing out onto the floor.

Outside her door, she finds a tray with a pitcher of coffee, another of warm milk, and some hard rolls with jam and butter. The complimentary copy of the Rotterdam paper confirms the date, Sept 10, 2001, the day of the opening.

A heavy bloated feeling, having something to do with dread, sinks into her chest then down into her bowels.

She's gone to great lengths to reach the Netherlands, but in the clear light of morning, she wants nothing to do with difficult girls in odorous apartments. She wants nothing more than a quiet day in the hotel like the one she would have enjoyed after the judging of the film festival, if she had been wise enough to refuse the fat Kraut's offer.

While pouring coffee and hot milk and spilling quite a bit on the table, she hears a knock on the door. Bothersome so early, though she has no idea of the actual time. Anyway, it's probably just Pedro, so she feels free to ignore it.

When the knocking starts up again a few minutes later, she puts down the coffee, gets her legs moving towards the door and finds Pedro standing outside with a grin on his face. With him are the young bellhop and an old man who also looks like a Turk wearing wrinkled robes.

"I've got them," Pedro announces with pride, "I've done what you asked."

The cloud on her face gets her message across. She's not ready to meet anyone.

Around noon, a more chipper old lady slips on one of her flannel shirts to meet the committee downstairs in the bar, wondering if she needs them after all. Four hundred Euros is a lot of dough, and while she's developed tolerance if not outright fondness for Pedro, she wonders if she can abide these two strange Turks.

Pedro can drive her to the opening himself (no Turks needed) and wait for her until she's done. He'll need to get her there unfashionably early, so she can guzzle enough white wine to settle her nerves before Tab appears.

On the elevator down to the lobby, the old lady projects tentatively into the future, her arrival at the opening.

She can certainly count on a former warehouse surrounded by dreary art pieces, installations they call them, as immature as their *épater le bourgeois* name, "Fuck Death." She sees a broken-down bed with fake shit, semen, and bloodstains. Didactic feminist rhetoric, probably in English, will be spray-painted upon it, "womyn bed," or, if that's too subtle for them, a coffin with a splattered female mannequin inside.

Downstairs at the hotel bar, she's sipping distractedly at the beer she's ordered when Pedro and the Turks show up.

Pedro tries to get her attention, but she's too stricken to pay him any mind.

"*Señora, señora,* we will take care of your trouble," he tries to reassure her, but she's busy watching herself cling to her three-pronged cane as the warehouse gets more and more packed with frivolous humanity: overwrought art critics cavorting in tight leather pants; overweight art patronesses, their miniskirts exposing their trunk-like legs; and no Tab anywhere, at least not at first.

The journey across the crowded room to the tepid Riesling at the bar will seem impossibly complex, so she'll have to endure glances as she takes out her flask and tipples publicly. And right on cue, Tab will emerge as young and fake blond as ever, on the other side of the room, in a crowd of fawning admirers.

The old lady will inch her way in that direction, but her legs will protest, twitching ludicrously and refusing to budge. She will smack them as hard and discreetly as she can with her cane, and, chastened, they will obey, leading her slowly across the room.

Several arduous minutes later, the circle of young Tab lovers will open reluctantly to allow in the old American lady.

Tab will be too engaged by her flock of fans to notice her, but a sullen glare settling on her face will reveal when she has. Shaking her head in disbelief, she will summon her admirers and march away with them through an unmarked door leading to a hidden room up several flights of impossibly steep stairs.

Punctured by disappointment, the old lady will shake her little fists in the air, wondering how she can come all the way from Spain only to be humiliated again.

No. Not possible. It just can't be. She can't enter *Fuck Death's* hallowed halls alone. Grabbing Pedro by the arm and ignoring the two Turks entirely, she whispers her new plan into his ear.

7:00 PM

At Boomgaardstraat 2343, less than a kilometer away from the port, there stands a warehouse with narrow flats for windows on its upper floors. Once a pit stop for hair pieces, clock radios, and other obscure materials arriving on ships, a large sign now wraps around it with an LED display á la Jenny Holzer proclaiming "American Shopping Mall" followed by a list of what a typical one is supposed to contain: McDonald's, Macy's, Walmart. The joke is that inside the warehouse one doesn't find an American shopping mall but its bold antithesis: a gallery opening for young Dutch artists.

The most *avant* of Dutchmen (with a smattering of Germans, Frenchmen, Englishmen, and Americans) line up in front of a fierce lip-pierced bouncer, and Pedro's white car parks across the street.

Only Pedro and the old lady are inside. They need no

Turks to help them watch for Tab coming out of the gallery. She and Pedro can follow her home once she appears.

Pedro sits at attention in the front seat, dressed in his same stained waiter shirt and black cotton pants a size too large, while the old lady—disguised in small sweat pants intended for a large child, a hoody, and dark sunglasses —slumps like a hunchback from exhaustion and osteoporosis.

Intensely, she scans the crowd in front of the gallery, both those coming in and those going out. Her legs twitch, then calm, then twitch again. In between bouts of twitching, she sips from a flask.

As seven turns seven-thirty, then eight, the atmosphere inside the white car grows blacker and blacker. It seems increasingly unlikely that Tab will arrive and even less likely that she is somehow still inside. She doesn't seem to have bothered to show up to her opening.

By the time the hour of eight has come and gone, the old lady's eyes (tear-stained behind her shades) begin to close. She slaps her face a few times to keep herself alert, but after several nights of little sleep, it's a losing struggle.

Wearily, she hands three folded photographs to her driver and asks him to take up the vigil. If he sees anyone remotely resembling the woman in the photos, he must immediately wake her up.

As the old lady dozes in back, Pedro tries to match the throng of people to the blond woman in the photographs. Checking to make sure his passenger is safely asleep, he takes a can of beer from the paper bag under his seat, opens it, and guzzles. Then (after another quick look in back), he reaches down and chugs a second. Then a third. Generally a responsible man, the buzzed Pedro has every intention of following his *señora*'s instructions, but the bad night in the French motel and the even more troubled one in the immaculate but uncomfortable Dutch hotel makes him vulnerable to alcohol.

He closes his eyes and dips briefly into half-sleep, then jerks them open again just in time to glimpse an eerily familiar woman with long, jet-black hair coming out of the doorway.

"*Señora*," he says sharply. The old lady comes immediately back to life.

"Tab!" she shrieks, almost loud enough to be heard across the street. "My *Nederlandse kutjehas*."

The black-haired woman waves tensely to her admirers and takes off by herself.

"Follow her," the old lady orders, but Pedro has already taken the car out of park and begun to inch forward.

Following her turns out to be difficult. In any case, Pedro is not very good at it.

They wait stupidly at a red light as she disappears into the distance and only catch up with her after several agonizing minutes circling nearby blocks.

A moment later, they drive past her and have to carefully back up in order not to lose the scent.

Which brings them dangerously close, only a few feet away, and gives the old lady her first real look at how lovingly the last decade has been written on Tab's face, the delicate lines around her nose and mouth.

Tab is deep in thought, her eyes pointed firmly at the ground. Has a younger admirer left her? the old lady wonders, flooded with a fuzzy, unfamiliar maternal feeling that's more than just schadenfreude.

From the fashionable neighborhood of the gallery near the port, its industrial roots torn up and replaced by cafes and boutiques, they slip into a northern European Arabia: several large minarets visible on the skyline and dozens of small stores with signs in Arabic advertising fruits, nuts, spices, and strange vegetables.

A travel agent offering packages to Morocco distracts the old lady by recalling Ornella, the little tramp being penetrated twice daily there by Dominique while her hung-over husband tosses and turns on a lumpy American mattress. Always complaining, endlessly pampered, then ditching dear sweet Tyler at the first sign of trouble, perhaps the little twat will finally get her comeuppance by the end of *Tyler's Last*.

Remembering where she is and what she's doing, the old lady finds Tab walking straight past a crowd of women in veils gathered in front of a *madrassa*.

She feels her bladder filling, as usual, but she must hold it in. She'd hate to be observed by Tab with the Johnny Walker bottle propped up under her sweatpants.

Tab takes another turn, but Pedro keeps going straight.

"Idiot," declares the old lady, "you've lost her again."

With the absence of curiosity one finds in better servants, he never asks who she is and why she must be followed but manages a quick series of turns that bring them back onto the block into which Tab has recently turned.

It is now well past dark. The few Arab markets on the mostly residential block are closing their shutters for the night. A solitary figure peeks out of a doorway and lights a cigarette. A mangy old mongrel growls listlessly nearby. The evening is ending, and Tab is nowhere to be found.

Which doesn't bother the old lady as much as it should.

Her heart no longer races quite so urgently. A faint calm overcomes her, the obsession starting to wane. She thinks of the comfortable hard bed in the Rotterdam Park Hotel, the even more comfortable one in her light-filled bedroom in Normandy. She can't waste any more of her life on a spoiled little Dutch girl who had the nerve to masquerade as Tyler Wilson.

And since that girl is no longer within eyeshot, she can finally pee into the empty bottle she's brought with her. That sensation relieved, she feels a mite better. But the problem with feeling a mite better is that the energy it gives her can only be spent on disappointment. They had been so close for so long.

And they are still so close. Tab is either walking down an adjacent street or entering the doorway of one of these buildings. The old lady can almost whiff her musky cologne. If she gives up now, she knows she'll never get near Tab again. Her own death waits impatiently in the wings.

Twice, three times, Pedro drives up and down the dark gloomy block, then slows down when she tells him to, one last resort.

Tab would never be so conventional as to have her name printed above her doorbell. Given her fame, beauty, and slatternly tendencies, she must have several other old lovers she needs to evade.

Nevertheless, the old lady wants to look for herself. Pedro gets out and opens the door to the back seat. Her legs don't protest as she lifts herself out onto the sidewalk with her three-pronged cane.

There are no signs anywhere on the concrete-block former daylight factory to indicate who may live or work there. That would be too pedestrian for the hip young Rotterdamians of the neighborhood.

The next few buildings seem more conceivable: a series of dreary brown brick apartment blocks that must have come up soon after the war.

In front of the first of them, just before the entrance hall, there are only numbers marking the buzzers: 1b, 12c, etc.

The next one has actual names, but none of them are hers. Tab (like Tyler) may not go by her real one anyway.

In the entranceway of a smaller, even more run-down brick tenement, she sees the name Tabitha Van der Kunst and a buzzer right below it, which she can ring if the spirit seizes her.

Something electric courses through her body.

"*Pedroçito*," she whispers, "I've found her again."

Rather than park the car, he has driven slowly behind her in case she falls down or has some new instruction.

The number of the apartment is six, the top floor.

The number of the building is 244.

Her cane takes her easily to the end of the block, where, unbelievably, there is actually a street sign.

Zaagmolenstra.

244 Zaagmolenstra, apartment six.

She can return whenever she chooses with Pedro and her two Turks and confront Tab in her own apartment.

Chapter 5
The Greenwich Train

September 9, 2001
9:00 AM
Tyler

Later that morning, Tyler boards a Connecticut-bound suburban train dressed more casually than the day before in blue jeans and a red flannel shirt that *La Moglie* had given him several Christmases before as a tribute to his latent Americanness.

Not long after rolling through Harlem—too far above the ground to glimpse the negroes and Puerto Ricans lolling on their broken-down stoops—and only a few stations past the massive condominiums of the northern Bronx, the train stops at a stage-set re-creation of a New England town: Greenwich, Connecticut.

Tyler finds a taxi stand once he's descended down from the station, but rather than a salty New Englander, the driver of the first available cab looks like an Incan warrior from the highlands of Ecuador.

"What is?" asks the accented cabbie once he's been given the destination.

"Thornton Hall," Tyler repeats, trying not to sound annoyed.

"Street address," the man insists officiously, "is not possible to find without street address."

Tyler slumps down into his seat. A place as elaborate as Thornton Hall should be a landmark that even a foreign driver would know. Who is this man, some sort of village idiot?

But when Tyler looks into the driver's deep-set Indian eyes, he sees reasonable intelligence and realizes that if there were actually such a place, the man would know it.

All those years ago, Cal must have heard the callow hint of Queens that Tyler hadn't yet tricked out of his voice and decided to make up a story about an impossibly grand old family mansion. Tyler's house of dreams was just that, an illusion. The affected young man he'd met in Sicily may have been lying to him from the start, though his father's money had proved real enough.

"What is the name?" the driver asks again.

"Thornton Hall," Tyler repeats dolefully.

"No, no, of person you visit."

Not as obtuse as Tyler had first imagined, the driver punches numbers into his mobile phone and learns from some sort of information operator that Christopher Thornton lives on 11 Rugby Road.

"Extra," he cautions Tyler as they take off, "extra for the call."

Rather than plunge into the quaint downtown, they merge onto a small highway, then exit into a neighborhood of expansive housing developments and an opulent golf course.

Fortunately, the guard at the entrance of the gated community onto which they turn seems to be off on some kind of bathroom break.

The driver, understanding the implicit instructions of the creased one-hundred dollar bill that Tyler's handed him, takes a sharp left. Once they've plowed through some boxwoods and what looks like a rose garden, they get back onto the road on the other side of the not-very-fortified entrance.

The house they pull in front of five minutes later is as absurdly grandiose as one might expect but not at all

Richardsonian. It looks brand spanking new. The fat white pillars in front and the brick and aluminum siding splayed out to the sides mock their colonial forbearers.

The place does not resemble Cal's description, not even slightly, as The Thorntons are as fraudulent as their so-called hall. Tyler growls gutturally. If Cal were still alive, he'd kill him again—just desserts for poisoning him with delicious-tasting lies.

But it turns out that the cab driver knows the place after all. He notes Tyler's expression as he pays and gets out of the cab and explains that the owners had torn down the old building to make way for the atrocity in front of them.

"Lovely," he says, gesturing grandly in its direction, "lovely edifice."

Old Cal might shed bitter tears if he were to see it, this mutated Thornton Hall. But on the other hand, he might get some pleasure from the ruination of his drunken dad's dominion, the crushing weight of Thornton history torn down and replaced by a *nouveau riche* monstrosity. In any case, old Cal may not have been lying about the place.

Tyler pauses to take in the façade behind which Thorntons have lived their lives for nearly a century. Peering up towards the higher floors, he tries to locate the spot where the young Cal had played with his toys and resented his father.

A shiver creeps up his spine as he approaches the front door. The place is far too modern to have an attic, but some mad creature may still lie hidden within its bowels.

Though there is a vehicle the size of a small bus in the driveway, one of the sports-oriented obscenities that were taking over America, no one answers when Tyler pushes the doorbell.

While the third ring still echoes through the house, Tyler starts banging on the door. He only has one chance to find the secrets of Thornton Hall, as tomorrow takes him to Washington on Delauney's errand, and the day after has him flying back to Spain.

No one responds to his knocking either, and just as Tyler is beginning to curse himself for not asking the driver to wait for him, he turns the knob and opens the door.

Instinctively, he covers his ears with his hands and tenses his body to make a dash for it, but no security alarm goes off.

The door opens to reveal an enormous living room with black vinyl chairs and couches surrounding a wide fireplace, folksy paintings of what look like Dutch peasants, and a great deal of wasted space, as if the Thorntons didn't know what to do with their riches.

Strange creatures may lurk in faraway corners of the mansion, but Tyler had better start things off right by addressing the man of the house.

"Christopher Thornton," he shouts as loudly as he can.

"Christopher Thornton, Christopher Thornton, please," he goes on like a public service announcement over an airport intercom. The ridiculous vehicle wouldn't be out front if no one were home.

As he sinks his feet into the Oriental rug and breathes the over-air-conditioned air, his nose catches something sour, sharp, and strangely suggestive.

11:00 AM
Chris

At that same moment, two flights of stairs and several huge rooms away, sixteen-year-old Chris Thornton Jr. is getting the hang of the video game prototype given to his father by one of his California clients. Metal Guitar has him jumping up and down with earphones attached to his ears and a guitar-shaped device in his hands. What he's playing isn't heavy metal but the Rolling Stones, who rock harder than anybody anyone listens to in tenth grade.

"Hey, you, get off of my cloud!" he wails.

The "you" he's got in mind are the bevy of boys who get all the attention from the delicate-faced blond girl who sits next to him in algebra.

Chris Jr. would also like his dad (Christopher Thornton Sr., nephew of the presumed-dead Calvin Thornton) to stop bugging him about leaving clothes on the floor and getting too many B's.

If Dad had even a little Keith Richards in him, he could have made his own son.

11:05 AM
Tyler

Downstairs, the sickly smell pierces Tyler's sinuses, and Christopher Thornton's Uncle Cal takes hold of his imagination: the second time they met, highballs in Taormina looking out over the bay.

The moment the fat girl had gone to the bathroom to freshen up, Cal had whispered, "*Andiamo a Stromboli, caro,*" so close into his ears, that Tyler could inhale the cologne from France, the whiskey from Scotland and the musk that was his alone. Jill was the name of the American girl. "Just us, *caro*. Old Jill can stick around here."

In the sway of sense memory, Tyler whiffs Cal around the huge oval table in the next room: sour, woody, fired off by the thousands of pheromones bouncing around his brain. The penetrating odor, which might actually be cleaning fluid, knocks him down onto the 50's-era circular couch right across from it, making him roll around on it like an itchy-backed dog. Then he gathers as much saliva as he can and spits up on the upholstery, Wilson genes mixing with Thornton ones for the first time since Stromboli.

A few moments later, once he's had his fill, Tyler wipes the tears from his eyes, rises to his feet, and starts moving forward again through the house.

Several rooms later, past a lecture-hall-sized kitchen, he takes a carpeted staircase up to a second floor of expansive bedrooms with downy king-sized beds as pristine as in furniture showrooms.

One room is stacked with unpacked boxes. Another is completely empty.

Behind the closed door of the next room, he hears a low electronic sound and the pitter-patter of lively footsteps like someone awkwardly dancing.

The same evening of the invitation to Stromboli, Cal had waltzed so gracefully with the fat American girl at the after-hours club, circling her occasionally towards where Tyler was sipping scotch alone and rolling his blue eyes magnificently.

Tyler puts his ear up to the keyhole and concentrates on the sounds: hard, fast, and distinctly human.

His hand slips instinctively into his coat pocket, but he no longer carries a blade.

He grabs the doorknob instead, his heart pounding, his teeth chattering, beads of sweat dripping down his underarms.

"Ohm," he says aloud, taking one long breath then several more.

"Ohm," he repeats helplessly as his heart races forward.

When he bursts through the door, he almost runs smack into the back of a smallish creature with stiff black hair.

A boy, Tyler observes once he's got a better glimpse, an early adolescent Oriental boy.

"Sorry, sorry to intrude," mumbles Tyler, trying to come up with something to say to the housekeeper's son.

But the palsied adolescent is too busy jumping up and down to notice.

Some ancient Oriental masturbation, wonders Tyler, intrigued by the thought.

But there are headphones attached to his ears and what appears to be a simulacrum of an electric guitar in his hands, connected by a cord to a computer.

Suddenly sensing Tyler's presence, the Oriental adolescent rips off his headphones, drops the pseudo guitar, and stares tensely at him, his body shaking like a frightened woods animal.

The kid is no Calvin Thornton, sighs Tyler, gazing down at the boy quivering in front of him. How had he talked himself into believing that Cal had survived blazing gasoline only to end up back at Thornton Hall? If only he'd been able to see the country code on his broken mobile when the FCT had called back in Spain, he wouldn't have suckered himself into thinking the man was in America. Clouded by wishful thinking, Tyler's trustworthy intuition has soured. The man torturing him over the phone in Spain could be just about anywhere, ready to pounce when he least expects it.

"Young man," says Tyler, "what if your mother finds out? You have absolutely no business sneaking into your master's house."

Panic overcomes the girlish face of the Oriental adolescent (who Tyler soon acronymizes à la Delauney, the OA.) The OA tucks his polo shirt into his blue jeans as if he'll be in less danger if he looks more presentable.

"I hope I don't have to tell her, or Mr. Christopher Thornton," Tyler goes on, that stentorian old man tone creeping back into his voice.

"But, but..." quakes the OA.

"But what, young man?" asks Tyler more kindly.

"But Christopher Thornton is my dad."

After a moment of confusion (how could this be?) Tyler remembers what he's read in magazines about middle-aged Americans and their Oriental adoptions. It gives him a good opportunity to introduce himself.

"I'm your Great Uncle Cal."

"Uncle Cal?" asks the confused or lying OA.

The OA (who Tyler now christens the AOA, adopted Oriental adolescent) still looks bemused but introduces himself anyway. His name is also Christopher, as it turns out, Christopher Junior, but he is known as Chris. He's heard of his Uncle Cal, but as far as he knows, the man died tragically long ago.

Tyler looks him up and down. He appears to be telling the truth. Whatever traces Tyler had sensed of Cal downstairs were ancient or not at all. His spirit lives on Stromboli, his ashes long dissolved into the atmosphere. Thornton Hall has no answers in any case, just a red herring that smelled like cleaning fluid.

At least he's escaped *La Porqueria*. Smiling to himself, he sees a shadowy man banging on the door of the empty villa, smashing it down, charging through room after room, and cursing in frustration when there's no trace of Tyler.

Tyler imagines him rushing up the stairs and rifling through the rickety dresser until he gets to Cal's white flannel suit from Stromboli, encased in tissue paper in the false bottom of the middle drawer.

He'll rip the thing to threads if he forces it over his burly body, but what if it fits him? The thought of that summer suit returned to its owner makes Tyler's eyes mist.

He looks back at the AOA, who looks to be pushing sixteen, old enough to indulge and more pliable if inebriated.

"I'll tell you about old Uncle Cal" Tyler informs him. "But we'll need a drink first, no?"

"A drink?" asks the AOA.

"*Bien sur*," replies Tyler. Even a second-generation adopted Oriental Thornton must know basic French.

The AOA leads his great uncle down flights of stairs through hallways with crisp modernist furniture and empty built-in bookshelves to a room with an actual bar: wooden stools in front and an impressive collection of first-drawer booze in back.

"Poison of choice?" asks Tyler, surveying the options.

The AOA, like the older Oriental the night before, wants a rum and coke, while Tyler finds an extremely fancy bottle of single malt.

The AOA warns him that they must finish their drinks in a hurry, as his father is due back in less than an hour, but Tyler slaps him on the back, his hand stinging from the contact, and leads him to another couch across from the bar where he tells the following story.

The third version of Cal Thornton to emerge in less than 36 hours more resembles the real Cal Thornton. The boy may know bits and pieces of his great uncle's story.

Naturally, Tyler's latest Cal was born during the glory days of Thornton Hall, long before it was torn down to build the monstrosity here today. A lovely but disaffected lad (adored by both chaps and chicks in school), he'd been so frustrated by Old Man Thornton's drunken dullardry and the general ennui of late 50's American life that he escaped to the continent in his early twenties. There he met another American fellow (Tyler chooses neither to name himself nor mention the awful American girl), and together the two men had rented a small villa on the far side of the island of Stromboli.

The two lads spent their first few days merrily recalling their childhoods, drinking scotch (Tyler waves his glass) and taking the old motorboat out for the occasional spin.

Then Tyler closes his eyes melodramatically, shakes his head and abandons his chirpy storytelling. Solemnly, he describes how the other man had fallen asleep smoking, creating the horrific inferno from which only he had escaped.

Then the story takes on the requisite soap opera styling. A beam had landed on his head in the blaze and given him terrible amnesia.

Not knowing who he was but finding he had some money in his pockets, he'd gone from Sicily to Rome and worked as a waiter at a café near the *Fontana di Trevi*. Did the AOA know of it?

Yes, of course, the already intoxicated young fellow tells him, his eyes bright with the memory of the trip he'd taken with his ninth-grade class that very spring.

Then Cal went to Paris (here Tyler takes the AOA's

musical enthusiasms as inspiration) where he played lead guitar in a band doing rock clubs on the Left Bank. Tyler knows no such clubs, but the words taste convincing in his mouth.

The AOA, now looking positively ecstatic, wants to know what their sound was like, and Tyler, more of a Mozart man himself, can only come up with that most obvious of chestnuts, The Rolling Stones, which the young man turns out to adore.

"How fucking cool, man!" he declares, so much better than dull Dad's corporate lawyering and fondness for madrigals. The real Cal Thornton's rebellious streak lives on in his nephew's adopted son, who Tyler has to admit is rather sweet.

Tyler takes in the young fellow's glowing face, the elaborate ebony bar and leather couches in back of him. Closing his eyes for a moment, Tyler tries to picture old Thornton Hall, still clearly delineated in his imagination. Gritting his teeth, he concentrates hard enough to superimpose it upon this dreadful modern mansion.

And it comes out just about right. The room upstairs where the boy had been playing his imaginary guitar fits perfectly into the expansive children's wing that the young Cal had had to himself along with his nannies and his governess.

As the AOA waits impatiently for the rest of the story, Tyler sees fragments of Cal's face in his Oriental features— the delicate nose, the high cheekbones, the hint of dimple. And the urgent way in which he stares up at him, the piercing curiosity of his eyes reminds him of himself as a boy, poor old Johnny Conlon.

Then Tyler is wrapping up the story as fast as he can by

describing the odd way in which his memory came back in bits and drabs over the years, how he'd decided to return to Thornton Hall as soon as he'd remembered where it was, before the sound of a car can be heard pulling up the driveway.

The AOA gulps down the rest of his drink and rushes into the kitchen next door to find something to conceal his rum breath. Tyler pours himself more single malt to steady his nerves.

The AOA has returned to the room chewing vehemently on a carrot, tensing his muscles like he's planning to make a run for it. Together, they hear the front door opening.

Heavy footsteps thunder towards them as the intruder seems to know exactly where in the house they are. The man still has several more rooms to stomp through, so Tyler has some time to think things through.

The easy ownership in his gait identifies him as Christopher Thornton Senior, the most recent lord of the manor.

A couple of huge rooms away now, the man knocks over something heavy in his hurry to get to his adopted son. One can hear him panting and cursing nearby.

The Christopher Thornton who walks in on Tyler and the AOA a moment later hardly resembles his lovely uncle but looks familiar nonetheless. Of medium height and quite a bit more than medium girth, a gray beard covers his jowly face, though he can't be far past forty. Back from an unsuccessful attempt to reduce himself at a local sports club, his running togs reveal his weak, milky thighs and his Yale tee-shirt is drenched with unpleasant-smelling perspiration.

After first taking in Tyler, single malt scotch in hand,

then his carrot-munching adopted Oriental son, he scowls in surprise.

"Who the hell are you?" he demands of Tyler, "and what the hell are you doing here?"

Only a few words of Christopher Thornton's patrician voice and one closer look at his ruddy face reveals him as the man on Court TV the evening before. He struggles to come up with an explanation of why he's there, but unfortunately the AOA beats him to the punch.

"He's Great Uncle Calvin," he says, "the one they interviewed you about."

"He's not actually dead," the AOA goes on. "He played in a rock band on the Left Bank of Paris that sounded like the Rolling Stones."

This has obviously hit some bitter chord. Apoplectic with annoyance, Christopher Thornton's body shakes violently.

"France in a rock band," he screams, "absolute rot. Burnt to a crisp in Italy in 1961," he declares with absolute surety like he'd been there himself.

"This man, this man," he pontificates, a rather Cal-ish drawl in his quivering voice, "is a complete fraud."

"In fact," he says, making impotent little fists, "the police need to hear about this."

More or less Samuel's last words, but Tyler feels too tender from the single malt, as well as the surprising charms of the AOA. Before he has time to say anything anyway, Christopher Thornton has dug into his pocket for his mobile phone.

"I wouldn't advise," stutters Tyler, "I wouldn't advise that."

"Dad!" goes the AOA, "what the fuck?!"

Which makes Christopher Thornton hesitate for a fraction of a moment before shrugging his shoulders and punching three numbers into his phone.

"Christopher Thornton here," he says.

Tyler jumps to his feet, his exhaustion dissipating, his old energies black-magically returning.

He slugs Christopher Thornton with his single-malt-bearing hand before the man can get out another word, sending him crashing head first down to the marble floor, blood spurting from his nose and glass-shard-punctured cheeks.

Whimpering pathetically, he can do nothing to prevent Tyler from reaching down and extricating the mobile phone from his fists.

Bringing it up to his ear, Tyler hears a bored information operator asking which number he's looking for, and still in the sway of angry energy, he winds up his arms like a pitcher and hurls the phone so hard it smashes through the window and skids painfully over the black-top circular driveway.

The AOA pants, on the verge of hyperventilating, his pretty brown eyes experimenting with emotions: terror as his world gets blown apart, excitement as his rock and roll Left Bank uncle takes control.

"Ohm," says Tyler, trying to calm himself, "ohm."

He could finish off Christopher Thornton easily enough but that might not help him much. After Samuels was suffocated, no one sniffed around the Delauney fund for years, and, after Martini perished, no more Italian types tried to swindle him. But knocking off Christopher Thornton won't get him out of his Delauney errand tomorrow nor stop the FCT from harassing him. Besides, while the child might appreciate a break from his dickish dad, he stood a fair chance of turning against Tyler if his father was snuffed out entirely.

Tyler grabs Christopher Thornton (by this point completely unconscious) by his arms, his nose and cheeks creating a small pool of blood on the carpet, and gestures for the AOA to take hold of his feet, guessing correctly that the lad is too deeply in shock to disobey.

"Nearest closet, son," he tells the child.

Who silently leads the way, helping to drag his father through the kitchen, its blue and yellow Portuguese tiles turning vibrantly red, into another empty room with a walk-in closet.

Then Tyler goes back for the chair he had been sitting on and jams it under the knob of the closet door.

Then he and the AOA find several large but transportable objects (lamps, encyclopedias) and stack them against the door.

Depending on the seriousness of his injuries, Christopher Thornton might not spend eternity in the closet, but Tyler has given himself a significant head start.

"Coming with?" he asks the AOA.

Teeth chattering and body convulsing, the boy disappears into the next room and reemerges a moment later, carrying the keys to the monstrous vehicle outside.

Chapter 6
The Rotterdam Park

September 11, 2001
2:00 AM
Eve

Deep in the night after Tab's opening, the old lady lies propped on pillows in her king-sized bed, the reading light trained on her *cahier*. She can't rescue Tyler from the crime scene he's created at Thornton Hall nor help him figure out what to do with the child he's collected along the way until she's worked out her own complicated tomorrow.

She's got Tab's address.

She's got her team assembled.

But she lacks much sense of how to proceed.

Uselessly wracking her brain, she covers page after page with senseless geometrical drawings.

Tab will slam the door in her face or flee down the stairs and onto the street if they force their way inside. And how can she convince her team of immigrants (for whom the slightest crime could mean deportation) to hold Tab by force, a local version of the martial law so dreaded in their homelands?

It's the memory of the atrocity attempted by Elizabeth Smalls two years before at the old lady's home in Normandy that transforms her doodles into words, the skeleton of an actual plan.

It was the summer of 1999, and she'd woken up from another demolishing afternoon nap in one of those blurry states in which Tab surrounded her everywhere.

And though no one was scheduled to visit her, there were voices coming from downstairs.

When the old lady climbed expectantly down the staircase, she found not just one Tab but a half dozen of them:

old and young Tabs, male and female Tabs, except for her two-faced evangelical cousin from Front Royal, Virginia, who wasn't a Tab at all.

The cousin, along with everyone else, had been summoned by Elizabeth Smalls. She called it an "intervention," but they just said the obvious about her drinking, and the old lady, who had more energy in those days, shooed them easily out of the house and told Elizabeth that she'd be completely cut off if she ever tried anything like that again.

Intervention. American culture was forever coming up with new banalities, but this one gives her an idea what to do about Tab.

She can just see Pedro and the two Turks nodding gravely as she describes the track marks hidden under Tab's clothes, the desperate lengths (sleeping with blacks and even girls) she must go through to relieve her desperate addiction. They will nod their heads in solemn agreement, eager to do whatever it takes to rescue this troubled damsel.

They'll have to threaten her with kitchen knives and tie her in place with a rope, both of which must be purchased by Pedro for the expedition. Otherwise, the Dutch girl will slip down the stairs to the street or lock them out of her apartment in her desperate quest to stay high.

Step by step, she lays it out in her *cahier*.

The Plan
September 11, 2001

Step One: 5:30 PM: Myself, Pedro, young Turk, old Turk (kitchen knives and rope inside his robes) pile into car.

Step Two: 6:00 PM: Ring Tab's door.

By that hour Tab's girlfriend-fucking and pretentious art-producing should be done, but she won't yet have left the house for her evening on the town. She won't just buzz them up to her apartment as they won't be expected, and one can't imagine her allowing any vagrant or déclassé into her hallowed inner sanctum.

The old lady will wear her most respectable outfit, the black woolen dress, albeit soiled. When the next inhabitant of Tab's building arrives or departs through the front door, she will take that sweet old American lady persona out of the musty closet in which she has been keeping her, maybe find a little Winchester, Virginia to put back in her voice.

Approaching them, she will explain that she has been staying with someone else in the building but has lost her front door key. She'll sound vague, foggy enough to have forgotten the person's name but not so demented as to be in the wrong place altogether.

Surely, they will let her inside the building before going on their way. Or at least won't force her outside after she's pushed her way in.

Once inside, she'll wait for the way to be clear, then wave her cane in a large circle to signal her team to be let in.

Step Three: 6:15: The younger, stronger Turk and Pedro will pick me delicately up in the manner in which I have shown them and carry me to the sixth floor.

Step Four: 6:18: We will knock firmly at Tab's door, then again more and more emphatically until we are admitted.

Then...

But the difference between jotting down this real life scheme and the outlines and diagrams she draws for her thriller books is the endless diverging of possibilities. One has to plan for breaking in and finding Tab present and finding her absent, which would lead to entirely different sequences of events. Why can't she bend her own fate like she does her characters? Of course, if that were the case, she would have long ago eliminated her nerve ailment as well as Elizabeth Smalls's tiresome interference and Tab's maddening lack of love.

Step Five: 6:18-?: When Tab arrives back or comes to the door having been home all along, Pedro and the Turks must grab her by her thin, delicate arms and tie her to something reasonably sturdy—a heavy chair perhaps—to prevent her from fleeing in search of more heroin. While tying her up, they must not (of this I must make crystal clear) refer to drugs or interventions or anything of that kind. If they do, the girl may convincingly deny it, my crazy old lady word against her younger, sharper one.

Step Six: Once she is good and tied, as my mother would have said, the Turks and Pedro must leave the apartment and walk down one flight of stairs. They should be close enough to hear me if I shriek for help ("aidez moi!"* will be the safe word), but far enough away so I can confront my* Nederlandes Kutjehas *in private.*

The Meeting
10:30 AM

Rather late the following morning, after her usual confusions and ablutions, she lets the Turks and Pedro shuffle into the room for their scheduled briefing. While they'd seen each other the day before, they've never been properly introduced.

The bellhop greets her first. Rather than his customary work uniform, he wears a shiny white tee-shirt, which shows off his rangy muscles. His slicked-back hair and prominent nose appear more Italian than Turk, which isn't a bad thing, as a little Brooklyn street thuggery might come in handy.

"Hamad," he says to introduce himself, sticking out his hand over-familiarly.

After shooting him a look to put him in his place, she shakes his hand anyway, as she doesn't want to run the risk of discouraging him. These Turks can be peculiar.

The older one greets her next. His distended stomach pushes pregnantly out from his traditional robes, and she wonders if he's in good enough shape to contain a struggling Tab.

Having noticed that Hamad's action was not well received (or being too devout a Muslim to shake a woman's hand) he bows deeply like an Oriental instead and picks a standard American name (Joe) for himself. Strange that the old man in traditional garb is Joe while a young one dressed as a street tough is Hamad, but the old lady plays along.

She sits down on one of the room's two rectangular-shaped modernist chairs, and Pedro (taking advantage of his role as corporal) takes the other one, leaving the two Turks on their feet.

"Gentlemen," begins the old lady, but bothered by the fidgety way that the Turks are standing, she gestures towards the only available place to sit, the bed itself, which feels wrong in several ways but will have to do.

When she gets out her *cahier* and begins to lay out the plan, they listen politely, thoughtfully scratching their bristly chins. They don't ask questions, which worries her, and don't appear puzzled or shocked, as if interventions were part of their daily grind and generally involved knives and cords.

The first few steps go smoothly. The white car winds its way towards Tab's neighborhood with the old lady and Italianate Turk in back, and the old Turk and Pedro in front.

But what if she's got some young girlfriend with her, the difficult lover occupying her mind on her lonely walk the night before?

"This is a private matter," the old lady will inform the simpering little thing, who resembles an *Umbrellas of Cherbourg*-era Catherine Deneuve in her imagination.

The car comes to a halt across the street from Tab's building. Pedro jumps out and opens the door for the old lady.

Who feels unnerved by the brevity of the ride. Though she hasn't discussed it explicitly with her *cahier*, she has imagined getting caught in at least one traffic jam, taking at least one wrong turn.

Once she's stepped from the car, the salty, noxious air from the factories and nearby port gets into her sinuses, leaving a mess of mucus on her face. Her chest lurches as she struggles to breathe. Outside the house of the live Tab, the bits of remembered Tab gurgle painfully inside her. She feels herself being slapped around again, then tied to the mattress with bungee cords. She feels her ego being pierced at the American-style bar.

The old lady wants to get as far away as she can.

To Spain, to America, to Normandy, to any place else but here.

In this troubled world with its Jews and its Arabs, its whites and its negroes, the communist threat eradicated but others vying to take its place, it is criminal to waste such effort on a girl.

"Gentlemen," she starts to say, but the words rumbling up her throat don't make it out of her mouth. Instead, the peculiar sound they create, which worries Pedro, may be a sign from above. Parkinson's, that mother of all cunts, may rob her of her tongue the way it she robbed that negro boxer who boasted so outrageously and danced so elusively throughout the sixties and seventies.

She finds the doorbell.

She rings it.

She rings it again.

Nothing.

Something acidic in her stomach shoots up her esophagus, tasting pungent on her tongue. Her obsession with Tab is as alive in her body as her nerve disease and as reluctant to budge.

Some electronic flatulence overcomes the door, but it takes the old lady a while to realize she's actually being buzzed in.

Her body shivers, her legs twitching maniacally, so that Pedro has to give her the customary push to get her moving.

Then he and the Italianate Turk lift her in their strong immigrant arms and begin the long journey up to the sixth floor. The banisters and landings pass slowly by, bits of blue paint flaking to the ground, the odor of mold and heavy Dutch cooking permeating the air.

They drop her carefully off in front of Tab's door and retire to wait for her on the landing below. So skillful are they, so gentle, that it's hard not to imagine they've done this sort of twisted favor before, that it's not listed in elegant calligraphy on their menu of services.

While her shaking hand approaches the splintery door, Tyler's Buddhist enthusiasm comes to mind. One should live entirely in the moment, not the one of encountering your little Dutch cunt but the one just before it, alone in her landing.

She hears the plaintive voice of her leading man begging for attention in the back of her mind but knows that she must concentrate on the scene unfolding in front of her.

"Ohm," she says quietly to herself while tapping lightly on the door, "ohm."

The door opens and there she is.

Flecks of gray have sprouted in her dyed black hair, and deep crow's feet have clustered around her eyes from decades of sleepless nights.

How old, the old lady wonders, attempting the math, nearing forty, the beginnings of middle age.

The old lady watches a series of easily legible emotions appear and disappear on her former lover's face.

First confusion. *Who is this odd-smelling old woman at her door?*

Then recognition, perhaps faint fondness. *Tyler's maker is looking so frail now, so weak, circling down towards her last.*

Finally annoyance, dismissal. *She had planned to sleep until six or so before going out on the town with her volatile young girlfriend, but something unpleasant has arrived from her past.*

Punctured by the scorn settling on Tab's face, the old lady's head spins, her throat constricts, her bowels ache, angrily.

The little bitch, the sarcastic little bitch.

The old lady watches in amazement as the three-pronged cane in her hand slams into Tab's thigh, half exposed in her raggedy nightgown.

She yells "*aidez moi!*" for reinforcements, but Tab already has got her clammy hands on the old lady's shoulder and begun to propel her back into the hall. Before the door can slam in her face, the old lady lands her cane again with deadly accuracy on Tab's right cheek, an elegant line of blood trailing all the way down to the top of her long neck.

While Tab is busy grimacing, the old lady's team enters the apartment.

When Tab yells in Dutch, the old Turk takes the long kitchen knife out from his robe to demonstrate what will happen if she doesn't shut up.

While Tab quiets and pants for breath, more pathetic puppy than rebel dyke, the Italianate Turk whispers reassuring words about cooperating and not getting hurt.

They use the rope they've brought to tie her quickly and efficiently to a small wooden chair like the ones the old lady remembers from grammar school and then tie the chair to a heating pipe in back of the room.

They are abandoning the old lady to her intervention, but her stomach is cramping, her heart creeping up into her throat.

She must sit on Tab's bed, where she'd once been fucked so aggressively, take out her flask, and guzzle it until she's calmer.

6:30 PM

Her legs twitching stupidly, the old lady struggles to get onto the paint-splattered metal chair across from where Tab is bound. The Dutch girl stares impassively at the old lady, as she lowers her bottom, leans back for just a moment, then loses her balance completely, falling onto the wooden floor with a terrible thud. The odd sound that the old lady hears midway down is not necessarily laughter.

Her back aches, her shoulders too, but if she yells "*aidez moi*" again so soon, her team may hesitate to leave her alone.

First, she pushes herself up to her knees, grunting indelicately, beads of sweat dripping down the arms of her black woolen dress. From her knees, she reaches the chair, which had stayed in place during the fall. Once she's got her breath back, she looks over at Tab. If the girl had been laughing, she's not anymore. She looks vacantly in the old lady's direction without taking her in, the three-pronged cane cut looking like a dueling scar, distinguishing her already distinguished face. She shifts position as best she can, yawns, then closes her eyes.

Which is the nearest equivalent, while being held captive, to ignoring phone calls, letters, and electronic mail.

Pulling herself back to her feet, the old lady leans close enough to smell her sweat, a hint of menstrual blood, her sour halitosis.

A delicate slap on her uninjured eye proves adequate. Tab opens her eyes and keeps them that way.

Sitting back down again, the old lady gulps the scotch and backwash remaining in her flask, clears her throat, and tells the following story.

An aging American had been living a placid life of the heart, the occasional lover passing inconsequentially through while she kept to her rituals—springs and summers in the brand new house built for her in Normandy, falls in Winchester where her melodramatic mother had recently died, winters in southern California with Eliza-

beth Smalls.

But when she came into Rotterdam on business, an extraordinary young woman broke into a bar bathroom to seduce her, kidnapped her for an earth-shattering week, and unceremoniously dumped her.

Of course, she should have been able to leave the whole bloody business behind, but the young woman refused to acknowledge her very existence, ignoring decades of attempts to reach her, rubbing toxic salt into the abscess around her heart.

Which got into her system, psychic septicemia.

"Which I just can't get rid of, " says the old lady.

"Don't you get that?" she goes on. "Don't you get that at all? Did the cunt factory that produced you fail to include a heart?"

She doesn't let on how she managed to locate her or her sudden appearance in her home with a battalion of immigrant mercenaries. The fact is she is there.

Tab looks down in an attitude of reflection if not contrition.

"Smoke," she asks a moment later, her voice calm and strong, like Tyler in his younger days.

The old lady shrugs her shoulders. It's the one vice she's managed to quit. Then Tab gestures with her long neck towards a dirty tile coffee table on the other side of the room.

The old lady pushes herself to a standing position, picks the cane up from the ground, and hobbles over to the pack of Gauloise and the matches. She takes one out and brings it back to Tab.

Her hands remarkably calm, she places it in Tab's mouth and lights it.

Tab inhales several times before the old lady takes it out of her mouth and stubs it out succinctly on the grainy

131

hardwood floor.

"Drink?" asks Tab.

The old lady gestures with her empty flask, but Tab points to the bookshelf in back of where she's constrained, on which stands a half-empty bottle of schnapps.

The old lady grabs it and props it against Tab's mouth like she's feeding a baby.

The drinking and smoking complete, Tab takes a deep breath and closes her eyes like she's praying for strength, then opens them again, a half smile on her face—wry, flirtatious.

"Sorry, baby," she says to the old lady, a delayed apology, the most inadequate in the world.

"Come here," she goes on, twisting her neck in a come-hither gesture.

Suddenly embarrassed, the old lady looks down at the floor. Doesn't it bother the girl that she's hit her twice with a cane and hired Turks to tie her to a chair?

Meekly raising her head again, the old lady glances furtively at Tab.

Who winks broadly back like she's Jean Harlow, Mae West, one of those sexy old-time vamps the old lady so adored when mother took her downtown to the Odeon.

Then Tab giggles and looks towards the door, where Pedro and the Turks are still lurking, as if she and the old lady are launching a merry prank on those foreign boys.

Encouraged, the old lady pulls herself to her feet. About halfway to Tab, she has to pause to insist that her limbs stop shaking, but the instant she arrives, the girl's thick, Schnappsy tongue is in her mouth, and her lower parts are catching fire.

Several moments pass this way, then several more, but

the old lady has forgotten how weak she is, how quickly she loses her breath. Adrenaline keeps both her little lungs going well past their breaking point, but it can't stop them from giving out all at once, right in the middle of the long kiss, leaving her gasping for breath.

Limping back to the metal chair, she collapses onto it, closing her eyes and doubling over her thighs. She respires as forcefully as she can, but her heart still pounds. She's resigning herself to suffocating in front of Tab, but then her heart starts to catch up and her breathing gradually becomes less encumbered.

After counting up to ten and back down again, the old lady straightens her back and looks over at Tab.

The girl smiles fondly and mouths something without saying it. She has to mouth it again because the old lady can't believe what she's lip-reading.

"Tyler."

Years ago, she got humiliating thrills from inhabiting Tyler's train station whores. But she had never been allowed to take on the man himself. Tyler wouldn't have minded. His words came from her mouth. But when she'd suggested switching up, Tab glared and hissed like an indignant tabby.

"Oh Tyler," Tab groans, a very particular sound the old lady remembers, surprisingly deep from the lips of a flimsy girl. It sounds pouty, impatient, and Tab keeps it going for what feels like minutes, an expert chanteuse maintaining a long note.

Once she's finally finished, she shrugs her shoulders and moves her right hand as far as it can go, just to show how trapped it is, how impossible it would be to pleasure anybody, until it is released.

Tab doesn't have to speak. The thoughts emerge in the old lady's head as if they've been telegraphed there. This was the upside of her tiresome obsession. Tab speaks so loquaciously in her imagination that she doesn't have to say anything to make herself understood.

The old lady jumps to her feet, unconcerned about her lungs now. It takes her just a second to free Tab's right arm. The old lady knows a thing or two about knots, from both her sex life and her novels.

Once freed, Tab's right arm slips under the old lady's black dress. She need not get her fingers under the old lady's panties to gently rock her lower lips.

"Tyler," Tab whispers ecstatically, "oh, Tyler."

Which immediately launches the familiar raucous feeling that Mother Parkinson's hasn't robbed her of after all.

The old lady grunts as it shoots up her abdomen through her intestines and into her heart. Drool soaks her chin, snot trails down her nose, and she feels ready to absolve the most horrific of sins.

Just before it reaches its gut-wrenching apex, Tab, in a drastic but efficient gesture, rips her hand out from under the old lady and smashes it against her shoulders, sending her careening, her little head bashing against the metal chair on the way down.

Then Tab's demon right hand tears at the rope, trying to free herself.

"*Aidez moi,*" the old lady thinks, but she can't get the words out. She's started to hyperventilate again.

Tab unties herself, stretches her long, lean body and begins to head towards a window.

Her chest calmer now, the old lady tries again to yell for help, but all that comes out is that same guttural sound she'd made outside of Tab's apartment when she was trying to call the whole thing off.

The third time her voice rings into the stuffy air.

"*Aidez moi! Aidez moi!*"

Tab has already begun to open the window, which must lead to a fire escape, when the old lady's team bursts in.

The Italianate Turk comes first. At lightning speed, he grabs Tab by the ass and pulls her back into the room. She hits him on the nose with her weak little art-girl fists, as he drags her back to the chair and ties her up again.

Rage, more powerful than any before in her angry life, pounds through the old lady's body.

She thinks of faggoty little Cal Thornton punched mercilessly to the ground in that villa on Stromboli, that fat negro Samuels gasping for breath under a pillow at Bel Vento, Martini thrown from a train in Austria in that book that never found a publisher, victims of an accumulating history of violence.

Chapter 7
The New York Train

September 9
2:00 PM
Tyler

The moment the train pulls out of the Greenwich station that effective double anesthetic (rum and shock) loses its effect, and tears splash down the AOA's pimply cheeks.

Tyler can't do much to comfort him. Violence is not a taste one can instantaneously acquire. His first time wasn't easy. Blackening the eye and cracking the teeth of a smarmy Cuban boy in eleventh grade had filled him with apprehension. But when the nasty boy ambushed him after school, Tyler grabbed his switch blade and plunged it into his shoulder, without a moment's pang of conscience.

What happened at Thornton Hall was necessary business, but it would take a while for the boy to see the sense in it. Christopher Thornton Sr. was unattractive and unpleasant, but he was all the boy knew. Surely the AOA had been taken from his habitat and brought to America at too tender an age to remember much else.

The little fellow clutches Tyler's arm and stares intently into his eyes, hoping against hope there is some way he can trust him.

"Well," says Tyler, trying to sound sympathetic, "the old fellow might survive." And he hears himself go on, like a robust British major wounded in the colonies.

"Not such a serious wound, breathing afterwards, one could hear that."

"But, but..." stutters the AOA.

Tyler presses his finger against the boy's lower lip and calculates carefully.

If Christopher Thornton Sr. doesn't get medical attention at some point, he could be in serious trouble, and while the AOA is providing surprisingly pleasant company, Tyler doesn't really want responsibility for him over the long term.

If he calls the police, they might make it over to Thornton Hall quickly enough to save him, but would they find anything incriminating? They could trace the sports-oriented obscenity to the station and figure them to be on a southbound train, but New York is far too large a place to search with effective speed.

The AOA's little fingers dig into his arms, but Tyler is still working out what to do.

For security's sake, he should wait to call the police until they've reached The Bronx, and he'll keep the AOA in his custody until he's left the country in case he decides to sneak off and contact law enforcement himself.

The little fellow may have a bit of a problem anyway, if his dad remembers how he'd helped drag him into the closet. Instant Stockholm syndrome is the best excuse Tyler can come up with.

By the time Tyler's processed this, his mind moving creakily, very unlike the old days, he notices the AOA reaching into his pocket, grabbing his mobile, and attempting to crawl over him to escape down the aisle.

Tyler delicately sticks his foot out just as the boy is getting free, so that he lands between the next rows of seats, bloodying his nose.

Tyler grabs him by his shoulders, gets him back onto his feet, then picks up the boy's mobile. He can tell from the tears on the lad's face that he thinks Great Uncle Cal is going to break his phone into pieces. But that is not Great Uncle Cal's intention.

"Poor little guy," says Tyler, wiping the AOA's bloody face with a tissue from his pocket, "you really have to watch your step."

Then he looks outside to confirm that they're now in The Bronx, punches 911, and reports the crime in a shaky society contralto.

Her name is Ethel Sampson, and she's Christopher Thornton's neighbor.

What has she witnessed? Three large negroes bursting into Thornton Hall and emerging several minutes later with Christopher Thornton's dear little adopted Oriental, gagged and bound, having left the master injured somewhere inside.

Then he hangs up and turns off the AOA's mobile, so they can't ask further questions.

"Just stick with me, kid," says Tyler, "and everything will be hunky dory."

9:00 PM

Frank Kim isn't around that night in the Hotel Pennsylvania bar, and the old Irish bartender doesn't seem to notice that Tyler keeps ordering two drinks (rums and cokes and Smirnoffs on the rocks) to take back to the weathered vinyl booth. He and the AOA have been sitting for hours watching the new American president talk Texan on the 24-hour news channel.

After the boy starts looking a little green, they go back to the room so he can vomit in the tiny toilet, and Tyler can try once again to catch the relevant episode of Court TV.

Apparently, the show is not on tonight either, but after slogging through an interview with a guilty-looking Jewish type wearing bifocals, he catches the beginning of the preview again. This time Tyler can see new Thornton Hall in back of Christopher Thornton and hear him specifically announce that the man who'd gone to Stromboli with his great uncle may have murdered him, stolen his money, and gone on the run.

"That man better watch his step," rails Christopher Thornton, shaking his meaty fists at the camera.

Tyler cleans up after the AOA in the bathroom, lays him tenderly out on the far side of the double bed, and lies down beside him. Christopher Thornton has no notion of what happened on Stromboli. He couldn't scare anyone, particularly now that he's critically wounded.

It's past midnight and his train to Washington leaves at half past nine. Staring up at the chipped blue paint on the ceiling and listening to the cars and car alarms outside, Tyler says "ohm" several times to himself.

How well he had slept in his youth, even those evenings in Catania after he escaped from Stromboli, even the night he'd buried Samuels. He was past forty by that point, but the insomnia monster hadn't yet secreted its dirty eggs in his brain.

One thing he's learned, at least, is to recognize a losing struggle. So he pulls himself up, the slicing pain in his knee making him gasp, and slips out the door. Downstairs in the empty bar, he orders a double vodka martini (without the bother of extraneous olives, twists, or hints of dry vermouth) and drinks it down like tap water.

Then he staggers back up the stairs and curls close to the drowsing boy.

September 10
8:30 AM
Chris

Tyler is still sleeping soundly while the boy is running from empty car to empty car of a stationary suburban train. Chris sits himself down when he gets to the back but still doesn't feel safe. All he can think to do is crawl under the last row of seats and cramp his small frame underneath.

His head pounds, his breath tastes like rum-and-coke vomit, but he doesn't think that anyone can see him there.

Of course, his back soon hurts, as do his shoulders and his knees. The spilled soda and rotting fried chicken on the floor of the car turn his stomach, and he still feels buzzed from the night before.

How old had he been (fifteen?) when Dad said that Grand Central was unsafe for children and insisted on picking him and Ezra up on the street outside the Ziegfield after they'd seen the new *Star Wars* movie? Being treated like a baby ticked him off, and he wouldn't speak to Dad for days, but now he wonders if anyone will ever worry about him that much again. Closing his eyes, he imagines Dad marching towards him, then beckoning him into the comfortably leather-padded world of his BMW.

He crosses his fingers as hard as he can, hoping that Dad is recovering safely in a hospital somewhere, then looks at his watch and sees that the train that will take him to Stamford should be leaving in twenty-five minutes.

Tyler
8:30 AM

Tyler wakes up with a dissonant hangover, the sun shining into his eyes.

His head pounding, he runs quickly to the bathroom.

After a satisfying shit and a quick shower, Tyler feels rather more like himself.

While he's never been much of a breakfast man, the AOA is a growing boy and needs to be fed.

"Chris," he tells the mound under the sheets, "rise and shine."

Receiving no response, he says it more loudly and lifts up the sheets, finding several blankets cleverly bunched together.

One has to admire the pluck of the little fellow, Tyler thinks, wondering where the shrewd Oriental lad acquired his resourcefulness.

While repacking his effects and climbing into a blue suit made for him by a Hong Kong tailor in Naples, he considers the difficulties presented by the AOA's nifty escape. It just won't do to have him wandering around New York. If he were to alert the authorities, they might catch hold of his trail and detain him at the airport when he tries to fly out tomorrow. *La Porqueria* is not his favorite locale, but it is far preferable to an American prison.

Slipping his hands into the sheets, he feels a lingering warmth. The boy hasn't been gone for long.

Tyler has thirty minutes to find the little fellow before his train leaves Pennsylvania Station for Washington D.C.

One hopes the AOA hasn't gone straight to the police. Surely, he'll head home first to Stamford to check up on his father. A logical kid, he'll spend the couple of fivers missing from Tyler's wallet on the next train from Grand Central Station.

Unshaven, his remaining hairs tangled, but in all other respects ready to go, Tyler tears out of the hotel room with his American Tourister, tromping down the peculiar-smelling, red-carpeted stairs. He almost smashes into a gaggle of rumpled Eastern European stewardesses checking in at reception and chooses not to shove them aside to pay his bill. That would expend too many of the few minutes left before the next Stamford train.

Seeing a cab driving by the hotel, he grabs the sticky old door and lands on the lap of an elderly Italian tourist wearing a woolen Yankees cap, despite the heat, and clutching several counterfeit Rolex watches in his hairy fists.

One strong pull on the man's shirt has him reeling out of the cab and into the gutter, but the driver, some sort of Arab type, deaf to the urgency of the situation, now claims to be "out of service."

"Well you're back in service now, buddy," announces Tyler, a bit of the old Queens coming back into his voice.

While the idiot driver brazenly searches for his phone, Tyler goes into his own valise for a blunt object, or anything, to get the man moving. His hands feel his toothbrush, toothpaste, comb.

Time is running out, and the bottle of shaving cream will have to do.

He pounds it savagely against the plastic divider separating him from the driver until it breaks on through to the other side. The next smash bashes the back of the man's head and explodes the bottle, so shaving cream, pinkish with blood, billows up all over the front seat.

Lucky for them both, the Arab drops his phone, puts the car in drive and screeches forward, careening in and out of traffic up Sixth Avenue then across town to Grand Central's 42nd street entrance.

Tossing a twenty into the front seat, Tyler charges out of the cab, his knees carrying him forward through the heavy doors and down into the main departure lounge.

On the large electronic schedule board, he sees that the next Stamford train leaves in five minutes from track seven.

Dashing through the hall, he slips through the open door onto the track, then into the train.

The first car has several pickled middle-aged guys returning to their Connecticut wives, and the second has only a solitary negro in a suit and a tie.

Tyler catches his breath, then runs through the empty third car into the equally empty fourth and last car. Cursing to himself, he's about to double back, except he hears an odd sound, a sort of rustle, like a tiny vermin must have snuck in, until it gasps, and then wheezes.

He goes to the front of the car and starts looking under each seat.

He finds some refuse—a greasy paper bag with traces of ketchup, an empty condom wrapper, then finally, cramped under the very last seat, a hyperventilating Oriental adolescent.

Great Uncle Cal grabs his nephew by the collar and looks into his dirty face. A hard smack on the nose, still fractured from yesterday, would make an excellent life lesson. But he doesn't want to upset the boy more than he already is.

Dragging him across the departure hall, Tyler explains what will happen if he tries that again. How his dear old dad, recovering nicely in the hospital, will be promptly smothered by his Filipina nurse; how the boy himself will end up with much worse than acne scarring his pretty little cheeks; and how at that inevitable moment in adulthood when he decides to seek out his birth parents, he'll find their lives have been mysteriously snuffed out in early September of 2001.

His head twitching side to side, the AOA bites his cracked lower lip until it bleeds. He watches commuters whose lives aren't in the hands of old men with funny accents that aren't exactly foreign.

"But all will be well," Tyler tells him beneficently, "in fact, perfectly splendid—if you just keep your head out of trouble." He just has to manage not to converse with friends, or family members, or law enforcement officials, and meet him back at track seven at six p.m. that evening.

Other than that, the day is his to enjoy. He can spend the three twenties Tyler hands him as he likes, on porno, beer, narcotics, or anything else his little Oriental heart desires.

Then Tyler lets go of his hand and races to catch another cab, this time to Pennsylvania Station to catch his Washington train.

9:28 AM

Stuffing another twenty through the partition, Tyler flies out of the taxi and into the station. Grazing some luckless tourists with his bag, he charges towards his departure gate, but the officious Indian Amtrak guard won't let him descend the elevator to the platform, as apparently the train has already started to move.

No, he can't just take the next one, as everything is carefully timed in the universe of Delauney, so he elbows the Indian in the stomach and charges down the escalator.

The doors have indeed closed by the time he gets to the platform, but the train only inches forward. With a strength Tyler didn't know he still had, he grabs hold of the metal grate between the cars, lifts himself up, and slips inside. His arm now aches along with his knees, but he feels quite pleased with himself.

Unfortunately, he can't simply find a seat. The ridiculous Indian may have reported the incident, and officials on the train may be watching for him. He has been looking forward to the pleasant ride, sipping miniature bottles of white wine while catching his first glimpses in decades of the good old northeast corridor, but he has to slip into the lavatory while the train pulls out of the tunnel and into the Meadowlands. If elbowing an Amtrak official were really considered so horrific, he hopes, they would have already stopped the train.

But in Newark, the first stop, he hears gruff voices with walkie-talkies boarding the train, the police.

As luck would have it, just as the officers are swarming outside, someone knocks on the lavatory door and demands to know (in a working-class New Jersey accent) what's been taking him so long.

Tyler gags eloquently, hoping to discourage the man.

Everyone is so damn sensitive in this new America. One can't give a recalcitrant official a simple elbow to the abdomen without a federal case being made.

The man outside seems to have disappeared, but a moment later, someone else knocks.

"Open up," says a different voice, "this is the police."

Tyler's only real option at this point is disguise, and, fortunately, his trusty disguise kit is readily available in his satchel. It certainly isn't subtle but has gotten him out of jams before. He finds a large black beard and some adhesive to adhere it. He puts it on as quickly as he can, and after one last soulful gag to show that he hadn't been kidding about being ill, he opens the door and walks right past the small group of police officers, finding himself a seat in the next car.

At Trenton, the next stop, five ruddy, sad-sackish police officers get off the train, having failed in their errand: the case of the elbowed Indian Amtrak official, another unsolved crime in the great metropolis.

A pretty young redhead sells him a half-bottle of tolerable white wine in the café car. He sips as slowly as he can as the train passes through Philadelphia, Wilmington, and Baltimore on its way to the capitol.

In fact, after the rocky start, his errand for Delauney goes remarkably smoothly.

The train arrives on schedule. Tyler follows signs to the parking garage, and easily locates the correct space on which stands a beaten-up old Cadillac with an empty manila envelope on its dash.

Tyler follows the implicit instructions, which are to place the travel drive inside the envelope, take the elevator back down to the station, and use Delauney's debit card to buy himself a seat on the next train for New York, leaving ten minutes later.

As he sits with his second half-bottle of white, watching the cities roll by in reverse, he wonders why Delauney has sent him all the way from Spain for this tiny peccadillo. Is there something else in mind for him to do? Or perhaps Delauney's baroque scheming is an end in and of itself. Why do something simply and easily when one can create an intricate intrigue? And Delauney can well afford it. He may have lost the fund, but he has fingers in dozens of even more lucrative pies.

Somewhere in between Wilmington and Philadelphia, Tyler slips into a sodden sleep but wakes up when he hears an electronic melody right nearby, *The Godfather* theme. It finally stops but starts right up again and seems to be coming from his jacket.

A few disorienting seconds later, he locates the Delauney mobile phone and answers it with a skeptical hello.

Still half asleep and mildly inebriated, he hasn't time to consider who it might be and is completely flummoxed to hear *La Moglie*'s voice.

"Oh Teelor, Teelor, *stai tu?*" she sobs.

"Yes, Ornella, *sono io*, Tyler, it's me," he responds, trying to get at least a little pleasure from this. She must be suffering a crisis of conscience out in Africa. All she has to do, and this she surely knows, is bid the simpering French girl *adieu*, meet him back in *La Porqueria*, and resume her wifely duties: no melodrama required. One so hated being apologized to.

"Whatever is the matter?" he asks, feeling immediately contrite about his sarcastic tone.

"*Rapito, sono rapito*," she moans.

"Yes, kidnapped," goes the FCT, "and the French girl as well." His patrician drawl is as aggravating as ever. "I'm afraid I've got both of them."

"Where the hell are you?" growls Tyler. The man wasn't at Thornton Hall, but Tyler can't believe he's really in *La Porqueria* despite his repeated claims to have been heading there.

"Hotel de Ville," says the voice methodically.

"Saint Louis," it goes on.

"Senegal," it concludes, bringing *La Moglie* back on the line.

"Oh, Teelor, *vieni qui. Aiuta me! Aiuta me!*"

But before Tyler can say the obvious, which is that, of course, he'll come rescue her, the phone goes dead.

How did they get this number? And do they know where he is now? He imagines Delauney in his trite French cravat; Christopher Thornton, surely out of the closet by now, dead or alive; and Cal himself—all of them in on some miracle of cross-conspiracy pollination.

Remembering how his Incan cabbie had summoned an information operator with his mobile, Tyler punches 411, reaches an American Express travel office and manages to book himself a flight for Dakar leaving late that evening. He's about to confirm that he is indeed the only passenger when he remembers the AOA, due to meet him at six back at track seven.

The little fellow will be more desperate than ever to find his awful dad, and one so hated disappointing children. Tyler might be able to talk him out of it if he issues another warning, but while he's busy traipsing after Ornella in Africa, the boy is sure to contact law enforcement. The safest course of action would be to take the boy down an empty Grand Central corridor and slit his throat. But Tyler simply can't abide the thought.

"How many passengers will be traveling," repeats the

testy Long Island Jewess on the phone, her accent recalling a long line of unpleasant homeroom teachers.

"Two," says Tyler, though he knows he'll have to field complaints from Delauney about abusing his debit card privileges.

He'll just have to accept that an Oriental adolescent on the loose constitutes an emergency. In any case, a moment later his reservation is confirmed.

The train from Washington arrives at Penn Station on schedule, and Tyler finds himself in a taxi for the third time that day (this one driven by a surly Russian with a prominent double chin) back to Grand Central and his six o'clock appointment.

The Great Hall's clock shows only a few minutes past as he hurries through the rush hour crowds towards track seven.

No immediate sign of the AOA, but, as it's too crowded to say for sure, he climbs up to one of the bars overlooking the hall to get a bird's eye view. After two methodical inspections reveal not a single Oriental adolescent, Tyler breathes a pained sigh, says "ohm" several times to himself, and feels bitter acid accumulate in his gut: another disappointment.

"The little fucker," he says aloud to himself (his voice channeling Queens), "the fucking little fucker."

Neither his ohms nor his outburst can calm him. He shakes like a hysterical girl, tears creeping down his face. The kidnapping of *La Moglie* must finally be hitting him.

Until he detects a distant pitter-patter, a smaller, sharper sound than the plodding progression of rush hour commuters. Then he catches a high-pitched voice—*excuse me, sorry, excuse me*—getting gradually closer.

The AOA wears a Knicks jersey and a Yankees cap on backwards, evidence of a day of jubilant tourism. Got carried away. Lost sense of time. One can hardly fault him for it.

As the AOA sputters his apologies, Tyler looks up at the clock and sees it's not yet fifteen minutes past the hour.

"Hardly late, dear boy," he assures him, awkwardly patting his sweaty shoulders, "hardly late at all."

Then the little fellow breathes a sigh of relief and stares longingly at track seven, where another Stamford train is about to leave.

"No, no, no," says Tyler a bit too exuberantly, "we're going somewhere much more interesting."

Which makes the AOA bite back into his bleeding lip, wipe the tear-inflamed acne on his cheeks, and try to explain how he's really grateful for everything and all but would just as soon go home.

Tyler shakes his head and considers how best to sell it to the little fellow—grandiose French administration buildings in only slight disrepair, handsome waiters in glimmering whites, gin and tonics on formerly colonial verandas —when the AOA starts swinging blindly at him.

After Tyler catches his harmless third punch with his hand, the little fellow springs another leak, yowling like a tomcat and frantically sobbing. Which hardly does justice to his inscrutable Oriental genes and causes several passing middle-aged matrons to shoot them concerned looks.

Tyler decides to behave like a typically sentimental American, giving the quivering boy a hug. He gets snot and tears on his dress shirt and a final muffled blow to his chest, but the AOA soon settles into his arms.

It would do no good at all to tell him that, back in Stamford, he'd inherit millions and a bother-free life if the old fellow died, and with Tyler, he was headed for an adventure on the dark continent, which might have its challenges but would surely, as Horace said, be a joy to remember.

Chapter 8
Tab's Apartment

September 11, 2001
8:00 PM
Eve

Tab is tied to the chair again, but the old lady can't stand to look at her. Pedro and the Turks lurk aimlessly, asking themselves the sorts of questions she's hired them not to. The pale Dutchwoman with the scabby eye and sweaty nightgown has gone quite a while without begging for drugs.

The old lady can't think straight with these smarmy men about. The words "go back into the hall" begin in her throat, but she waves dismissively at them instead.

Which seems like a basic signal, but these immigrants are too dense to understand it. After a second, more vociferous wave, the Italianate Turk, the least imbecilic of the bunch, leads them outside to the landing below.

Finally alone with Tab again, the old lady sinks on her chair and chugs at her empty flask until she notices that the schnapps bottle hasn't leaked out entirely. The finger or two feel good in her throat..

"Ohm," she says helplessly, "ohm."

She closes her eyes and concentrates hard enough to see a little into Tab's murky mind.

The girl probably feels miffed that her escape attempt has been foiled. She may have been slapped around and tied up. But that hardly equals splintering the old lady's heart, then returning years later to ruin her last chance at pleasure.

Worldly, blasé, a professional cynic, Tab couldn't have imagined her the day going like this. If she really suspected that a former lover was planning to come out of the woodwork with a team of immigrants and tie her to a chair, wouldn't she have gone to visit one of her aunts in the country?

Just when the old lady is ready to look back into Tab's eyes, she hears a rasping sound, a wheezing.

Tab has fallen asleep again, snoring obliviously.

She drains the dregs of her schnapps, then takes her cane and taps the girl on the forehead.

Tab wrinkles her nose and mutters some unpleasant Dutch colloquialism. She yawns and looks around at her hands (now tied more tightly to the chair), the painfully empty Schnapps bottle, and the old lady peering at her from her nearby chair.

Then the last several minutes of her life roar back: the wound on her face, the cord around her torso, the insipid carrying on about a mediocre love affair nearly a decade past.

The memory of that nauseating week after the film festival makes her especially pissed: the endless drinking; the flaccid little body orgasming hysterically whenever you even looked at it; the arrogance of taking personal credit for Tyler's accomplishments like she'd been there herself. Generously, she had kept up their affair a day or so after she'd lost interest, only to be rewarded with a deluge of calls and letters when she finally ended it, some of them psychotically angry since the old lady kept confusing her life with her thriller books. Eventually, she'd had to change her phone number and move to another neighborhood without leaving a forwarding address.

Just last month, she had made the foolish error of allowing the pompous *Fuck Death* curator to list her name on the Internet only to be invaded by the same old woman now accompanied by some sort of Turkish Stasi.

The indignity of what's just happened hits her all at once. Her fingers and toes tingle with rage, adrenaline surging through her body. If she pushes just a little harder, the ropes will snap away, and she can fight these cretins out of her apartment.

When the ropes refuse to budge, she bites her lip so hard it bleeds. She can't come up with adequate curses, so she shrieks then releases a quiet volley of malicious cognates in Dutch.

The more Tab carries on, the more angry Tab becomes, her voice growing loud and shrill again, her body shaking along with the chair like they're suffering grand mal seizures.

Which makes the old lady close her eyes and peer back into the middle of the 1960's. A little girl with a bow around her waist and pigtails in her blond hair pitches a monumental fit at a family dinner (she'd been given the wrong flavored ice cream, the wrong kind of doll), her voice screeching through the upper bourgeois Dutch country home.

Tab switches languages and starts in on her again.

"Feeble, lame, pathetic," she tells the old lady, experimenting with her English vocabulary and sighing morosely, "pitiful."

Forgetting that she's being held captive, her life hanging in the old lady's hands, she gathers as much spittle as she can and fires an unwieldy globule right into the old lady's left eye.

"*Dood*," growls a guttural, barely human voice from deep inside her innards, "*dood, dood, dood*."

Which sounds like *tod*, German for dead, which the old

lady recognizes from Wagner.

Dead.

You should be dead.

You're practically dead.

Why don't you just die?

Yes, the old lady is dying, but Tab remains alive. She will recover from her minor injuries and go back to her life, all the better for the humiliating story she'll get to tell.

The lady knows full well that Tab will talk to friends, then newspapers, magazines and eventually talk shows, that it will inspire a whole new series of installations; *Death and the Maiden*, she'll call them, after the Schubert quartet.

The old lady's last has never felt closer; Parkinson's, laying easy for her Rotterdam adventure, will roar triumphantly back. Just a few more miserable, barely functional months is all she can look forward to, under the stringent care of Elizabeth Smalls, whose stern face will be the last she'll see as the world fades before her eyes.

The newspapers will not mourn the passing of the mother of the classically handsome sociopath (who she prays will find a way to live on) but will rejoice in the final humiliation of the crazy old lesbian who could never get over a *frivolous frolic* and had to stalk her younger ex-lover and hire immigrants to imprison her.

The old lady looks around the room, the threadbare rug; the stubbed-out cigarette on the coffee table; the empty bottle of schnapps within easy reach.

The old lady takes it in her hand and caresses it thoughtfully. Taking a deep breath, she pulls it fluidly in back of her shoulders like a golfer swinging backwards. Then, after toppling briefly, she drives it forward and watches it slip from her hands and shatter into Tab's forehead, creating a terrible sound. Has she meant to throw it at the girl? She just can't say.

In any case, she feels queasy, like she's overindulged, and she lacks the stomach to look down at the ground.

It can't be too bad, or wouldn't the girl be whimpering?

"Ohm," says the old lady hopefully to herself, "ohm."

But something damp and sticky around her foot interferes with her concentration, and she wonders what she's spilled on herself.

The pool of blood spreading over her shoes is from the open wound in Tab's forehead, and the gaping hole in which she can see something grayish must be her brain.

Tab's eyes are open, and she shallowly breathes.

Highlight it, the old lady remembers Elizabeth Smalls' instructions for erasing, *then push delete*. The trouble isn't an awkward sentence on her computer, though, but a girl bleeding on the ground near her feet. The pistachio nuts she'd munched on the drive fight their way up her esophagus, but she swallows them back down again and gazes upon Tab, looking unexpectedly innocent in the early evening light.

"Tab dear," she says as sweetly as she can, slipping a little Winchester into her voice, "are you okay?"

She gets no answer, so all she can do is sit back down and wait for the cavalry, who must have heard the crash.

Then she remembers how she'd shooed them from the room.

"*Aidez moi!!*" she yells, "*aidez moi.*"

They finally burst in, led by the Italianate Turk who cries out in his native tongue when he sees the girl.

"Look what happened," says the old lady. "Look what

happened to her."

The Italianate Turk takes off his shirt and presses it to Tab's wound.

"No, no," says the older Turk, "that could make it worse."

Then the old Turk takes Tab's delicate little hand in his bearish paw and feels for a moment until a shudder of relief ripples through his body, a pulse.

The old lady's heart palpitates—would that it overstrain itself and stop altogether. Tab's last wish would be granted, and the old lady could escape the crime scene she's just created.

Her legs quiver as Pedro joins the Turks by the girl's body. Pedro looks into Tab's eyes and puts his ear up near her mouth to see how well she's breathing. Then he peers at her head and groans when he sees the extent of her wound. Rising to his feet, he takes a few angry steps in the old lady's direction before regaining control of himself.

The old lady shrugs. There's really nothing she can do now. Her heart is calming, beat by slower beat, and, once it's relatively normal, she realizes how desperately she needs to pee.

Of course, her legs can only shake in place, and when she looks towards Pedro in hopes of his customary little push, she sees the questions on all three of their faces.

10:00 PM

Several minutes have passed and several minutes more but the two Turks and Pedro can't wrench the old lady away from the wall at which she's been peacefully staring, apparently not too concerned about the bludgeoned girl bleeding on the ground.

Tab shudders periodically, her body twitching like she's being shocked with electricity while blood from her head still seeps into the carpet.

Which may be leaking into the apartment below, turning the neighbor's herring dinner salty red.

"Señora, please," says Pedro more firmly than before, "we can't just let her lie there."

The lady looks at him as if he's making no sense.

"We were supposed to help her and look what you've done," says Pedro.

The old lady waves her index finger at him, then turns her attention to Tyler and his Oriental companion, efficiently getting them another cab, which scoots them from Grand Central towards Kennedy Airport and their flight to Africa.

But then Tab suddenly gasps, her chest clenching as she struggles to breathe. Blood dribbles down from her scalp onto the carpet, but the gashes on her forehead, which the old lady is only now noticing, are thankfully clotting.

The girl twitches then gurgles, then lies quietly for nearly a minute, her pallor turning from bright red to faintly blue.

The old lady looks at Pedro and the Turks. They look back at her.

From the research for an early novel, the old lady has some notion of CPR, but can only administer it if she gets down to the ground where Tab lies. Grabbing hold of her three-pronged cane to brace her fall, she gently lets herself go, landing on her hip in the slippery pool of blood that's collected around the bludgeoned girl.

When Pedro and the Turks rush towards her, fearing she's had some sort of seizure, she waves them fiercely away until the pain in her hip subsides.

Tab gurgles again, peculiar yellowish foam coming from her mouth, but the old lady can't do anything for her until she catches her own breath.

The moment she does, she smells something funky that doesn't seem like blood and realizes that she's landed in the least convenient position, her head nearer Tab's filthy bare feet than her struggling torso.

She manages to get up on her hands and knees, but when she tries to turn around in order to crawl towards Tab's face, she can only flail uselessly on the bloody floor. She looks up at the Turks and Pedro, but they look too disgusted to do anything for her. She finds her cane but tosses it away because it won't help her move forward.

Tab gurgles ever more pathetically, drowning in her own juices, but the old lady can still only slither on the ground. After looking around her one more time, she grabs the only thing she can find, the girl's narrow thighs.

Which work like a pulley, propelling the girl slowly towards the old lady and rousing nervous gasps from Pedro and the Turkish peanut gallery.

By the time she gets Tab's face close to her, she's lost her breath and has to rest her head on the girl's boobs to re-gather her strength.

A final pull on Tab's shoulder brings her mouth right above Tab's mouth and makes her imbecilic team titter nervously.

"No, I'm not fucking her," she informs them.

She wipes off the foam around the girl's mouth, then sticks her hand inside to make sure nothing is obstructing her breathing. Then she clamps her own mouth over Tab's mouth, pushes in Tab's chest with her hands and exhales as muscularly as she can.

The first couple of breaths yield only bloody halitosis, but the third time, she feels stronger, healthier air coming from Tab and rolls off onto her side.

In the several moments it takes the old lady to get her own breath back, she registers the sordidness of the whole scene: the blood-drenched girl, the dingy drop ceiling, her mismatched team of badly dressed immigrants. But when she tries to get back on her feet, she just slips around in the blood. However petulantly she thrashes her little legs, she can't get them off the floor, and her team—on some sort of strike, she supposes—still refuses to help.

Her body trapped for the foreseeable future, she closes her eyes and allows her mind to go where it pleases.

Rocking delicately from side to side, she wonders if she's been picked up by a trolley car or a rickshaw, maybe a gondola. She recognizes a smell, the boiling of many, many pots of tomatoes. Then she curses out loud. Her treacherous brain has taken her to the last peaceful place it can find.

Mother is downstairs, canning her autumn tomatoes, and she's upstairs in her little closet of a bedroom, trying to remove Raggedy Ann's tunic to see what's underneath.

This can't be a dream because it's happening just how she remembers it.

She's removed the tunic with the cherries sewn onto it and little pants as well to see what it tastes like when she licks it.

Stupid beyond belief, she becomes preoccupied with Raggedy Ann's nonexistent cloth titties, then rocking back and forth on her bed with Raggedy Ann's curly-haired head between her little legs. She doesn't hear Mother's footsteps coming up the stairs, and now Mother has opened the door and caught her at it.

She doesn't think she's defied Mother's instructions—like when she begged to move to Atlanta with Father—but Mother rips the doll from her hand, nevertheless, and slaps her hard in the face.

The old lady hears not very Mother-like Turkish whispering and opens her eyes a crack to see the face of the Turk. Mother is still telling her how dirty and disgusting she's behaved. Then she's taking her to the bathroom and scrubbing her all over with a bristly sponge, including the place between her legs where the dirtiness originated.

And worst of all, she takes the kitchen scissors and cuts Raggedy Ann into several pieces.

The next sound she hears is the fat Turk opening the door and running down the stairs, though he's only been paid half his fee for the evening's work.

The old lady makes sure Tab is still breathing. Yes, she is, but when poor old Owen Sinistra (one of her most pathetic characters) broke that Chinese water pitcher over his wife, Eliza's, head, she had breathed normally, talked normally, even fucked her Italian lover normally, until the subdural swelling reached a certain point and her lights went permanently out.

But the Italianate Turk is also losing patience. He grabs her by the arm and pulls her to her feet. He looks her in the eyes to try to see if she's in any way *compos mentis.*

But the old lady has already flipped away from Eliza to Christopher Thornton, in his private room in Stamford General hospital.

Christopher Thornton sleeps on his back, his body attached to a series of IVs. The Filipina nurse, who Tyler has warned the AOA about, is taking his pillow in hand, but rather than strangling him with it, she is fluffing it and placing it in back of his head.

Her characters hardly ever die of natural causes, but after taking a sharp breath and twitching like he's been shocked by electricity, Christopher Thornton slips away into a hopeless coma.

Meanwhile, at her feet, Tab's complexion looks a little better, at least for the moment, as if she's benefitted from Christopher Thornton's passing.

The old lady says a prayer, as she always does when she knocks off one of her characters, and the Italianate Turk shakes his head and bounds down the stairs.

"Some sketchy-looking Turks," she explains to the dispatcher at the emergency number written on the pay phone across the street. "They just ran out from 244 Zaagmolenstra all covered in blood."

It shouldn't take long for Rotterdam's finest to search apartment by apartment until they find the bludgeoned girl and take her to the hospital.

Her poor little Dutch girl has been dealt a terrible blow, and the old lady has fled the scene of the crime. She can now turn her mind to Tyler's departure for the dark continent with young Chris in tow.

Chapter 9
The Flight to Dakar

Fortunately, the plane to Dakar is configured more favor-
ably than the one from Spain, allowing Tyler and the AOA
an aisle and a window together without the bother of a
middle seat and a nosy stranger.

Tyler has given the AOA the window in case he wants
to look out, but once the plane takes off into the night,
the little fellow gets restless, unsettled. Every few moments
he's up to something else.

Sometimes he sleeps but only for minutes at a time.

Sometimes, he weeps quietly to himself.

At other times, he has claustrophobic little fits, twisting
and turning, stretching and kicking, his shiny new Nikes
knocking into Tyler's vulnerable knees.

Tyler's mission in the dark continent will be challenging
to say the least, and he can't possibly succeed if he doesn't
relax on the plane over. But he's not always afflicted with
bad luck. Two good things happen at the same time. First,
the AOA disappears to the bathroom, then the drink cart
comes back by.

Tyler gets another glass of white for himself, and a rum
and coke for his companion. Then he rummages in his valise for the last two Ativans from the *Sant'Agata* pharmacy.

Grabbing a foil gum wrapper left on the seat by the
AOA, and two quarters from his own pocket, he ducks
under his seat like he's misplaced something. Then he slips
the Ativans into the foil gum wrapper and crushes them
between the two quarters.

Finally, he pulls his head up and takes the rum and coke

from the AOA's upright table. After looking around to make sure no one is watching, he dumps in the white powder and stirs it around with his index finger.

He's just got his finger out of the AOA's drink and his attention back on the men's magazine he purchased at the airport when the boy returns from the bathroom, glaring sorrowfully at Tyler as he gets up to let him back into his seat.

"Figured you could use a drink," Tyler announces too buoyantly.

Which makes the AOA wince and shake his head, rejecting anything his torturer might suggest.

But, thankfully, better sense prevails, and he drinks it down hungrily, without comment on the bitter taste or chalky consistency.

Within fifteen minutes, he ceases to knock about. Within half an hour, he's checked out for the remainder of the flight.

September 11
7:00 AM (Senegal time)

Tyler has tasted the tropics before—Morocco, India, that unpleasant Delauney errand in Mexico City—but West Africa is virgin territory.

The Dakar airport is packed with negroes in flowing robes and odd little Muslim hats, and there's no sign anywhere telling one where to go. While Tyler and the sleep-sodden AOA wander in search of a *cambio*, an old man with a trustworthy face pulls them into a ramshackle version of an airport gift store, which smells of incense and cigarettes and is packed with batik shirts and wooden masks.

He pours them black tea and offers to exchange money at a reasonable rate. Before any transaction can occur, the AOA, lacking proper tolerance for benzodiazepines, closes his eyes, dips into sleep, and nearly falls off his chair. Then he bolts to his feet and stares wildly around him.

The shopkeeper shoots Tyler a concerned look and asks what's wrong with the boy.

Tyler shakes his head gravely and wipes his brow to show how difficult this all has been for him.

Both the mother and the father, he dolefully explains in French, were killed two weeks ago in a terrible car crash, some Chinese driver barreling into their BMW on the Brooklyn Queens Expressway.

As the godfather and a longtime family friend, he's decided that visiting a new locale might take the boy's mind off his loss.

The concerned shopkeeper sighs and finds several pieces of licorice candy in a drawer near the register. The AOA delves immediately into them. Chewing gloomily, he wipes his tear-stained eyes with his sticky fingers.

The little fellow looks up from his candy when the large pile of West African francs are handed to Tyler in return for his dollars.

"What's the currency here?" he asks. The brightness in his voice is a relief.

"Can I have some for my foreign money collection?" he asks sweetly, and ingenuously. Tyler, seeing no harm in it, hands over a few bills.

Looking less than absolutely miserable for the first time in more than a day, he studies them carefully before slipping them in his pocket.

While counting bills and sipping sugary tea, Tyler asks

the man advice.

From eavesdropping on one of *La Moglie*'s phone conversations with her French girlfriend, Tyler remembers that Saint Louis, where he's supposed to go, is somewhere up the coast near Mauritania and was the former capital of French West Africa, but neither bit of information helps him get there from the airport in Dakar.

What the pleasant old storekeeper suggests, after pouring more tea and thinking hard on the matter, is getting his good friend, the taxi driver, to take them there: an air-conditioned ride with solid brakes and good pickup, not lasting more than four hours.

And the cost? Tyler learns that "the very special price just for them" would still take nearly half his pile of francs. These people like to bargain, but he doubts he can bring it down far enough.

The old storekeeper looks pensive, terribly worried, when Tyler says he can't afford it. There are no passenger trains heading north, and he's sure to be robbed if he gets anywhere near a bus.

The best alternative the old man can come up with would be for them to allow the taxi driver to take them someplace in Dakar called the *Gare Routiere* where there are *sept places*, moderately comfortable station wagons headed for particular destinations. When one gets filled with seven Saint Louis-bound passengers, it will go there directly for a reasonable sum.

9:30 AM

Soon they're riding down a bumpy highway full of potholes. Vendors wearing raggedy western clothes or garishly-colored African robes pour from the early morning sidewalks into the streets, hawking hubcaps and condoms, peanuts and dried fish.

The *Gare Routiere* turns out to be a murky parking lot adjacent to an underpass in which huge ancient Peugeots lie quietly like sleeping elephants, surrounded by hundreds of dubious-looking natives, drinking tea, smoking cigarettes, and sleeping on the dirty ground as they wait for their rides to leave.

True to his bargain, the taxi driver takes them to find one of the *sept places* bound for Saint Louis. The AOA peers skeptically around him as he gingerly steps through the crowd, trying not to tromp on excrement and rotting food or brush against anything skeevy or contagious.

He looks to his right, then to his left, tensing his leg and arm muscles like a cartoon character about to make a run for it, but gloomily relaxes once he realizes that there's no place to go.

The taxi driver introduces them to a nervous-looking man in his early sixties with a pert gray beard and a traditional Muslim cap, whose old car has had its trunk removed and replaced with cramped little seats and whose hands hold up a small sign with the words "Saint Louis" clearly written in black magic marker.

Tyler and the AOA are passengers five and six, so the wait shouldn't be terribly long. Taking advantage of the pause, Tyler slips behind a broken-down cement wall, pisses where thousands have pissed before, and takes a furtive tug at his whisky flask, hoping that the sanctimonious deity worshiped by the poor wretches surrounding him won't strike him down for violating his sanction against alcohol.

Tyler returns from his nip and his pee to find the AOA being assaulted by a dirty-looking beggar. Probably about the same age as the AOA but dwarfed by malnutrition and disease, its hair is covered by lice, its skin is full of hives, and its body is barely covered by a raggedy Miami Dolphins tee-shirt. The awful creature has its face right up to the AOA and keeps complaining how hungry it is.

The AOA pinches his nose with one hand and holds his other one away from his chest, trying to keep the creature at bay.

How obnoxious they are, thinks Tyler, resenting the whole pathetic lot of them, ruining everything decent the French had set up.

Taking his handkerchief from his breast pocket and covering his hands with it to avoid contagion, Tyler grabs the vagrant by his collar and smacks him soundly to the ground.

The bloodied vagrant lies on its back, moaning to itself, and several of the restless natives surrounding them begin to move closer, as Tyler appears to have broken some sort of primitive code of conduct.

Then the not very grateful AOA clutches his stomach and vomits up some gooey green leaves, the remains of the salad that was all that he'd managed of his airplane meal.

Thankfully, before more trouble can befall them, the *sept-place* driver returns with the seventh passenger, a not unattractive female. Tyler climbs into the front seat, the AOA gets crammed into the doorless far back, and they are off to Saint Louis.

Noon

Driving out of Dakar takes over an hour in deadening traffic, with Tyler in front and the AOA and the five other passengers (or seven if one counted the two babies) crammed into the back. They inch in and out of traffic circles: vendors surging onto the road to hawk their wares through open car windows, the air thick with dust, exhaust, and the fumes of rotting garbage.

Once they get out of the suburbs, if one can call them that, they bounce along towards Saint Louis on a fairly well-paved road, watching the scruffy bushes and long, dry African plains passing by on either side.

The driver pulls off the road every half an hour or so to pay respect to groups of old men in white robes sitting in solemn circles from whom he receives crinkled pieces of paper, tickets that must be presented to the baby-faced, sub-machine-gun-bearing military policeman at the many roadblocks along the way.

The uneasy journey keeps Tyler's mind away from the FCT and his captives, but each time they bounce back he has another question. How can the FCT manage hostages inside a hotel? Have Ornella and her little French girlfriend been indoctrinated into his cult? Can the AOA ever be counted on to help?

He stretches his legs as best he can and stares dully out the window. But he can't stop trying to puzzle out the identity of the man waiting for him in Saint Louis.

Most likely, he's a random stranger who chanced upon incriminating information, but there is also no harm in imagining he is who he says he is.

When the Samuels incident had gotten under his skin

and his screaming in his sleep had started to bother *La Moglie*, he'd seen a Neapolitan psychiatrist who quite reasonably ascribed the problem to the stymieing of his childhood imagination. It hadn't been right of his mother to make him slave the afternoons away delivering sausages and chops for that grimy Italian butcher when he was barely eleven years old.

Closing his eyes and resting his hands in his lap, Tyler releases his imagination. A newer and sleeker Peugeot drops himself and his little Oriental in front of a grand colonial hotel in an amiable town square that seems rather *Provençal*. The man drinking Pernod and soda at a table in front looks better than the Spanish girl's computer program had suggested, his bald head covered in an expensive blond toupee and his cheeks made ruddy by the African sun.

And it turns out that things between them had pretty much evened themselves out, Cal's kiss-trickery and bitch slap equaling the burning of the villa, which hadn't killed him after all. It was as good a time as any for a fresh start.

Upstairs in his suite of rooms, Ornella and her awful little French girlfriend are both bound and tied, ready to be released after the two old friends have had a chance to catch up.

But just as he's imagining falling into Cal's arms, the car hits a rock and lurches into the air. Something sharp penetrates the small of Tyler's back. Just a broken seat spring, but it can't help but remind him of Cal's merciless machinations.

With about eighty kilometers to go, the driver takes a left turn onto a dirt road, dropping one of the passengers off in their village and picking up several more at a local *gare routiere.*

After several minutes bouncing uncomfortably up and down the rough dirt road, Tyler starts hearing whispering coming from the back seat. Along with several incomprehensible African words, he recognizes *pluie*, French for rain.

The blazing sun has been covered by threatening clouds, and more resentment is brewing in the back seat.

Tyler hears the phrase "*rue mauvaise*," bad road, repeated *sotto voce* by several of his fellow passengers. They don't like the detour any more than he does. Why can't the pretty young woman with the grayish teeth just walk to her village from the highway?

The stakes get higher when the rain starts pouring, and all the passengers (except the girl getting door to door service) move from mumbling into mutiny. He can hear the cackling sounds of their language.

As larger and larger sheets of water come down from the black sky, the teenager right behind the driver (wearing long short pants and a dirty Colonial Williamsburg tee-shirt) starts delicately, then not so delicately, banging the driver's shoulders with his fingertips. Which only seems to encourage the obstinate fellow who fords deeper and deeper puddles with almost no visibility through any of his windows.

He swings off the road to avoid a particularly cavernous one only to clip off a large tree branch.

After that, the car goes dead.

When all the male passengers except for him and the AOA leap immediately out of the car, Tyler closes his eyes, not wishing to witness the mauling of the driver.

But looking in back of him, he sees that they are trying to push the valiant old Peugeot out of the puddle into

174

which it appears to be sinking.

While Tyler understands that he won't make a good impression with Ornella (or the FCT for that matter) if he arrives soaking wet and covered in mud, he doesn't want to be a bad sport. Besides, he can barely breathe the heavy air inside the Peugeot.

So he opens the door, allowing in a lot of rain and some pleasant cooler air, and searches around with his foot in the puddle below for solid ground. He expects water to come up somewhere around his calves, but soon they're submerged along with his knees and the beginnings of his thighs. He splashes his way to the back of the Peugeot and inserts himself into the mass of negroes pushing it forward.

After a few minutes of shoving, they manage to get the thing moving, but the engine refuses to catch, and the car sinks into an even deeper pool of muddy water.

As he catches his breath, there's another commotion. No longer trapped, the AOA is fighting his way out from the back of the car. He jumps out of the car, the puddle coming up almost to his navel. At first, he splashes towards Tyler but skids off to the side, back onto what's left of the road.

Before Tyler can think to run after him, he's disappeared.

Hang it, thinks Tyler. The obnoxious little fellow can drown in the flood for all he cares.

Everyone climbs back into the steaming car, talking all at once.

Taking the flask from his coat, he finds that he'd finished the last of his liquor back at the *Gare Routiere*. Here it is, the most hellacious afternoon of his life, and there isn't a drop to calm him. Water must be seeping in. It tastes salty on the sides of his mouth.

Tears.

The rain splashes more powerfully. The driver takes off his hat and buries his face in his big black hands. Both back seat babies decide to crap themselves, further thickening the air. When Tyler closes his eyes and listens as hard as he can, he hears only raindrops and heavy African breathing.

Hotter, clammier, smellier than ever inside the car, he wheezes and rasps but can't fill his lungs.

Opening the door, he slides into the deep water and hears that peculiar little melody from the inner pocket of his jacket, the *Godfather* theme. Picking it up, he catches the FCT's sarcastic voice, warning him of the terrors in store for his wife and her girlfriend if he doesn't come immediately to Senegal. Before he can explain that he's already there, the phone fizzles in the rain.

Muddy water creeps up his abdomen and Tyler remembers *La Moglie*'s feathery arms, the way she'd held him after Jackson's letter had arrived, announcing that Mother had passed. Or Mother's own arms. She'd never shown him much affection, but it would be a good time to start now that he's old and drowning.

He lolls around in the filthy water quite a while before he hears the creaking of a primitive engine. Then sees a vehicle emerging in the distance, which turns out to be a tractor. After some sort of negotiation with the driver, they tie it with rope to the Peugeot. Within moments, Tyler is climbing back inside the car and is being towed slowly out of the flood.

3:00 PM
Chris

Chris feels the old grime, which has been collecting for days, getting covered by new grime, a dark green mud covering his bottom half.

Then his ankle gets caught by something deep in the water, and he topples into the enormous puddle .

His spits mud out his mouth and remembers what Dad used to say: "If there's ever an emergency, and I'm not with you, make sure not to panic and call me on my private phone."

That phone now lies on a black-top driveway, badly cracked and thousands of miles away.

Chris gets his legs moving, as close to running as he can. He keeps his eyes half closed to stop the rain from blurring his vision and takes himself to task for growing up too slowly. The credulous little shit who used to be him accepted the bull about rock clubs on the Left Bank and got so trashed on one rum-and-coke that he helped drag his father into a closet. Hardened by the last few days, he knows that if he gets to do it over again, he'll tackle that old fucker by his bad knees or stab him in the abdomen with a knife from the kitchen.

The rain begins to dwindle and Chris gets a better sense of his surroundings. Rudimentary concrete structures start emerging on both sides of the road, the beginnings of a town.

3:30 PM
Tyler

Tyler stands in front of a weathered wooden counter, asking the teenager with the harelip if he can have something they probably don't sell. Across the street, some miracle mechanics are working to resuscitate the *sept place* and send them on their way.

"*Une bierre. Une bierre, s'il-vous-plait?*"

"*Je suis désolé,*" repeats the harelip, and Tyler winks back at him in that "can't something be arranged" way that generally works in these countries. He takes out his wallet to show his billfold, but the little fellow shakes his head.

He hasn't drowned in the deluge, and he may even see his wife again, but his life, with its pennilessness and infirmity, its loss of enthusiasm and lack of self-respect, has gone completely to shit. One has to admit that.

The AOA was right to take off.

Until the boy with the harelip pulls him towards the back, into a room knee-deep in water. The young man's face is surprisingly intelligent, as he smiles and splashes towards a stack of wooden crates. From the top one, he pulls out a glass bottle of murky yellow fluid, which must be moonshine.

Tyler grabs some bills from his pocket, but the boy shakes his head.

Then Tyler takes the bottle and guzzles down as much as he can, gasoline-like but calming.

He clutches the boy's hand and wraps his body around him, a desperate, grateful embrace.

His head now buzzing, Tyler checks to make sure the mechanics are still working, then strolls down the main drag of the grubby, one-horse town, thinking he might run into the AOA, who is damn good company when he isn't weeping, vomiting, or trying to pummel him.

If *La Moglie* were to meet the little fellow, she'd find him charming despite his peculiarities and might even broach the topic of acquiring one of their own. That idea would have to be nipped in the bud, but Tyler enjoys the image of Ornella in her nightgown, the morning sun streaming into Bel Vento's expansive kitchen, feeding himself and their own little Oriental a healthy American breakfast of pancakes and bacon with a spot of brandy to brace them for the day.

Of course, the AOA may have drowned in the storm or wandered hopelessly away from civilization, but since the tractor hadn't had to pull the Peugeot terribly far, he may have made it into town on his own.

So far, Tyler sees only negroes and negresses, and a few blocks from the Peugeot, he passes a row of junky *car rapides* painted in vibrant primary colors. They look like the hippy buses of the seventies, except with *al hamdu lilah*, the stern motto of the Muslim Brotherhood, etched on the side. Why anyone would want to praise God for these clunky conveyances, he doesn't understand.

Tyler peers inside the cars at the natives in their robes and torn western clothes, not immediately registering a fleeting glimpse of his little companion deep within the sea of bodies in the third one in the line.

Covered in greenish mud that's beginning to cake his hair, his reopened nose wound bleeding down his chin, he clings determinedly to a pole.

The *car rapide* engine revs, and, without further thought, Tyler puts as much weight on his knees as they can stand

179

and catapults himself inside, feeling several arms pulling him out of harm's way.

"*Arretez, arretez,*" screams Tyler at the top of his lungs, "*arretez cette car rapide.*"

The vehicle shrieks to a stop, then Tyler ducks down and plunges through the crowd in the direction of the AOA. By the time he's made it to the pole in back, the little fellow is scurrying on his hands and knees. Tyler grabs hold of him, but he slithers out of his grasp, leaving only mud in Tyler's fingers.

The *car rapide* engine revs, the driver losing patience.

"*Aidez moi, s'il-vous plait,*" Tyler begs his fellow passengers. "*Aidez moi,*" he groans again, knowing he can't catch him on his own.

"*Mon fils est echappé,*" he has the good sense to bellow a moment later, as the AOA is too filthy and the bus too crowded for anyone to notice that the boy can hardly be his son.

"*Mon fils, mon fils,*" he mumbles gloomily one last time while retreating towards the door, praying that one of these people will show at least a little conscience.

He's climbing down to the street when he happens to catch a glimpse of a man in white robes grabbing the muddy boy and dragging him towards the front, just in time for Tyler to pull them both off the vehicle before it takes off into the night.

They tumble down into another puddle, but Tyler manages to get them both up to their feet again without losing hold of the boy, no particular harm having been done.

Striding back in the direction of the Peugeot, he sees a piece of plastic in the little fellow's hand, a phone card that he's bought with the francs he'd been given at the airport.

Dangerous enough, but he can keep it for now. He won't be using it any time soon, as he won't be let out of Tyler's sight.

The little fellow smirks at him, as if the entire episode were some sort of prank.

"Try that again, young man," Tyler hears himself roar, "and I'll slit your throat."

The AOA looks at him, bluntly, and Tyler cracks a smile, like he's really just kidding, but he does rather fear for the boy if he escapes again. His patience is spent.

5:30 PM

Tyler begins to drift off as Saint Louis approaches, his head resting on the grimy Peugeot window.

Hotel de Ville. He conjures waiters in formal whites, gin and tonics on the veranda, that pleasant neo-colonial side of life in the tropics.

Which he can enjoy once he's liberated his wife.

Like Dick Tracy, his childhood hero, he can take care of the FCT with one solid punch, just like he'd taken care of Christopher Thornton at the *nouvelle* Thornton Hall. Tyler will show up in their hotel room and *bam!* If the man turns out to really be Cal, Tyler can knock him down easily. He's bested him before.

Then they'll repair to the bar for needed sustenance. Yes, the little French girlfriend can come too, but her role will be drastically reduced: no longer the mistress's mistress but the master and mistress's au pair. So what if her father was a baron? A few years spent in service would be just desserts for meddling in their marriage.

The AOA, now drowsing in the back seat, can come too.

While the whole precarious business is working itself out in Tyler's imagination, he feels the car draw to a quick stop and hears the sound of voices. The highway is thronged with angry young men wearing the usual mixture of African and western clothes and shouting incomprehensible slogans.

Some sudden civil war, worries Tyler, trying to factor this problem on top of his other ones. *La Moglie* and her girlfriend had picked Senegal as a destination on their *Tour Nostalgique de L'Afrique Coloniale* for its relative stability; it really wasn't right for anyone to start overthrowing the government.

The protesters have surrounded the windows, so Tyler can no longer see out of the car. They rock it gently back and forth like a children's carnival ride.

"*C'est une situation très grave*," says the nervous driver, "*très, très grave*."

"*Un coup d'etat?!! Une guerre civile? Une revolution??!?*" Tyler is getting himself more and more worked up.

The driver scratches his little beard, shakes his head, and curses the protesters under his breath.

Though weaker, older and completely outnumbered, he jumps out of the car and starts arguing with the young men.

Back in the Peugeot, Tyler's heart patters, his legs twitch, and the undigested beef bits, still fermenting in his stomach from his airplane meal, fight their way back up.

The air feels so thick, Tyler can barely breathe. His aching body rebels against his small seat and his foolhardy hands keep reaching for the door handle. After several more intolerable moments, he closes his eyes, grits his teeth, and pushes his way out into the dangerous outside.

Keeping his eyes firmly closed, he says "ohm" four times and waits to be smacked or knifed or shot. When he opens them again, he sees one of the protesters, a lanky lad in a Manchester United tee-shirt a couple of sizes too small, going into the trunk of the *sept place* and grabbing his satchel and American Tourister. Tyler is still debating whether or not to fight him, when the lad hands it over to him.

Tyler taps on the window to get the AOA's attention, but the surly boy just slumps into his seat. Once the other passengers have leaned to the sides to clear the way, the AOA reluctantly complies, allowing himself to be led by Tyler out of the car and down the road in the direction of Saint Louis, which can't be far away.

Tyler says some more "ohms" for insurance (along with a few "Hail Mary's" that come back to him from Catholic school) as he fears being tackled from behind and dragged back to the Peugeot.

A few moments later, ambling more confidently, his foot lands in a pothole, and a sharp pain slices through his knee. Yowling and cursing, he grabs the AOA's shoulder to stop himself from crashing down. He glares at the sky, then down at his treacherous knee. Back and forth across the Atlantic without complaining, it's waited for the worst possible moment to fail him.

His soaked clothes, which had begun to dry, are getting damp again, this time from sweat as the sun blazes down He feels excruciatingly thirsty with no potable water in sight.

As waves of pain pulse through his knee, he closes his eyes and a moment later finds something missing from the scene.

He's got his satchel, his American Tourister. His wallet and travel documents are in his pocket, but his adopted Oriental adolescent has succesfully escaped him.

Chapter 10
The Road out of Rotterdam

September 11
11:45 PM
Eve

After hanging up with the emergency dispatcher, the old lady collapses in the back of Pedro's car, and directs him towards the Rotterdam Park to collect their belongings and begin their journey.

Not back to Spain where her business is done—and Elizabeth Smalls and her Spanish girlfriend still lurk—but to her home in Normandy, which she misses with all her heart.

Before hitting the road, they have to pay the hotel a princely sum and create more attention than the old lady would wish in order to convince the bartender to fill her flask with decent scotch.

She feels reasonably relaxed as they dart through Rotterdam, but begins to feel uneasy once they've left town and begun to approach Belgium, worried about ID checks at the border. She doubts, though, that the police could act that quickly.

She asks Pedro to turn on the radio, but all he can get in is a Dutch announcer carrying on hysterically about something in America: buildings, planes and terrorists.

About ten miles before the border, the traffic stops dead, and there appear to be roadblocks after all. She reaches to the driver's seat and pokes Pedro with her finger. If he'd driven a little faster, they could have gotten through.

"Patience, patience," he says, forgetting his place altogether.

The Dutch officials wave them over the border once they finally get there nearly an hour later, but the Belgians take one look at Pedro, order the car to pull over, and drag him forcefully into one of their concrete immigration buildings.

The old lady's shrinks in relief when he finally returns—nodding reassuringly and resuming their drive into Belgium—until she considers how easily she could be extradited within this so-called European Union.

None of the trip is easy. She gets weaker and weaker on the journey to France, scotch provides little comfort, and a few hours in, the complexities of the kitchen funnel and the peeing bottle become all too much, and she begins to wet herself at will.

It's unpleasant for Pedro, but she smells nothing, her senses no longer properly functioning. And it's far from clear, she thinks, as she wobbles back and forth in traffic near the French border, if the man is really still in the front seat as he's stayed silent for hours.

In the dead of night, he starts to speak.

"*Señora*," he asks, "who was that girl?"

The old lady ignores the question only to have it asked again a few minutes later.

"You must tell me who she was. Who was that girl?"

There's an edge in his voice, almost threatening. He could pull off at any point and toss her out of the car. She owes him money, but that might not stop him.

"You mean the girl in Rotterdam," she says, hoping to buy herself a little time.

"Of course, the girl in Rotterdam," says Pedro. "There is no other girl."

But what can she say? The truth is just too awful.

She sees Pedro looking back at her, his meek little face now dour and determined.

"I met her at a bar for women," begins a story that her driver can't possibly understand.

The old lady has never asked Pedro about his country but feels reasonably sure that he comes from a mountain village where men tend to llamas and kill each other in brawls and women produce broods in their teens and wizen in their twenties. He lives in Europe now but in a narrow immigrant corner.

"A bar for women," he repeats neutrally, just to make sure he's got it.

So as the morning sun begins to fill the sky and the lovely Norman farms emerge from the fog, she tells him a tale of love and hate, the ending of which he had witnessed for himself.

They drive in silence for several more miles.

Telling the story, getting it off her chest as they say in America, has relieved her. She's old and sick and must surely be at least slightly senile. No one would expect her to remember it exactly. The old lady takes a long pull on her scotch and drifts pleasantly towards sleep.

But it soon turns out that Mother is driving her in the family Ford. They must have been on their way to Richmond to see Aunt Mabel but have made some drastic wrong turn, ending up far south of the border in a place that hardly resembles North Carolina.

But in fact, the little Incan is driving. And he's talking to her. She is suddenly awake again, and Pedro is taking the liberty of telling *her* a story.

The story takes place in another continent altogether, the continent of his birth. He doesn't describe the *puebla* in which he was born as it isn't relevant to the terrible point he means to make.

It's all rather complex.

First his father dies of some disease one doesn't catch in the civilized world.

Then his mother, at this point living in a tiny shack with Pedro and his six sisters, meets a reasonably pleasant fat man who runs the *lavanderia* in the center of town. It makes good money. Tourists go there sometimes. But despite how useful it will be if Pedro's mother keeps the fat man as her lover, her heart just won't allow it.

The "act of love" with him, Pedro's strangely formal phrase, plain disgusts her.

Pedro doesn't describe it, but the old lady can well imagine: odorous and suffocating. So, despite the economic risks to her family, she tells the fat man it's over.

The *lavanderia* owner weeps washing-machine loads of tears and makes troubling fists with his meaty hands.

The mother agrees to think it over, and makes a plan to meet him in two days. Instead, she packs the whole family into the next *colectivo* bound for Cuenca, where her older sister lives.

In Cuenca, they are even more cramped and even more poor, which is why they sent Pedro off to Spain to stay with a distant uncle who has lived there, since Franco days and mail money back home, as he has been doing faithfully for years.

Then time passes, quite a bit of time. The old lady gathers from the story that what she's suspected is true. Pedro must be well into his thirties, his forties perhaps.

Hace tres años, says Pedro, losing his English in the thrall of the story.

Three years ago.

Three years ago Pedro receives a call from home.

The *lavanderia* owner has shown up in Cuenca.

Has found where his mother lived.

He hasn't actually killed her, but the beating is severe, and now the money arriving from Pedro is spent almost entirely on medical bills, plus the wheelchair, as she can no longer walk on her own.

The story is over, but details are missing. Is the *lavanderia* owner in jail? Will the old lady be? They better incarcerate her fast, as she plans on dying soon.

In more primitive places, one hears of women being beaten by their lovers. One just doesn't think of it happening in the civilized world.

Except it had.

In Rotterdam.

Chapter 11
Saint Louis

September 11
6:00 PM
Tyler

Tyler's maddening knee gives out once again, but while tumbling back to the ground, he feels a hand grabbing him back up. His little Oriental back so soon? No, it belongs to an infuriating teenager in dark blue robes. He's about to head-butt the interloper to kingdom come when sees the boy holds a rope connected to a donkey and a small wooden cart and has an appropriately solicitous expression on his narrow face.

Taking advantage of the implicit offer, Tyler grits his teeth and limps to his feet. He tosses his bags into the back of the cart and hurls himself on after them.

Despite the bumps in the road and the pain in his knee, Tyler quite likes being carted around like a *memsahib* from the days of the *Raj*. The driver looks back and catches him smiling goofily at the thought.

A moment later, Tyler pulls himself up on his satchel and sees that they're approaching an enormous wrought-iron bridge. Rusty and precariously tilted, the structure retains a certain *fin de siècle* exuberance, which must have seriously impressed the natives at the time it was built.

"*Fait, d'Eiffel,*" explains the donkeycartsman.

Yes, of course, Tyler remembers having heard about the colonial African city with a bridge designed by the famous tower man.

"*Quel hotel, Monsieur?*" asks the donkeycartsman about halfway over the bridge.

He can't go straight to the Hotel de Ville. He needs to make himself presentable before confronting the FCT and his fashionable hostages. *Besides*, he thinks, remembering his finite collection of West African francs, *it's probably too dear.* All he can think to do is to ask for a recommendation.

"*Je ne sais pas,*" he says, "*un bon hotel, pas chère.*"

The façade of the definitely *très chère* Hotel de Ville comes into view at just that moment: a grand, early 20th-century colonial building painted in cheerful blues and yellows with a café right out of Tyler's wishful imagination, happily imbibing sun-burnt tourists being served by formally dressed waiters. He ducks down in the cart to conceal himself in case the FCT and his captives are watching, then keeps his head down the rest of the way as it's actually more comfortable that way.

About fifteen minutes later, the cart draws to a halt. Tyler pulls himself off and hands the driver one of the smaller denominations of West African currency from his pile. Looking around as the cart shuffles away, he sees that he's at the far end of a long dirt boulevard: a Tobacco Road *Champs Elysees*. There is an area of trees and bushes in the center, rows of dilapidated nineteenth-century buildings off to the sides but nothing that looks like lodging until a small hand-painted sign with *Hotel Senghor* written upon it comes out of hiding to his left. An arrow beside it points down a path, which goes straight through an enormous puddle. In back of the puddle is a concrete-block building looking out over the same river he had crossed earlier in the afternoon.

Tyler looks at his watch, which had somehow survived the flood, and finds that it is only seven p.m., the long day not nearly over.

Looking more carefully around him, he sees a handwritten sign with the word "reception" safety-pinned to a dusty sheet that seems to be operating as an entrance way into the concrete building.

There's no place to ring or knock, so all he can think to do is yell.

"*Excusez moi!*" he bellows.

A strikingly beautiful young woman with long, curly hair and light mulatta complexion opens the sheet and gestures for him to come into a small room with a cot full of rumpled sheets and a broken-down black-and-white television.

Tyler takes note of his attraction, arousal even. It would certainly be impressive to bed a local beauty before rescuing his stray wife. More attractive than the small-faced French girl, surely one could say that.

But the hotelier gets quickly down to business, grabbing Tyler's bags in her powerful arms and taking them in the direction of what she claims to be one of their best riverview rooms.

They climb two flights of crumbling stairs to the top floor, where there are rooms with actual doors. The great Senegal River drifts stagnantly in the hazy afternoon sun, and like some cut-rate Venice. Pontoons motor slowly back and forth to the land mass on the other side, seagulls dipping in and out of the viscous brown water. The hotelier hands him a rusty old key and disappears without telling him the nightly rate.

The room has a bare mattress raised on milk crates and some threadbare sheets folded at its foot.

Enough room for the AOA when he crops up, thinks Tyler, banging his chest to keep wistful feelings from creeping back into his throat. While the constant escape attempts got on one's nerves, one does feel sorry for the little fellow—filthy, wounded, quite possibly orphaned.

The disintegrating mosquito nets around the mattress remind Tyler of all the inoculations and medications he'd taken in preparation for his Indian jaunt the decade before. He'd had no time for them on his way to West Africa.

Behind a sheet in back of the room, there is a primitive bathroom: a fetid squat toilet and a hose with a drain, which functions as a shower.

The dank, steamy air makes it hard to breathe, and he's grateful for the little fan across from the bed. But nothing happens when he flicks it, nor when he turns on the light bulb hanging precariously from a wire. The Hotel Senghor's power is out, at least for now.

What he wants most in the world is a drink, but there is none to be had. What he wants second most is a nap, but the moment he lies back on the lumpy mattress, he hears a familiar voice kvetching nearby.

The voice grumbles on, warning him about his wife and her little French girlfriend. He slaps himself on the head, but it just won't shut up. Only after he's inspected the crumbling veranda outside can he feel reasonably assured the voice is only in his mind.

Slipping back to the mattress, he falls into a sleep, which takes him deep into the night.

When he wakes up with a start, it is pitch black, and he has no idea of the time.

He can find neight his clothes nor his money in the darkness and trips over the American Tourister, landing (by some lucky chance) not on the concrete floor but back on the mattress.

When he wakes up again, it is light outside, well into morning, and he sees in his mind the desolate, dirty corner of town in which the AOA had likely spent the night.

But Tyler's first order of business is to confront whoever it is at the Hotel de Ville and get *La Moglie* and her little French girlfriend out from his insidious clutches. He'll lose the element of surprise if he lets himself be recognized, so he hopes his travel disguise kit has survived the journey.

The black beard had ripped a bit back in the Amtrak lavatory, so he chooses one of his Hercule Poirot curlicue mustaches. This is, after all, one of the godforsaken corners of the French-speaking world.

He's pulling off his jeans and searching in his American Tourister for something more presentable to wear to meet *La Moglie* for the first time in months when it occurs to him that keeping on his filthy clothes will make him look even less like himself.

Hang that, he decides; there are standards one has to maintain. Besides, it might all be some terrible trap, the FCT planning to do immediately away with him. Decades spent looking reasonably presentable only to be sent to one's death looking like hell, absolutely not.

He slips on some Chinos and an only slightly wrinkled Italian shirt. He's also caught quite a bit of color in his weeks in Spain and his afternoon in Africa, as well as dropping some pounds and shaving his head.

So when he meets the FCT, he'll be bald, thinner, and will sport an absurd mustache.

The grand boulevard that leads to the Hotel de Ville

is lined with dilapidated villas that once housed French statesmen. The dying grass and dirt in the middle of the road must have been a tropical *Tuileries*: a perfect strolling ground for their wives and mistresses.

There are very few people around, but he sees legions of adorable goats. They crawl on the broken-down benches and inside the abandoned cars and trucks, whole families of them with sweet-faced kids ambling purposefully from place to place.

After about fifteen minutes of limping forward, the grand boulevard disappears into a maze of smaller, more densely populated streets. Tyler plunges into them, figuring the Eiffel Bridge and the Hotel de Ville must be somewhere on the other side.

In the center of town, young men are milling about dressed in the long short pants and obscure tee-shirts he'd seen in Dakar. Older women in traditional robes sit silently working on the sides of the street, cleaning fruit and vegetables and selling pungent snack foods.

A few steps further, Tyler is discovered.

Young man after young man approaches him, offering national lottery tickets, big wooden sculptures, and freshly caught fish.

The slicker ones go through several languages in search of his own: *Français*, English, *Italiano, Español.*

Tyler nods vaguely at them and keeps on going.

Until a particularly aggressive tout with dreadlocks and a long black beard blocks his path and tries some more obscure languages.

"*Russky, Polsky, Portugues.*"

If Tyler comes into his shop nearby, he can buy the best tourist items at the most favorable prices: African robes, shirts, and masks, which would impress his more travel-timid friends back in the United States of America.

If he wants to sightsee, a guide can be found to show him traditional villages or the Mauritanian desert, or the nearby bird preserve featured in *National Geographic* magazine.

The man stands firmly in between Tyler and the street ahead, keeping the lesser touts away. He pauses when he finishes each category to give Tyler a chance to refuse. As he flies from item to item with impressive speed and dexterity, Tyler decides to let him reach the end of the long list before explaining that he's in a hurry and in want of nothing at all.

The man proceeds to dodgier categories.

Drugs: ganja, cocaine, ketamine, oxycodone.

Girls: young, old, dark, mulatta, white, fat, thin, petite, buxom, hairless, hirsute.

The list of boys varies slightly: young, old, dark, mulatto (no whites available at present), all with big cocks.

"Anything you want, anything at all," pleads the man, a bit miffed at Tyler for finding nothing to his liking, "all available pronto."

Tyler is feeling sorry about wasting the man's time by making him go through his whole menu of services when he thinks of something that might actually come in handy.

"A pistol," he hears himself request. "With a silencer."

The salesman looks dismally back at him. *Not really anything you want*, thinks Tyler, *but anything you want except white boys and guns.*

The French word (*"pistolet"*) does nothing to soothe the poor man. He understands full well but has just given away his last one. Not to the FCT, hopes Tyler.

Shrugging his shoulders, the man solemnly shakes Tyler's hand and leads him to an enormous ramshackle gift store. They walk through rooms of masks and figurines, sex toys and pornography. In a small box, hidden under a statue of an African god with a huge penis, he pulls out a collection of identical silver pocket knives.

Tyler can tell how sharp they are and reaches for his francs to pay for one, but the man shakes his head. It turns out to have been a kind of game, and the man plays fair. If he doesn't have what you want, he'll give you something second best for free.

Delicately, Tyler strokes the blade with his thumb until it almost breaks his skin, then grips the cool handle in his fist. Bursting at the seams with newfound energy, he slips his prize into the comfortable old knife spot in his left shirt pocket.

A few blocks farther, the street runs into a small plaza near the river. The Hotel de Ville looks even more pleasant in the morning light. Tourists and foreign officials on dubious errands smoke cigarettes and drink coffee at the tables in front, served by handsome negroes in white. It hardly seems a place to hold anyone captive, and Tyler only has the FCT's word that they are actually there, the word of someone burned in a terrible fire who claims to be alive decades later.

First, he scrutinizes the people strolling down the waterfront for signs of the AOA.

Then he settles himself into a table, orders a Stoli martini, and breathes a sigh of contentment.

After it arrives, cool and delicious, he realizes what a fool he's been.

More than a lie, it's a trick, a hoax.

A few tables away, past a group of ruddy Germans and an insolent French couple, he sees Ornella and her little girlfriend.

He's too far away to catch their words but can hear them laughing, not kidnapped in the least.

A man sits with them, wearing a trite white linen suit and a black fedora. Tyler can only see his back but recognizes his snotty patrician voice.

The False Calvin Thornton.

Noon

After the people at the table nearest the FCT and his captives pay their bill and leave, Tyler gulps down some more of his drink, mutters "ohm" several times in his mind, and sits himself down there.

The little French girlfriend, wearing a native scarf from the Marrakesh souk, is in the middle of a dramatic story. She tells of the mayor of New York City diving heroically into some apocalyptic wreck she refers to as "zee ground zero." Ornella and the FCT, whose back is still to Tyler, nod their heads in solemn agreement, ignoring the man at the next table.

Which makes Tyler wonder if he might actually be dreaming. But if he's dreaming that means he's sleeping, which seems unlikely as he feels utterly awake. His knee twangs suddenly, but his groan attracts no attention from them. That careful but random combination of weight and hair loss, tan and curlicue mustache means he no longer resembles himself.

Then the FCT bombastically announces that their

"changing" world with its "civilizations at war" exhausts him. He suggests they repair to their room for a drink.

Tyler could take out his knife right then and there. With a bit of luck, he could have it stuck into the FCT's throat within seconds. *Basta, ça suffit,* problem solved, but even in Senegal, public violence is probably discouraged, and he may not have enough francs in his pocket to bribe his way free and bring the two women back to Europe. Besides, how can he kill a man when he doesn't know who he is?

When they're almost out of sight, Tyler chokes down the last of his martini and follows stealthily after them.

By the time he's made it inside the lobby, they're climbing a wrought-iron spiral staircase up to their rooms. Ornella goes first, looking quite lovely in a silk dress he remembers from Bel Vento, then the French girlfriend, then the FCT whose face in profile (though not necessarily familiar) makes his heart pound: high cheekbones; a small upturned nose; a kind of artificial tightness of the forehead one associates with plastic surgery. And something is wrong with his right ear, barely visible under his fedora, small and misshapen as if it had been injured and ineptly put back together.

After counting to three to give them a little more of a head start, Tyler creeps up the stairs, but after only a few steps, his knee mutinies once again, sending him sliding back to the ground, banging his nose and creating an undignified clanging.

Thankfully, the FCT and his captives don't come down to see what the trouble is, but by the time Tyler has stood up, stuck some damp, mud-flood-stained tissue into his nostrils to staunch the bleeding and pulled himself back up the staircase, they've disappeared, leaving nothing to indicate which room is theirs.

As Tyler limps desolately back down the spiral staircase, one of those enormous mosquitoes one finds in the tropics starts buzzing around his head.

It lands first on his shoulder.

He almost nails it when it flies to his scalp, which has gotten bristly since he'd shaved in Spain.

It wanders off for a moment in search of a juicier victim but ambushes his upper lip once he reaches the lobby.

Tyler feels something enormous and hairy that turns out to be his Hercule Poirot mustache. It had gotten tangled during the fall.

Of course, he should find a lavatory and restore it, but he has no adhesive and lacks the will.

In one powerful, painful move, he rips it off and sneaks it into the pocket of his Chinos. Pulling the skin around the nose restarts the bleeding, but there's really nothing he can do about the pathetic spectacle of himself he must present to the tall, elegant, rather sexually attractive young mulatta at the reception desk, dressed in green silk pants that must be from the latest Paris couture.

She looks at him skeptically but pulls herself together, smiles artificially and asks what she can do for him.

"You see, *madame*, I have a package to deliver to Ornella Wilson, and they failed to give me the number of her room."

"Ornella Wilson?" asks the girl, dubious about what is, after all, a supremely silly name. It was already the seventies by the time they had married. Why hadn't Ornella thought to keep her own name?

"*Nous n'avons pas une Ornella Wilson ici, Monsieur,*" she says, wagging her index finger censoriously.

"Perhaps it's under her friend's name," suggests Tyler, "Dominique..." What the devil is the little French girl's last name? He just can't come up with it.

The woman at the desk is turning her back to him to attend to some contrived business on the computer when Tyler makes one more try.

"Calvin Thornton."

She turns around, says something incomprehensible in French that could be a room number and announces in English that Calvin Thornton is a "charming man."

"What did you say before that, *madame?*" asks Tyler anxiously.

"*Deux cent trois,*" she repeats.

Great at numbers at Saint Joe's Academy, winning *Le Competition des Numeraux Françaises* junior year, Tyler freezes completely nevertheless.

Or rather, he chokes. His French fails him. The FCT and his pseudo captives are right above him if he can only get the right room number.

"Two hundred and three," she finally says in exasperation.

Tyler clears his throat, thanks her with as much dignity as he can muster, and begins to limp back up the spiral staircase.

The door to room 203 is at the end of a long hallway with a moldy, salty-smelling carpet that squishes as he walks over it. He hears no sounds coming from any of the other rooms. All the other residents must be down at the café or busy with their dubious enterprises around town.

He goes down on his good knee once he gets to the right door and sticks his ear up to the keyhole. What he imagines at first is the murmur of voices turns out to be that same miserable mosquito greeting him warmly after their time apart by biting back into his bristly scalp.

No one answers when Tyler knocks on their door.

Before rapping more firmly, he tries the doorknob, which, like its nephew in Greenwich, Connecticut (*nouveau riche* Thornton Hall), turns out to be unlocked.

It creaks slightly as it opens.

His eyes take in a king-sized bed with an elegant lace mosquito net, several grand old chairs from the colonial era, and the dyed blond hair and white tropical suit of the FCT, who is gazing out the balcony at the river below, his arms draped delicately over the shoulders of *La Moglie* to his right and her little French girlfriend to his left.

Tyler takes a deep breath and skulks towards them. He reaches for the knife in his pocket, even though he doesn't generally stab from behind.

When he's about halfway through the room, just in front of the bed, the FCT and his captives turn around and face him.

They gasp in surprise, but it seems like an act.

In fact, *La Moglie* looks remotely pleased.

"Teelor," she says, coming up to him and pecking him lightly on both cheeks, "*come stai?*"

"*Bene, grazie*," he murmurs under his breath, as if he's found himself in an introductory Italian lesson.

The French girlfriend, tanned black from the African sun, smiles inscrutably at him, and the FCT, after a moment of quiet contemplation in which his eyes close briefly in what looks like prayer, gets suddenly chummy.

"Cal Thornton," he says, pumping Tyler's hand like a fraternity brother, "how the hell are you?"

Bewildered, Tyler limply shakes his hand and smiles

vaguely at his wife and her girlfriend.

He should get the inevitable confrontation going, but he's losing himself in the FCT's minty breath, his sweetly perfumed aroma. Familiar? He still can't tell.

The FCT breaks the spell by running to the mini-bar, taking a bottle of champagne and grabbing four glasses from a nearby shelf.

"To the future," toasts the FCT, presenting each glass filled to the brim.

"And the past," he goes on, looking around him.

The champagne restores Tyler. A taste of civilization.

And past the balcony, the great river runs below them. It must meet the Atlantic somewhere not far away. Eventually, it goes to America, or *La Porqueria*, or Rotterdam if one took the English Channel and got involved in those infernal canals.

And somewhere below them, much nearer by, lurks the adopted Oriental adolescent.

Tyler takes the knife out of his pocket, flips open the blade, and listens to the music of gasps.

Bringing it up to the FCT's prominent Adam's apple, he leads him into a bathroom and locks the door behind them, pushing the FCT onto his hands and knees. With his knife still pointed firmly at his throat, he sits on the toilet and rests his weary legs.

Then he sighs a deep and satisfied sigh, as he's about to get to the bottom of the business that's been troubling him since that first phone call in Spain.

Chapter 12
Saint Louis

September 12
Noon
Chris

On a dusty street not far away, Chris searches for a public phone that will accept his calling card so that he can reach Stamford General Hospital. He shadowboxes the air around him as he walks, punching so hard that his arms nearly fly from their sockets.

He has more energy because he actually slept through the night. The dreadlocked man had cleared out a space for him in between boxes of sex toys and fertility goddesses. The man had treated him to some gamey-tasting charred meat and had loaned him an African batik-print shirt with matching pants a couple of sizes too large. He couldn't get him a shower because the store's pipes were clogged.

He'd approached Chris just after he'd arrived in town, patted his greasy head, and offered him a discount on Angel Dust. Something about his warmth, the first human touch in days that didn't creep him out, made Chris want to trust him. People were kind in Africa, but you didn't understand their motives. He didn't know what the dreadlocked man wanted in return.

Which is why he'd left early that morning before the man had finished opening his store.

He'd stuck the man's present in his pocket and can figure out how to use it if he needs to, as he's been getting more and more savvy since his fake uncle smashed his father's head in, forcing him out into the world on his own. Chris Jr. remembers the supercilious voice and bullshit stories, but all the insults he comes up with now—cocksucker, dickwad, fuckface—seem too kind, and soon his body is spasming , his teeth chattering, his heart banging inside his chest cavity.

The *dickbreathed dumbfuck* had tripped him on a train, embarrassed him on a bus, and threatened to slit his throat. He can't afford to think about what he did to Dad or he'll have to remember how he'd gotten so blitzed on rum, coke, and shock that he'd helped drag him into the closet. Just getting away from the man is no longer enough. Ideally, Dad would get better soon, fly over to Africa and hold his fake uncle in place while Chris uses his sunburned face as a punching bag.

In his mind, the more he shadowboxes, the redder his fake uncle's face turns, until it gets black and blue. He sees cuts and scratches opening on his cheeks and forehead, blood draining from his nose. He sees him stumbling to the ground, begging for mercy in his faggoty little voice.

Kicking his head like a soccer ball, Chris loses his breath, and the steamy sun slips towards the center of the sky, blasting his bruised and filthy body.

Something warm and soft brushes up against his thighs, which turns out to be a goat kid wandering away from its family.

It points its pretty little face up like it's smiling at him, but when he wraps his arms around it and sinks his face into its fur, it brays and prances off.

A few blocks later, near the stairs leading up to the rusty bridge, Chris finally finds a public phone.

When he enters the numbers from his plastic phone card, a recorded voice comes on to tell him that there are no connections available due to the situation in America. He gets it to work on the third try but has to talk to an information operator first because he doesn't know the number of Stamford General Hospital.

He's surprised by how fragile and childish his voice sounds as he asks the hospital switchboard about the status of Christopher Thornton.

"Hold on," the woman says after she's looked up his name, "I'm connecting you with Critical Care."

A few moments later, the nurse's station phone starts to ring, then keeps ringing and ringing.

No one is picking up, but his phone card minutes are still getting exhausted, and he has no money to buy a new one.

After about five minutes of useless ringing, he hears that same officious voice telling him that his time is up.

Chapter 13
Normandy

September 13, 2001
Eve

Two days have gone by, and her fears have come to pass. The old lady is now drastically ill, the nerve disorder sucking her down towards her last. It could be months or weeks. They talk of hospitals, but she refuses.

La Madame has returned from Rouen to cook the meals and attend to the house, and Henri takes care of the garden.

The old lady drifts in and out of consciousness, hearing people on *La Madame*'s kitchen radio carry on about planes and buildings, Arabs and Americans.

When Elizabeth Smalls and her awful Spanish girlfriend arrive from Spain, they turn it off in case it upsets her. Besides, they need to focus on playing nurse—a nurse from some late Victorian tale: tough, persistent, and always right. They refer to the old lady in the first-person plural and berate her sharply when she fails to comply: not eating when she has no appetite, peeing into her sheets instead of the nearby commode, demanding to be taken to Virginia, Italy and other places impossibly far away.

In better moments, she gets out her *cahier*, reads the notes from the trip to Senegal that Ellen Winters took on her behalf last spring, and sketches Tyler further into that unfortunate country, bracing him as best she can for his showdown in the bathroom of the Hotel de Ville.

One night, she slips out of bed and wanders the house, managing (without her cane and with only the occasional fall) to stay one step ahead of her keepers as she searches for stashes of salted pistachios and single malt.

But most of the time, she lies feverish in her bed: her

little body sweating, her little head aching, her tender innards writhing.

Mother visits from Winchester by way of hell to make sure her daughter is sufficiently miserable.

"When you come down here," she announces, "you'd better act more proper than you did as a girl."

The old lady screams in horror, but the sounds don't make it out of her throat.

Tab also makes the occasional social call, insisting on doing herself up as a sort of postmodern corpse: white make-up applied to her face like in an amateur theatrical, a sheet hanging over her body, stained with something red that doesn't properly resemble blood.

"Please go away," the old lady begs her, her voice cracking, her heart pounding "please leave me in peace."

Sometimes younger, more peaceable Tabs visit, several of them at once, sitting around her bed and peering at her. They read Dutch art books and sip Dutch gin. The old lady tries to hide under her sheets, but they lift up the covers and breathe on her with their rotten breath.

September 14
8:00 AM

The next day, it is clear and unseasonably cool outside, and the old lady feels as lucid as a child.

She sits up in bed, pulls her obedient legs out of the tangled sheets and remembers exactly what it is she's been trying so hard to forget.

"Have the police come by?" she asks Elizabeth Smalls when Elizabeth Smalls tries to steer her back into bed.

"No, dear, no police," says Elizabeth, shaking her head

at the delusional question.

Elizabeth Smalls is hopeless, of course, so the old lady summons *La Madame*, Elizabeth Small's Spanish girlfriend, and Henri, still sweaty from mowing the lawn.

Her voice strong, her mind still clear, she makes each of them promise her that they have neither received calls nor correspondence from law enforcement.

Which could mean several things.

It could mean the Dutch police can't locate her. That makes sense, until she remembers the web of the world that she's used to find Tab, and the stupid interview in the German magazine in which she described exactly where she lived, sending several overzealous Tyler lovers to her Norman front door.

It could mean that Tab is comatose.

It could mean that Tab is *dood*.

The old lady ponders her own last as the morning's clarity starts to slip away. How peaceful can it be when she may have taken someone's life? If that turns out to be the case, she can ask *La Madame* to run down to Saint Terese and fetch Father Jacque to come absolve her. But he won't be able to stop the story from ruining her reputation, and she can't properly protect Tyler with it hanging on her mind. And, however much she fights it back, that vision crops up in her mind when she least expects it, the Dutch girl on the dirty wood floor gasping for breath, her sticky blood leaking onto the old lady's shoes.

The old lady looks pleadingly at Elizabeth Smalls. If she consents to go to Rotterdam and investigate for her, the old lady will be relieved of her presence for at least a spell and will learn if the Dutch girl is still alive. But Elizabeth smiles her usual killjoy smile, reminding her how little she can be trusted.

The old lady looks towards *La Madame*, who couldn't possibly manage outside of France, then at Henri, who couldn't possibly manage out of *Hemavez*, and finally at Elizabeth Small's Spanish girlfriend, who could manage anywhere but was devoted to Elizabeth and therefore treacherous.

But the old lady does have an ally, if she can only reach him.

She asks Henri, the most obedient of the bunch, to go down to her study and bring up a *cahier*, the one from *La Herradura*. Somewhere in it should be the number of Pedro's mobile phone.

Henri goes downstairs and comes back up with it only moments later, but the old lady's energies are already starting to fail.

Then she announces, her raspy voice sinking back into her throat, that if it isn't near her bed when she wakes up, if someone (like Elizabeth Smalls, for example) has removed it, there will be hell to pay.

Her legs failing, her heart pounding, she creeps back into bed.

Dear God, she begins to pray.

But which one? There are so many, and she doesn't trust any of them.

Dear God in heaven, she starts again, picking the one she knows best, her mother's ornery Baptist god.

Please help me reach Pedroçito.

And also, Lord.

Please keep Mother out.

And then, after a pause, in which sleep almost overtakes her.

And protect poor Tyler for me.

Baptist heaven is far away, and the message takes a while to reach God.

The first time she wakes up, she can only move her head. It flops helplessly around the pillow.

She knows the message hasn't reached there yet, because the next time she wakes up, she sees Elizabeth Smalls and her Spanish girlfriend wearing dusty jailor's uniforms from the 1950s.

But the third time, she is alone and fairly lucid. She pulls herself up to a seated position with her achy little arms and sees the right *cahier* where it should be, at the foot of her bed.

Leafing back through several pages to the *La Herradura* section, she finds Pedro's name and mobile number.

There is a phone on the bedside table.

Picking it up, she manages the sequence of numbers necessary to reach Spain.

Pedro sounds distracted when he answers. Perhaps he has been drinking. The old lady must get straight to the point.

Money is no object, she tells him, promising hundreds, thousands, enough for the miracle surgery that will help his mother walk again and plenty for the tactful rubbing out of a *lavanderisto* walking scot-free around Ecuador.

In order to get all this money, Pedro must do the following:

Drive to where they had been, Rotterdam.

To *Zaagmolenstra.*

And find out what happened to Tab.

"But the borders are still jammed after what happened in America," says the little weasel, making no sense whatsoever. "And also the *policia*; I don't know if it's safe."

"Two hundred thousand," says the old lady, remembering the advance she's due to receive for *Tyler's Last* if she finishes it.

"Enough," she goes on, "to buy your fucking little country."

"Please," she begs, "you're all I've got."

Soon, she's carrying on to the little man about poor Tyler in the Hotel de Ville bathroom, but he makes no comment, like *she's* the one talking gibberish.

"Please, please, please," she begs as tears splash down her face, and Elizabeth Smalls's footsteps walk towards her up the hall.

Chapter 14
Saint Louis

September 12
12:00 PM
Tyler

Only inches away, Tyler gets his first good look at the False Calvin Thornton's face, which indeed has a reconstructed quality as if it had been taken apart and put back together. And, yes, there are those disturbing little ears: pink, elfin, looking like rubber or plastic, some material more pliable than skin.

When Tyler flips off the FCT's fedora, he is shocked to discover that the man still has his hair—cheaply dyed some outrageous blond only natural on Nordic children but full, even bushy.

When Tyler takes a bunch of it in his hands and pulls as hard as he can, the FCT winces but only loses a few strands. The damn thing is real.

Either he's not who he claims to be or *What They Look Like Now*, the computer program operated by the Spanish girl in *La Porquería*, has some serious bugs.

What should Tyler do with him now that he's got him?

Play with him like a cat with a mouse and see if he trips himself. The knife against his throat should make a pretty good truth serum.

There's certainly pleasure to be found here—popping open a bottle of decent champagne, cracking a succulent lobster tail. Tyler has been waiting since that first phone call in Spain to expose the man, and he might as well savor the moment.

"So, Cal," says Tyler as casually as he can, figuring he should start with a pleasantry, "nice digs you got here."

The bathroom glimmers spotlessly—shining toilet, optimistic blue wallpaper—while the FCT looks suspiciously back at him.

Then the interrogation gets going in earnest, Tyler asking the False Calvin Thornton questions that only the Real Calvin Thornton could answer.

"What were you wearing that last night on Stromboli?"

"What were you drinking?"

"Weren't you burned? What happened to your ears?"

And finally.

"What the hell do you want with me after all this time?"

"Please let me go," the FCT says, gesturing towards the knife. "Get this thing away from me, and I'll tell you anything you want to know."

Tyler chuckles as the FCT looks around the room, scratching his peroxide locks.

The man's next move is peculiar.

Grabbing hold of the sink, struggling on his own feeble knees, he kneels in front of Tyler like a petitioner.

Then he delicately rubs his chin against the zipper of Tyler's pants.

Tyler can't help but feel a certain warmth, arousal one has to call it, even though he's had mixed feelings about this sort of thing ever since that shameful eighth grade afternoon at the Lusty Lady. His mind and body don't agree, the mind finding this development presumptuous, but the body, starved for so long, enjoying the stubbly warmth of the FCT's chin, the delicately applied pressure.

And the cock expands rebelliously.

Well, of course, there were the occasional times even before his and *La Moglie*'s retirement from this type of business that the pressure would grow unbearable, and he'd have to wander in back of *Napoli Centrale* to hire a strapping foreign boy or a willowy girl to relieve it as quickly and suc-cinctly as they could. But there had been nothing like that since the Delauney fund had started to unravel a year ago.

Meanwhile, the cheeky FCT has taken it a step fur-ther. Grabbing Tyler's zipper with his yellowish teeth, he attempts to unzip it like he's bobbing for apples, which proves difficult, as it keeps slipping out of his mouth.

Tyler considers putting a stop to what could become a colossal misunderstanding: accused of using a knife to make the FCT go down on him. Still an attractive man even in these trying circumstances, he hardly needs to go to such desperate measures. He'd find a willing partner eas-ily enough, a local negro perhaps, or pay for one if that proved laborious.

Finally, the grimacing FCT manages to grasp the zipper and open it with his teeth.

Then, after an unsuccessful attempt to dig around in Tyler's briefs for his cock, he chooses the simpler method of taking its head into his mouth through the conveniently threadbare cotton.

Causing Tyler to groan sharply and ejaculate immedi-ately, perfuming the air with semen.

Once he's caught his breath, he steers the FCT's mouth away from his groin with his knife, sighs in heartfelt annoy-ance, as if he's just been terribly inconvenienced, and zips himself back up again.

"Calveen, Teelor, *state bene?*" goes the nervous voice of *La Moglie* from outside the bathroom door.

"*Bene, grazie,*" says Tyler stiffly.

"*Bene,*" agrees the FCT in his frightful patrician voice.

The two look rather sheepishly at each other like

schoolboys caught misbehaving as Tyler's knife-bearing hand grows more and more tired.

He wonders what would happen if he put the knife back in his pocket. The FCT had greeted him quite peacefully when he'd entered the hotel room, but, now inflamed, he might grab the knife himself or try to pummel him with his weak little fists.

Or run away like a scared little boy and hide behind the big girls outside.

One thing seems clear. They can't waltz back to Europe like a big happy family. There is room for only one man.

When Tyler moves his knife away from the FCT's throat for just a moment to rest his arm, the FCT looks desperately around him but makes no immediate attempt to escape. Then Tyler switches the knife to his left hand and puts it back up to the FCT's throat.

"Teelor, Calveen, *cari*, stop the funny business," goes *La Moglie* from outside, employing one of her favorite old-fashioned English expressions.

"*Vieni qui.* We are lonely here," she goes on, "we need our men."

Something about her sentimental tone reminds Tyler of the drippy Italian television programs she used to watch in the afternoons at Bel Vento, variety shows with vacuous European pop songs and even more vacuous banter between those tiny men with their silly names (Pippo Baldo was his favorite) and those bottle-blond Amazons with enormous breasts. He remembers one of them carrying on about an elaborate epiphany she'd once experienced at a *festa carnivale*.

Approached from behind by a masked man, she'd recognized the kissing style of her first lover despite the passage of decades.

"*I baci*," Tyler hears her words in his mind as Ornella, and now her little French girlfriend as well, beg them in unison to come out from the bathroom, "*non sono mai dimenticati.*" Kisses are never forgotten.

It is in this spirit that Tyler rises to his feet and stands toe to toe with the FCT, face to face.

He moves his knife away from the FCT's neck and kisses the FCT's lips. Hearing a faint gasp, he opens his mouth to allow in the FCT's tongue.

Which tastes warm, sour-sweet from champagne, salty from sweat and fear.

The FCT grabs hold of the back of Tyler's head as they entangle, making Tyler forget for the moment about his knife, which drops from his hand, chiming discordantly on the tile floor.

He feels the hardness of the FCT against him, not easily faked, unless he's spent his lost years in pornography.

Playing with the FCT's dyed blond curls, he concentrates carefully.

A certain déjà vu, yes, but when was the last time he'd been kissed at all? Not by *La Moglie*, God forbid, nor by any of the hustlers outside of *Napoli Centrale*. That Dutch boy who'd approached him in the Plaza Garibaldi on that unfortunate errand in Mexico City? But that was over a decade ago.

Feeling the thickness of tongue and hardness of teeth, he listens to the scratchy music of bristly cheek on bristly cheek.

Lost in those sensations, living entirely in the moment like the true Buddhist he knows he's not, Tyler fails to notice the first signs of disengaging, the separating of the FCT's body from his own, and therefore loses the jump in the mad pounce for the knife on the floor.

But Tyler is faster, of course. He always is. Despite his troubled knees, he springs down to the floor and grabs the knife.

When he doesn't sense the FCT anywhere near him on the bathroom floor, he figures the old fellow's knees just weren't up for the journey down. Feeling his own knee twinge as he pulls himself back to his feet, Tyler wonders if the FCT may have been too clouded by their kiss, too lost in the moment, to notice the falling knife.

But then something cold and metallic pricks him through his sweaty shirt, and he sees the FCT again, standing right across from him, tickling his stomach with a knife identical to his own.

Which he must also have bought from the dreadlocked salesman.

And treacherously slipped out of their kiss to remove from his pants pocket.

He wants to stick his knife into the FCT as far as it will go, just like a stuck pig, though that would only lead to his being stuck-pigged himself and create an unholy mess for *La Moglie* and her little French girlfriend.

Instead he takes the knife and makes a delicate incision around the FCT's left nipple, causing the front of his ridiculous tropical suit to turn immediately red.

The FCT clutches his chest, watches the manageable spillage of blood accumulate on the tile floor, and stabs right back into Tyler's stomach, harder but less accurately.

Tyler groans, breathes in deeply, reaches back into the stoic strength of his youth and manages not to collapse onto the slippery ground.

Chapter 15
Normandy

September 15
6:00 PM
Eve

Time passes with preternatural speed. The old lady lies in a trance, her left breast hurting like she's somehow sliced herself, the unlikely odors of blood, bathroom detergent and semen making it hard to breathe.

Until she is distracted by the voices surrounding her, particularly Elizabeth Smalls's, with a touch of hysteria.

There is more talk of airplanes and buildings, that business in America.

Elizabeth Smalls speaks to her Spanish girlfriend just outside the old lady's room, loud enough to be heard.

She'd been determined to keep it from the old lady, as the shocking news might hasten her last. The more Elizabeth has thought about it, though, the more upset she has become. She really must return home as America needs her in its time of trouble.

But how can she abandon the old lady when the old lady can't survive without her?

The answer to that starts in the old lady's throat, but gets wrapped up around her thick-feeling tongue. It is Elizabeth Smalls's patriotic duty to return to her homeland and take her Spanish girlfriend with her.

"Don't worry, my dear," says Elizabeth Smalls, rushing to the old lady's side and grabbing her hand, "I'll never abandon you."

If she goes home, a plane might have sense enough to crash into her, too, but Elizabeth will insist on staying with her in France until her last.

The doctor who comes to see her claims she is rapidly failing.

Every few hours, she wakes up. Sometimes, she can barely move, so she closes her eyes and prays for more sleep. Other times she thinks she's somewhere else.

La Herradura.

Winchester.

Bel Vento.

Rotterdam.

Only very occasionally is she sharp enough to grab her *cahier* and help Tyler withstand his knife wound in the Hotel de Ville bathroom. She worked out exactly what happened to Cal in the fire on Stromboli in the old days on Greenwich Street when she was living with that fiery Italian girl and being forcibly befriended by the young Elizabeth Smalls, but it's hopelessly hidden among her papers in the basement. She remembers full well, on the other hand, that the man besieging poor Tyler in Spain hadn't been in Thornton Hall, and that Cal himself never returned to the place after escaping his drunken father in the middle of that stormy August night in '58. She'd also worked out the identity of the cretin calling Tyler on his various phones before she'd even started work on *Tyler's Last*, but the facts of the case float tantalizing just outside her recall like an itch she can't quite scratch. It infuriates her but also keeps her going because it would be criminal for her to die before figuring it out.

Sometimes in the middle of the night, she wakes up with bountiful energy, slips down the stairs to the kitchen, and eats ridiculous foods: raw eggs, cold beans, little bits of stale bread slathered in oil.

Several times she has fallen, creating deep bruises that she tries to hide from Elizabeth Smalls by keeping her body under the sheets.

Elizabeth Smalls, by the way, has come up with several unsuccessful techniques for the prevention of these nocturnal escapes.

The old lady cuts the bell attached to her ankle with shards from a drinking glass she's broken.

When they lock her door, she tries to get out the window.

She puts the heavy sleeping pills into her mouth but spits them out into her sheets.

Elizabeth Smalls has tried several times to remove the phone (on which Pedro might call) from the old lady's night table, but each time, the old lady finds her voice and screams bloody murder.

The phone doesn't ring often, but the old lady manages to pick it up each time that it does.

Once it is her Jewish literary agent, on whom she happily hangs up.

Her editor (wondering about the past-due *Tyler's Last*) receives the same treatment.

Elizabeth Smalls's sister in Massachusetts learns from the old lady that Elizabeth Smalls is dead, which causes a whole hullabaloo, as one might imagine.

Finally, three days after the old lady had telephoned, Pedro rings back.

He's in a car on his way to the Netherlands.

"*Señora*," he calls her, sounding respectful again, the way he had before she'd bashed in Tab's head. The promise of $200,000 has bought back his devotion.

"What do I do if I find her?" he asks.

"It doesn't matter," replies the old lady. If she turns out to be alive, Tab will have to stop haunting her .

Pedro begins to sign out.

"I will talk to you when I get there," he says. "*Adios.*" But the old lady can't stand to lose him on the phone.

"Don't hang up on me. I can't stand to be alone with them." She's getting sentimental in her dying, and the characters in her immediate vicinity are the worst she's ever known.

September 16
4:00 PM

Elizabeth Smalls is attempting to feed the old lady some horrific low-sodium chicken broth with a spoon. The phone rings, and when they both rush for it, the old lady spills hot soup all over her.

Elizabeth Smalls is in one of her furies. But the old lady holds the phone close. Pedro is calling from Rotterdam.

"I've parked," he says, "across the street."

The old lady stays silent—saving her voice for when she may need it—but can picture it exactly, almost like she's back there herself, next to the Turk in Pedro's car.

"I'm approaching the building... I'm ringing the bell."

The old lady closes her eyes, so she can concentrate on Rotterdam. But Elizabeth Smalls is more concerned with spilled soup. "Lourdes and I have waited on you hand and foot without receiving a single kind word in return. In fact, you've been a terrible little woman all your life."

Through the phone, she hears the sound of the buzzing of the door and Pedro's footsteps clomping up the first few flights.

She hears his breathing, then his footsteps again. A moment later, she hears a tentative tap on Tab's door.

An older woman with a deep voice says something in Dutch.

A torrent of Elizabeth's pent-up histrionics is breaking loose in her bedroom, though the old lady has lost sense of the words.

"Just shush, " she tells her in a clear, calm voice, "can't you see I'm on the phone?"

Pedro doesn't seem to understand, so the Dutchwoman switches to a heavily-accented English.

"May I ask what you're doing here, young man?" the Dutchwoman asks.

The old lady hears a muffled crinkling sound, which must come from the slipping of Pedro's phone into his pocket. He keeps it on, though, so the old lady can hear what transpires.

"*Señora,*" Pedro stumbles, not sure how to explain himself, "you see...I'm...well..."

If even a drop of Tyler's blood could be introduced into the simpleton's veins, he'd improvise something credible.

But has the girl changed apartments to elude her? Or perhaps Tab's died, and her apartment has been turned over by some efficient Rotterdam housing authority.

"Does Tabitha, the lady with the long black hair, still inhabit this house?" Pedro asks over-formally, explaining that he's an "acquaintance from the world of art."

Meanwhile, the old lady hears suitcases in the next room, the room Elizabeth Smalls shares with her awful

Spanish girlfriend.

"I just don't see," the Dutchwoman replies, "I just don't see how that can be right."

The packing sounds in the next room have been replaced by tense whispering. Elizabeth Smalls and her girlfriend are having one of their serious conversations. The old lady can't make out the words but can recognize Elizabeth's smarmy tone. Is she losing her determination to march back to America? The old lady hopes not.

Pedro and the Dutch woman have reached an impasse. She wants him out, but he stays in place. If he leaves without learning what happened to Tab, he'll lose 200,000 Euros.

She's trying to close the creaky front door on him when more footsteps can be heard, from the back of the apartment. Tab's voice comes all the way from the Netherlands through the mobile phone in Pedro's pocket.

The old Dutchwoman must be Tab's mother. The old lady can't believe Tab has allowed her mother anywhere near her apartment, as she'd called her a "shitty old cow" the one time she'd mentioned her, or was it a "shitty old sow," the old lady can't quite remember. The girl doesn't sound in the least bit *dood*.

She'd tied up her share of girls and smacked them plenty hard in bed, as well as knocking off legions of deserving characters, but she's never fatally injured anyone in real life. If she'd learned she'd accidentally rubbed Tab out, she'd have gone shaking, shivering to her grave with Mother, Tab, and other ghosts haunting her every hour. Smelling of rot and raw onions, they'd slip into her bed and nip at her mercilessly. Instead of escaping Elizabeth Smalls's clutches in search of scotch and pistachios, she would have had to look for pills, guns, anything to make her last come quicker.

"My name is Tab. What is your name?" asks Tab again, but Pedro must be too stunned by the sight of her to come up with anything to say.

Recovering from her own initial shock, the old lady focuses on Tab's words, her tone.

Sweet, innocent, kind. Some fake Tab. Some alien Tab.

"My name is Pedro," says Pedro gently, like he's addressing a child.

"Do you remember this man?" asks Tab's mother dubiously. "Look at him closely and tell me if he looks familiar."

Then Tab's mother whispers the same question in Dutch.

"He says he used to be your friend," Tab's mother goes on, beginning to lose patience with the girl, "could that really be the case?"

"I'm sorry, Pedro," says the girl who used to be Tab, "I'm sorry I don't remember you. I had a little accident, you see. Can we still be friends?"

Of course, thinks the old lady, beginning to figure out what this is, what has happened.

Meanwhile, her own door is opening and Elizabeth Smalls and her girlfriend are coming towards her, tears in their eyes.

Brain damaged. The blow to her head had been expertly

aimed. No surgeon could have more skillfully removed the nasty, the cruel, the sarcastic.

"Okay," says Pedro, "I will be your friend."

Leaving the trace elements of sweetness buried under the piles of bile. Which is why she needs her mother's care. There is so little of her left.

The old lady wonders whether she should ask to speak to the girl herself. She won't remember the schnapps bottle, but might she have retained some traces of their love affair? If Tab remembers so little, though, it would hardly be worthwhile to talk to her. She'd just ask if they could be friends or some other sweet-natured inanity.

Along with the unpleasantness and cruelty, the frisson that got the old lady's attention in the first place has also disappeared. She just can't imagine having anything to say to a brain-damaged forty-year-old in her mother's care.

But what happens when her mother gets too old to care for her, the old lady finds herself suddenly worrying. She sees the naïve new Tab wandering aimlessly through the seamy port of Rotterdam, getting kidnapped by longshoremen or Arabs, sold into white slavery, pimped by perverts. When her mother can't handle it any more, the old lady resolves, Elizabeth Smalls will take over. Elizabeth will need someone else to foist herself upon after the old lady has had her last.

This little frolic, thinks the old lady, rapt by the changes she's wrought in Tab, has gotten dull.

Meanwhile, Elizabeth Smalls and her Spanish girlfriend are apologizing profusely for Elizabeth's outburst and swearing to stay with her until her very last.

The old lady says her goodbyes to Pedro on the mobile phone as he descends the stairs of Tab's building, wondering how little she can get away with paying him, surely not the entire advance for Tyler's Last.

Her Dutch girl has been damaged beyond repair, but Tyler's life still hangs in the balance, the dyed-blond man looking for any opportunity to stab him again more lethally.

"Get me my *cahier*," she frantically orders Elizabeth Smalls and her girlfriend as a knot of fatigue pulls her head back down into the antiseptic-smelling pillow.

"Then get out of my sight," she mutters as she fades away.

Chapter 16
Normandy

For a long time after Pedro has hung up the phone, the old lady sleeps deeply and dreamlessly. When she finally awakens, she sees Elizabeth Smalls's horrible Spanish girlfriend looking down upon her with a quizzical expression.

She is clearly trying to decide whether the old lady's last will be a boon or a curse.

On one hand, they will no longer be able to stay in the Norman house, as it has been willed to Tyler. Her fat British estate attorney had cried foul when she had insisted upon it. She can still hear his pompous Oxfordian tone: "One cannot leave one's house to one's character, Madam."

When the old lady goes, the awful Spanish girlfriend will get more attention from Elizabeth Smalls, since Elizabeth Smalls will be liberated from her lifelong obsession. It's fortunate that Elizabeth is not the old lady's "partner"— that absurd term that's floated in from America. If that were the case, Elizabeth would wear widow's black after the old lady dies and wail away the rest of her days.

Obsession binds the three of them together (her, Elizabeth, and the Spanish girlfriend) like deluded musketeers, failure to give things up. The old lady might not have put up with Elizabeth Smalls all these years if she hadn't sensed herself the object of a Tab-like fixation. But while Elizabeth has tended conscientiously to her, the old lady has brained her obsession with a bottle of schnapps. Not one of them has had a great deal of love returned, though she, at least, has Tyler. On that happier note, she begins to fade out.

But she fades right back in again with that same question preying on her. It would be better, she decides, for the awful Spanish girlfriend if she manages to postpone her last. Without the old lady to obsess about, Elizabeth will smother the poor girl to death.

The old lady looks up and sees beautiful green Spanish eyes. She'd never noticed them before.

"Lourdes," she tries to say, "you must leave Elizabeth after I've had my last."

But no words come out. Not stuck in her throat this time, but gone altogether, not a hint of them anywhere. She tries to move her head, her hands, her lips, but can't. She no longer senses the sheet under her legs. Cool wind blows in from the open window, but she doesn't feel it on her face. So this is what a coma is like, she thinks, sympathizing just a bit with the characters upon whom she's inflicted them.

The next time she wakes up, she can pull herself up onto her pillow at least a bit. A circle of chairs surround her. Death-watching has turned into a spectator sport. It reminds her of the wake for her mother in Winchester, everyone sitting around the whorish red velvet funeral parlor, looking down upon her face, sour even in death.

The chairs around the old lady now are filled with the usual suspects. There is Elizabeth Smalls, of course, and next to her, the awful Spanish girlfriend. There is a slightly overweight Tab, looking sweet and docile in ironed jeans and a churchish white blouse. Sitting next to her is the ghost of Tab past, wearing a Girl Scout uniform with a pink mohawk, plus piercings around the nose and lip, which look equally dreadful.

Next to her is Mother, looking like she did in her coffin, then Henri, who actually appears to be crying, though it might be allergy season.

"Dear friends," says the old lady, figuring she might as well get the dreadful eulogy business out of the way while she's still alive.

But she finds herself still voiceless, slipping into a new oblivion. Buoyant, bracing, it reminds her of the magic mushrooms she took with the Jewish girl of the enormous bosoms in the 1970's. They don't generally give those to the dying, and when she looks up, she sees the IV that the doctor has just inserted into her arm.

Morphine.

The next time she wakes up, they haven't been giving her half enough. Her body aches, and her innards burn.

The row of chairs still surrounds the bed, but no one sits in them.

Have they left her to die alone? She knows she should appreciate the gesture, but she resents it nevertheless. Since this whole dying business has gotten going in earnest, she's come to miss hearing people's voices.

There is no bell to ring anywhere near the bed, and she doesn't think she could move her muscles far enough if there were. She must resort to yelling and can only think to yell for Elizabeth Smalls. Whatever one thinks of her, she's the one person remotely paying attention.

"Elizabeth," she cries, not sure if sound is coming from her mouth, "Elizabeth, I need you."

Two figures shuffle forward who apparently have been lurking in back of the room.

Neither of them happens to be Elizabeth.

In fact, they are awkwardly conjoined like some new-fangled version of Siamese twins and point melodramatically at each other.

It's only when they've gotten very close that the old lady sees the knives.

"You're supposed to be working this out amongst yourselves at the Hotel de Ville," she scolds. "What in God's name are you doing in France?"

Tyler looks considerably worse for wear: bristly white hairs sprouting adjacent to the dyed black ones around the crown of his head, deep pouches under his eyes, bits of skin falling off his face from an unhealthy-looking sunburn, not to mention the blood leaking from his stomach wound. The FCT looks outrageously tacky with his bottle-blond hair and bloodstained tropical suit, a damaged version of the provincial queers she'd glimpsed around Winchester in the 1970's.

"Can't you see I need your help?" whimpers Tyler. "There's so much I don't understand."

He goes on, sounding more and more aggrieved: "You place me in these situations, and then just abandon me... I simply can't allow you your last without some basic answers."

The old lady is finally meeting the man of her dreams. There would have been no need to trifle with Elizabeth Smalls or big-titted Jewesses or even Dutch girls for that matter, if he hadn't waited so long to come out of the woodwork, but now he's aggravating her. She's been concentrating as hard as she can on his situation since resolving the business with Tab, and you'd think the man would have a little more patience. Her plots are worked out with her pen and *cahier* in any case, and in their absence, she just doesn't see how she can help.

First, Tyler wants to know what happened with Christopher Thornton in the hospital in Stamford, and then the adopted Oriental now loose in Saint Louis.

Recalling her *cahier*, she knows the pompous older Thornton has been pulled off life support. And his Oriental son has snuck into the Hotel de Ville bar before anyone noticed his appalling appearance. He manages to befriend a plastered Englishman, and, while the man is busy trying to get the bartender's attention, grabs enough bills out of the wallet hanging loose from his cargo pants to buy another phone card.

The new card almost runs out before he learns the terrible news from the Filipina nurse. Not whining nor weeping, the boy glares at the sticky phone receiver and bashes it so hard back into its cradle that some nearby goats prance away.

Tyler is moving on to other pressing questions, but the old lady is busy puzzling out the arc of the Oriental boy's grief, which has quickly transformed into the blackest of rage.

He breathes deep, bites his lip, and careens off in search of Tyler, the one familiar face in the entire dark continent.

The beautiful black lady at the Hotel de Ville admits that there was indeed a "*vieux Americain*" staying there, but she insists the man is blond and doesn't have a gimpy knee.

He refrains from smashing the fake ivory statuettes and counterfeit Cartiers on the reception counter and embarks on a long day's afternoon, banging on door after door, asking for an old American fitting Tyler's description.

He gets no after no, until he meets another pretty black lady at the scummy Hotel Senghor. She confirms that the white man staying at her place isn't blond and walks with a limp.

She directs him upstairs, where he bangs on the door until his knuckles bleed, then kicks it open with his calloused feet.

Tyler's specter sighs in impatience, tired of being ignored, and the fake blond groans in pain, but the old lady can't wrest her attention away from the spectacle of the boy entering the filthy hotel room.

The stench of cheap cologne and old-man sweat make him retch. But the flickering bulb in a lamp near the bed reminds him of the holiday season with Dad.

Mrs. Murphy would cook them a huge turkey, and they'd sit around eating it on Christmas Eve. Then Chris would wake up early Christmas morning and stuff himself with the fancy foreign chocolates in his stocking. Dad wouldn't make him start rationing until later in the day. At nine sharp, Mrs. Murphy would be sent back to her own family in Stamford, and Chris would open his presents in front of the enormous Christmas tree while Dad sipped eggnog.

Chris's lungs heave, the knot in his throat slipping down to his chest. He bawls like a two year old, and a few minutes later has to accept that the pretty black lady from reception isn't coming upstairs to comfort him.

Another whiff of cologne penetrates his broken nose, and he starts shaking all over again. He smashes his fist into his palm, then kicks the weird-looking metal box that he sees on the floor . Fake noses, eyebrows, and a container of some perverted-looking putty fly out onto the floor.

Gingerly, he dips his finger in it then brings it up to his

nose.

It smells like the make-up they gave him when he played Pippin in seventh grade, and confirms his suspicion that Uncle Cal isn't who he says he is.

He hasn't peed all day, but when he unzips himself and aims at the man's pillow, nothing comes out. He has to piss in the squat toilet behind the curtain.

It goes on for a while, and once it's done, he takes a deep breath and tries to calm himself in order to wait for the man to come back, but after a few more minutes in the stagnant air, he's feeling in his pocket for the dreadlocked man's gift and taking off back into the night. He'll prowl around looking for his fake Uncle Cal, and if he can't find him, make his way back to the Hotel Senghor.

At the old lady's bedside, Tyler still stands glaring. All he wants to know is the identity of the FCT.

"I just don't know. Ask him," says the old lady, pointing to the other pathetic character with a knife held up to him.

Who just shrugs his shoulders and looks quizzically at her. Apparently, he has no idea either.

The answer is in one of her *cahiers*, but she has no way to retrieve them.

Besides, she may well still be comatose.

Her improvised explanation is byzantine and unconvincing. The FCT was a half-brother of Cal, fathered by the old man with a scullery maid in some drunken incident in the 1940's, burned terribly in the ears in Vietnam, and cast out of the family when he turned out to be homosexual. He had seen the fateful episode of Court TV that featured his half-sibling's murder, found Tyler's whereabouts on the web of the world and begun to stalk him from afar, waiting for the perfect moment to blackmail. How had he known about Samuels, the big black man knocked off by Tyler in the 1980's? The old lady figured it had to be a lucky guess.

Tyler looks hopeful, like maybe there's some sense to her answer, but the FCT rolls his eyes.

He and Tyler look down on her as she searches for a better ending, the outline of their figures growing dimmer and dimmer. As the rest of them fades and finally disappears, their disappointment lingers..

"Don't worry, darling Tyler," the old lady declares. "I promise I'll get to the bottom of this."

When next she opens her eyes, the circle of chairs is filled again, this time only with living people. Elizabeth Smalls, Elizabeth Smalls's Spanish girlfriend, *La Madame*, Henri. Tab and Mother are absent, but her cousin from Winchester and her literary agent have taken their place. Given her agent's cheapness and busyness (no time for not-quite-dying writers), the old lady can assume her last is fast upon her.

Elizabeth Smalls has noticed that the old lady's eyes have opened again, and she is running over to the bed, tears draining down her dour New England face.

"Calm down, Elizabeth," the old lady hears herself say, weak but audible.

Stunned by the old lady's voice and her return to consciousness after God knows how long, Elizabeth Smalls tries to get decades off her chest in between sobs.

She confesses the obvious, that she's been in love with the old lady since the late 1950's. What she had claimed in the early seventies—that her love had matured into fondness—had been patently false.

The Spanish girlfriend grumbles—though this can't really be news—while Elizabeth Smalls begins to apologize for all her scolding, her criticizing, her generally possessive behavior. Apparently, she knows the old lady has never been in love with her but has found it impossible to let go.

This sudden self-knowledge grows more and more tiresome.

"Forgive me," begs Elizabeth, "please forgive me, my darling Eve."

Which tugs, slightly, on the heartstrings of the old lady —whose given name is Eve. It might just be the sentimental properties of the morphine, which they seem to be giving her more of now, but a certain regret about taking Elizabeth Smalls for granted flits through her mind.

It is true that Elizabeth should consider herself lucky to have spent time with the old lady at all. But she also remembers the horseishly handsome girl with the severe haircut and practical clothes, looking nervously around that Greenwich Village lesbian bar in the mild winter of 1955. She has to admit that she would not have coped so well all these years without her help.

"I forgive you, Elizabeth," she says, sounding cross despite herself. It's the only way she knows how to talk to Elizabeth Smalls.

And while Elizabeth sobs with renewed conviction, the uneasy feeling of unfinished business sweeps over the old lady.

Tab? She stares at the telephone on which Pedro had been calling and fights the image of Tab bloodied on her apartment floor from her mind.

Tyler?

First Tyler's spectral visit knife-on-knife with the FCT

comes back to her, then her promise to him.

She looks at the literary agent, who toys with some sort of electronic device. It would be good to take away her cut of the advance for *Tyler's Last* by dying before completing it, but where would that leave Tyler?

She tries to reach for her *cahier* but can barely move her arms, not near enough to chicken-scratch an ending.

Elizabeth moves her head closer to the old lady. There's more she wants to confess.

"Now, now, Elizabeth," says the old lady, her voice remarkably clear and composed. "You've got your forgiveness and now you must take dictation."

"Eve, darling Eve," wails Elizabeth Smalls until Eve manages to get her hand out from under the sheets. Her little finger clutches Elizabeth's dowdy arm, compelling her to obey.

After reaching for the latest *cahier* at the foot of the bed and being handed a pen by her Spanish girlfriend, Elizabeth Smalls begins to take down the end of *Tyler's Last*.

Chapter 17
Saint Louis

September 12
2:00 PM
Tyler

FCT and Tyler are still locked in a stand-off when Ornella and her little French girlfriend burst through the bathroom's feebly locked door.

Ornella quickly sees that not only does her husband still hold his knife up to the FCT's throat, but he seems to have made an incision in the FCT's chest.

"Teelor, Teelor," she scolds, "why always do you do these things?"

Which hardly seems fair, as the FCT holds an identical knife and has made his own even deeper gash into Tyler's stomach.

The little French girlfriend, not at all squeamish about the sight of blood, goes straight over to the FCT, delicately unbuttons his tropical shirt and pulls it out of the way to reveal the wound. Perhaps she was a nurse in some prior life before she started sleeping with wives.

The injury turns out to be worse than Tyler had intended. A large flap of pudgy flesh hangs loose as blood trickles down the FCT's flaccid chest, so different from the tanned musculature that still pleasures Tyler's imagination.

The little French girl goes into a large walk-in closet and pulls out an elegant leather valise from which she removes a travel sewing kit. Finding a pair of small but sturdy scissors, she walks over to the bed and cuts off a section of sheet.

Tyler can't figure out what she has in mind, until she's brought it over to the FCT and begun to make a tourniquet.

It's a tricky operation. She doesn't want to interfere with the knife the FCT still holds to Tyler's heart nor does she want to get wounded by the one Tyler's still got attached to the FCT's throat.

Once the tourniquet has stopped the bleeding, she goes into the bathroom and emerges a moment later bearing a damp towel, which she uses to wipe off some of the blood drying on the FCT's torso.

Once he's been bandaged and cleaned, the FCT shoots *La Moglie* a look and declares that if she can't make her husband surrender his knife, the least she can do is fix him a drink.

And *La Moglie*, who would pout for hours when Tyler snapped at her even slightly, smiles at the FCT and goes off to the bar.

While she's off, the French Florence Nightingale, humming some inane pop tune to herself, puts the scissors back in the sewing kit, the sewing kit back into the valise, and the valise back into the closet.

La Moglie returns from the mini-bar with a glass full of ice and a bottle of tolerable scotch. After pouring a healthy quotient, she delicately places the glass in the FCT's non-knife-bearing hand.

"Really, ladies...?" Tyler protests.

But his voice comes out weak, and a jolt rips through his stomach. He yowls pathetically.

The little French girl sighs, goes back to the closet, grabs the sewing kit from the valise and the scissors from the sewing kit then rips off a smaller, messier piece of sheet.

The tourniquet (though hasty and painful) stops the blood from dripping into Tyler's underwear.

"One little drop," whines Tyler. "What's the harm in

that?"

Shooting her girlfriend a knowing look, *La Moglie* hands him the whole bottle, shaking her head.

As he's draining as much as he can (while trying to keep the knife in the same position), he ponders this unjust world where one fellow is handed a proper glass with ice and another tossed a whole bottle like a dreadful drunk.

The FCT coyly sips his drink. Still pointing his knife, he retreats a step.

Tyler takes another swig and moves back as well.

Together, still poised, they move onto the balcony looking over the river. They sit across from each other, slipping their knives from one hand to the other, and listening to the distant calls to prayer, the chortling of old car engines, the buzzing of mosquitoes.

Tiny black birds that may be bats circle around them, a warm sewery breeze drifts up from the water, and distant dark figures pass back and forth below them.

Then the FCT begins to talk, describing languid afternoons in the distant past.

Back in Taormina, the fat American girl was showing signs of over-attachment. The touristy town was beginning to wear on him, too. He was still young, and the world demanded to be explored.

They had been approached at their hotel bar by a pretty but guileless stranger with a touch of Queens in his voice and an immediately besotted look in his eyes. Cal thought he might make tolerable company as he escaped the American girl and tourist town for somewhere more exotic and isolated.

Stromboli was the logical choice: enchanted enough to lure Ingrid Bergman into Roberto Rosselini's arms. And the first few days weren't half bad. They rented a small villa on the almost uninhabited far side of the island from which one could climb down a steep path to an empty beach.

The unrelenting sunshine was turning them negro, and the absolute isolation grew tiring fast, in part because of his companion's constant drinking. By sunset, they were already hammered, and there wasn't much else to look forward to. For their meals, they had to walk to a homely *trattoria* where they were served the same local fish night after night. It could have been a tropical paradise, but he began to feel shipwrecked like Robinson Crusoe, except that Friday was insisting on falling in love with him.

"What was I wearing that last night on Stromboli?" The FCT directs his gaze at Tyler, his hard blue eyes slicing through him.

"Frankly, I have no idea."

"What were we drinking?"

"That rotten local wine plus martinis without olives or ice made from the vodka you dragged with us from Taormina."

Those magical first days on Stromboli, the only time Tyler can say he was absolutely happy, turn out to be an act, a posture. The False Calvin Thornton remains the False Calvin Thornton even if he happens to be the real Calvin Thornton because nothing about him turns out to be sincere.

Wiping his eyes with his right hand while clinging to his knife with his left, Tyler travels back to Stromboli before things went so sour, watching Cal emerge from the water after a swim, then snipe at absent friends with a drink in his hands. In the heat of the afternoon, Tyler remembers shuffling over to where Cal lay sleeping on a towel and gazing soulfully into his delicate features.

The series of losses that Tyler has suffered since the collapse of the Delauney fund has stripped him of pretenses. In Sicily, he had been inexperienced and impressionable. For a young man who'd only seen the ocean at Rockaway Beach, the coast of Stromboli was magic. One was young. One fell in love.

When Tyler tunes back to the FCT, he hears him claiming to have been sitting on the divan, minding his own business, when he was jumped and sexually assaulted.

"Just like what happened here," says the man, gesturing in the direction of the bathroom. As the crass young American had been sensitive and in need of affection, he was charitable enough to put up with a few moments of fondling before finally slapping him away.

And all he can remember after that is waking up with his head pounding, his lungs aching, and his eyes watering, as blazing gasoline surrounded him.

He burned his hands on the white-hot tile table, using it to pull himself to his feet. Then he stumbled out the door just in time to glimpse Tyler in the far distance creeping away with his money.

After jogging a few steps after him, he'd called out angrily in his smoke-damaged voice, but the fellow was long gone.

It was upsetting, of course, to be robbed and left for dead—but even through the haze of throbbing hands and aching lungs, he recognized it as the opportunity it was.

He could disappear.

Grandfather Thornton had a tender spot in his tough old heart for Cal and didn't want his drunken son or the

IRS to get hold of all of his fortune. So he'd left a not particularly frugal lifetime's worth of money in large bills and gold in several safe deposit boxes throughout Europe. He slipped his grandson the keys before his lung cancer immobilized him completely.

Where did the old fellow get so much dough? Well, there was the original Thornton fortune plus the wise purchases he'd made from those desperate German investors while their war was going south, all that confiscated Jewish jewelry.

It was while running back inside and grabbing the valise that contained the safety deposit keys that Cal's right ear got so terribly burned.

He no longer had to return to the tiresome girl in Taormina, his awful drunken dad in Greenwich, nor anyone anywhere for that matter: his mother was dead already, and everyone he could think of in America was dull and disappointing.

So he took off to Switzerland to have his ear reshaped and, while he was at it, decided to have an elaborate nosejob, along with a slight reshaping of his cheekbones. For the last many years, he has traveled the world like a cursed Dutchman, except with an aristocratic, German-sounding pseudonym, Eric Von Erminheimer, EVE for short, investing his grandfather's money in real estate, and buying and selling murky industrial buildings at considerable profit.

For several years, he'd lived in Goa, for several more in Macau. There were, of course, his Montevideo days and his periodic retreats to the condo in Copacabana.

When an overzealous investigator in Paris traced a confiscated eighteenth-century Jewish necklace to him, he got hold of one of his dodgier Belleville friends, who hooked him up with Tyler's old colleague, Delauney, who had the investigator rubbed out for him, easy as pie, as they say in America. It was Delauney, of course, who had christened him EVE.

He had admired Delauney's rascally charms, particularly his penchant for photographs. And one of the many images on the walls of Delauney's house off the *Parc Monceau* turned out to look eerily familiar.

Closer inspection revealed it to be a side view of old Thornton Hall. Delauney's great uncle, the baron, must have attended one of his grandfather's house parties when he visited America between the wars.

Tyler pounds his thigh with the handle of his knife in frustration. How had he managed to miss the photograph the several times he'd been over to the house?

EVE looks at Tyler and giggles at his expense, before explaining that he and Delauney palled around quite a bit. Just last spring, Delauney had invited him for a weekend of excess at his Swiss chalet.

The mention of which upsets Tyler even more, pain slicing through this abdomen.. Taking a sharp breath, he glances nervously at *La Moglie* and shakes his head. Assuming himself to be on the guest list, he'd tried to distract her from her little French girl by buying her a vintage Fortuni gown and carrying on about the grand soiree outside of Lausanne where she'd get to wear it. When he learned they weren't invited, he left a cowardly note on the kitchen table. The moment she came back from having her hair done in Positano and read what it said ("Swiss trip off"), she started referring to him as the "disappoint man." The next day she took off with her French girlfriend for a long weekend of shopping and screwing in Rome. They plotted their colonial nostalgia tour in a cafe on the Via Veneto, while back in Bel Vento, an Italian financial cop showed up inquiring about the Delauney fund, everything tumbling down on Tyler all at once.

"And imagine," says EVE.

"Just *imagine*," EVE repeats, the shock he experienced when he found himself once again looking at Delauney's photographs, this time at the chalet, and discovered among the snapshots of his operatives a grainy image of the man who'd molested him and left him to die, wearing that same unpleasantly sanguine look on his grubby face.

From Delauney, he learned the whereabouts of the little *finnochio*. EVE shudders and explains that Delauney was half *pied noir*, Algerian Jewish on his mother's side, and therefore easily bought. With a small contribution, Delauney also told him what he knew about Samuels, more good dirt.

Delauney willingly gave him Tyler's number and allowed him the use of the chalet house phone to harass him to his heart's content.

Tyler moans to himself. If only he'd made out the Swiss country code on his broken Italian mobile when he was getting the calls in Spain, he might have figured out what was happening to him. He might not have had to wander from continent to continent in an ignorant daze.

It was EVE's idea to send Tyler off to America on some trumped-up mission that local operatives could just as well have taken care of, something along the lines of a practical joke. He had gotten a particular kick from sending the awful man right back to his childhood train station in Howard Beach. He'd remembered the dreary drunken stories he'd told on Stromboli about his terrible early life. And, upon learning that Tyler's wife had gone to Africa with her friend, EVE could not resist the opportunity of showing up there himself and calling up the old fellow, claiming to have nabbed them.

First, he charmed the pants off the two ladies at the hotel bar and, after more than several cocktails, got them on board, quite a delightful gag. Since his wife turned out to be rather missing the dreadful man, it had the added benefit of forcing him to make a command appearance.

He was never planning on harming Tyler physically, despite what Tyler had done to him. He'd gathered that Tyler had done a fair job ruining himself: drinking slowly to death in crummy surroundings, remaining Delauney's errand boy late in middle age, allowing his wife to abandon him for a French girl.

Which makes *La Moglie* groan, her little French girlfriend shrugging matter-of-factly.

"And the insanity of traveling to America under my name," complains EVE, beginning to lose his cool, "as if trying to burn a man to death then taking his cash gave him rights to his identity."

So Delauney had told him that, too, Tyler grumbles to himself, noting his absolute lack of discretion.

EVE shakes his head, rolls his eyes, and swears once again that before he'd had the knife pulled on him, he'd been planning to leave after only making a "minor nuisance" of himself, as he'd decided that another surprise visit was in order, this one to Thornton Hall, where he was considering spending his twilight years.

"This awful, awful man," sputters EVE, waving his knife at Tyler, "wanders about like an aging gadabout, but has the heart of a working-class brute."

True, in a sense, admits Tyler to himself, slipping briefly back to those hot summer afternoons during his teen years delivering meat on Northern Boulevard to those sweaty Italians and crass old Jewish ladies who'd suspiciously stick their beaky noses into perfectly good chicken entrails.

Not so many years after that, he'd been humiliated by a queer little rich boy in Sicily. Tyler gestures with his blade, then tries to smile it off when he sees the horror on *La Moglie*'s face.

The FCT's allegations cannot have taken her completely by surprise. She certainly had doubts about Samuels's disappearance, for one thing. For months afterwards, she'd asked Tyler leading questions about the black man who'd asked for Tabasco sauce to pour on her carefully prepared *risotto* and guzzled *amarone* like water. He'd been very much in evidence, clanging drunkenly around when she'd gone to sleep after midnight, but nowhere to be found when she'd arisen at seven o'clock that morning. Had he really woken up that early to catch the *circumvesuviano* to Naples? *La Moglie* had never seemed convinced. And, of course, however carefully Tyler had strangled the man, Samuels had still let loose the odd yelp, and it seemed impossible to dig a grave in an unfinished basement without making something of a ruckus.

But if knocking off a nosy negro was one thing, setting fire to a villa around Calvin Thornton was quite another, particularly after having assaulted him with homosexual intent.

Tyler should explain what really happened on Stromboli, but he only has the strength for another pull at the scotch bottle and a wary stare across the street at the night-time river. Putting the bottle down, he places a hand on *La Moglie*'s knee. She lets it rest for a moment before shivering suddenly and jerking away.

The old lady, having valiantly dictated for more than an hour, loses her voice, this time for good.

The room spins around her as her heartbeat slows, and she feels herself being sucked away.

Elizabeth Smalls sobs again, as does her Spanish girlfriend, as does the curly black-haired literary agent.

A little bit pickled, his life story now complete, EVE looks more relaxed but shows no signs of putting down his knife.

Tyler could charge him like a bayoneteer but would just get wounded again himself. He could dash from the balcony, down the spiral staircase, and out into the night, but where would that leave him? Wounded and humiliated by a prissy little queen who'd lost the first round on Stromboli.

Helplessly, he looks over at EVE, who stares sardonically back at him with his knife still planted. The French girlfriend had effectively staunched EVE's wound, but he's bound to pass out eventually. He looks alert, while Tyler feels quite shaky, but there's no question who has the greater endurance. EVE had been gallivanting in Macao or Copacabana while Tyler was shooting down Italian types for hours in the Villa Borghese with a bullet lodged in his shin.

La Moglie yawns loudly, rises to her feet and grabs her little French girlfriend's shoulder, nodding her back inside the room.

Tyler recognizes their conspiratorial whispering.

Then he hears the little French girlfriend pick up the

phone and dial reception.

"*Nous partons*," she says in her snotty little voice, "*maintenant*."

They'll still pay for the night, Tyler hears her explain, but they are leaving right away.

Tyler looks back at EVE's smile, sips again from his bottle, then gazes down at the dark sleeping city, wondering where his dear little Oriental (who *La Moglie* may not meet after all) might be lurking.

Then he hears his wife and her girlfriend removing their clothes from the closets and dresser drawers and cramming them into their suitcases.

Tyler's gut stings, and he feels like he's about to vomit. He grits his teeth, closes his eyes, and wills those sensations away. But when he tries to open them again, they appear to be stuck. He pulls one open a crack, but it closes back up again when he sees the world swimming torpidly around him.

He wakes up again with a start, feeling EVE's knife plunging back into his stomach, except the man's still sitting across from him and Ornella and her girlfriend are saying their goodbyes.

"*Bon soir, mes amis*," says the girlfriend.

"*Buona notte*, dear friends," says the wife.

And then they are gone.

Another knot of exhaustion descends on Tyler, and his head collapses onto his chest.

When he pulls it back up again, he feels something

missing in the pit of his stomach.

EVE still sits there with that eerie smile, but Tyler feels layer after layer of skin sloughing away. And then a lump melts in the back of his throat

More than just Ornella and her little French girlfriend have abandoned him, more than just Delauney, who had so cheaply sold him out, more than the adopted Oriental adolescent who couldn't wait to get away. What's missing is that ineffable sprite who smelled of scotch and urine and watched his back for as long as he can remember.

Then a snore comes from EVE, a thin line of drool trailing down his mouth towards his chin.

Chapter 18
Saint Louis

September 12, 2001
8:00 PM
Tyler

Leaning back on his chair, Tyler takes another pull of scotch and gazes down at the robed men, donkey carts, and goats ambling by on the dark street.

A quick glance confirms that EVE is still snoring. *Let the man rest,* Tyler decides, *he'll need his strength for his dying.*

Down below, a small, solitary figure in African clothes paces back and forth. Then he looks up in Tyler's direction and darts across the street.

Tyler's heart skips a beat. A ray of light from a hotel window catches the boy's dusty black hair, kinky from the accumulation of filth.

Tyler listens to the dull murmur coming from the lobby, followed by the climbing of spiral steps, pleased to hear that the dear boy has figured out where he is.

Tyler hears the last few steps being climbed, then sweet and tender little legs tromping across the soggy wall-to-wall carpet.

The firm knock a moment later makes Tyler jump, worried that Cal may wake up.

The second knock is followed almost immediately by the opening of the door.

A rank odor of mud, sweat, and sewage follows the AOA into the room. His ripped polo shirt and filth-encrusted blue jeans have been replaced by a batik-print African shirt and matching pants already tainted by grease and mud. Several sizes too large for him, his new clothes hang loosely from his frame, revealing bits of his chafed and bruised little body. He's gotten some of the green gunk out of his hair, but it sticks straight up like a mutant mohawk.

The odor gets worse as the AOA approaches.

"Dear boy," Tyler chortles, "I'm afraid we'll need to get you some better threads."

The little fellow glares back, his nose still black and blue from the accident on the train, his pimples seared by sunburn, his lips twitching involuntarily.

The AOA slips his hand into the pocket of his batik-print pants and pulls out a small revolver.

He looks from one bleeding old man to the other. He clears his throat like he has something to say, but cocks his gun instead.

"Ohm," says Tyler helplessly, wondering why his heart pounds so momentously, his underarms and upper lip sweat so profusely. He'd taken that gun away from Martini and knocked off nearly a dozen Italian types with it. How can he be so worried about a pampered and broken little adolescent?

Slowly rising to his feet, he steps towards the AOA, extending his arm within grabbing distance.

The AOA grips the gun and pulls the trigger.

The deafening report makes him yelp in surprise, and the kick from it sends him flying back towards the king-sized bed in the middle of the room.

The bullet ricochets off the balcony, missing Tyler, but almost catching Cal Thornton's thigh.

Tyler thinks of Italian types again, nearly a dozen of them, firing bullet after bullet as they chased him down the Spanish Steps, useless against him despite all their years in the violence business.

The AOA cocks his pistol again.

"Dear boy," begs Tyler, "you've got everything wrong. Put down the silly pistol and give your Uncle Cal a hug."

Switching the knife so the blade no longer points outwards, he opens his arms. Then he closes his eyes. No one is going to shoot a man who doesn't have his eyes open.

The next report is even louder, or maybe it's just intensified by the excruciating pain in his gut and the blood pooling on the floor where he's just landed.

"*Et tu*, AOA," Tyler mumbles, as the little fellow gets up from where the kick has sent him.

The boy smiles in recognition, as he'd just read the play in ninth grade, then cocks the gun and fires again.

Meanwhile in France, Tyler is being discussed by Elizabeth Smalls and her Spanish girlfriend while the people from the funeral parlor remove the old lady's body.

"Such a pathetic figure by the end," says Elizabeth, who has already delved into the unfinished manuscript.

"Ridiculously in love with the man," says the Spanish girlfriend.

"Someone needs to come along and put him out of his misery."

The pain has disappeared along with the eerie sensation of blood seeping into his clothes, but Tyler can move only his eyes.

He opens them and sees the adopted Oriental, looking just as dirty but no longer so angry, and his Great Uncle Cal, who'd been awakened by the gunshots, gazing down upon him.

The boy's revolver is back in his pants.

Uncle Cal's knife is back in his pocket.

Tyler watches as they turn and walk out onto the balcony.

Don't listen to him, Tyler tries to warn as the world slips away.

It didn't happen like that on Stromboli.

Don't listen to a word he says.

Acknowledgements

I would like to thank readers and editors of the previous drafts of the novel: Cara Diaconoff, Dave Hughes, Kathy Lavezzo, Mat Lebowitz, Angela Starita, Robert Schirmer, Janet Steen and Jon Roemer. And particularly my father, Anthony Winner, who read it several times in several stages.

I would also like to thank Felicia Eth, for her humor and unwavering support, and Jon for his tremendous backing, imagination and infectious enthusiasm.

I beg forgiveness from the nations of Spain, Senegal and the United States, countries I've been in but recklessly reimagined. And particularly from Rotterdam and its early 90's lesbian bar, a victim of a terrible flight of fancy.

My thanks to Elise Tak and Liesbeth Nieuwenweg for telling me some Dutch words and straightening me out about Schnapps drinking in the Netherlands and Patricia Highsmith for sparking this whole insanity.

About the author

David Winner's first novel, *The Cannibal of Guadalajara*, won the 2009 Gival Press Novel Award and was nominated for the National Book Award. A film based on a story of Winner's played at Cannes in 2007. His writing has won a *Ledge Magazine* fiction contest and been nominated for two Pushcarts and an AWP Intro Contest. His work has appeared in *The Village Voice, Fiction, The Iowa Review* (upcoming), *Chicago Quarterly Review* (upcoming), *Confrontation, Joyland, Dream Catcher*, and several other publications in the U.S. and the U.K. as well as being included in *Novel Strategies*, a Pearson/Prentice Hall anthology for college students. He is the fiction editor of *The American* (www.theamericanmag. com), a monthly magazine based in Rome.

CPSIA information can be obtained at www.ICGtesting.com
Printed in the USA
LVOW10s1600030915

452709LV0000

31192020950786